P9-CFJ-466

INVINCIBLE

Also available from Diana Palmer and Harlequin HQN

Magnolia
Renegade
Lone Star Winter
Dangerous
Desperado
Merciless
Heartless
Fearless
Her Kind of Hero
Lacy
Nora
Big Sky Winter
Man of the Hour
Trilby
Lawman
Hard to Handle
The Savage Heart
Courageous
Lawless
Diamond Spur
The Texas Ranger
Lord of the Desert
The Cowboy and the Lady
Most Wanted
Fit for a King
Paper Rose
Rage of Passion
Once in Paris
After the Music
Roomful of Roses
Champagne Girl
Passion Flower
Diamond Girl
Friends and Lovers
Cattleman's Choice
Lady Love
The Rawhide Man
Outsider
Night Fever
Before Sunrise
Protector
Midnight Rider
Wyoming Tough
Wyoming Fierce
Wyoming Bold

Coming in November 2014

Wyoming Strong

DIANA PALMER

INVINCIBLE

HARLEQUIN® HQN™

Recycling programs
for this product may
not exist in your area.

ISBN-13: 978-0-373-77880-5

INVINCIBLE

This edition published by arrangement with Harlequin Books S.A.

For questions and comments about the quality of this book, please contact us at CustomerService@Harlequin.com.

Printed in U.S.A.

HARLEQUIN®
www.Harlequin.com

Dear Reader,

Carson, the hero of *Invincible,* is one of the Oglala Lakota people. For many years, the Lakota have had a special place in my heart. During World War II, our mother dated a Lakota man and spoke of marrying him. Our father came along before that could happen. But my sister and I grew up hearing stories about the Plains tribes, especially the Lakota (whom most people outside the tribe refer to as Sioux).

I wrote a book once called *Paper Rose,* whose hero had Lakota blood. I thought at the time how nice it would be to do something useful for the nation I held in such esteem. I contacted the Oglala Lakota College in Kyle, South Dakota, and asked about founding a nursing scholarship there in the name of our mother, who was a nurse. So the Eloise Cliatt Spaeth Nursing Scholarship was born.

Over the years, the scholarship has helped a great many people with families afford to go back to school. My friend Marilyn sends me letters from them, which I keep and treasure. I can't tell you how proud I am to be contributing, even in a small way, to such a grand cause. I grew up poor. I can tell you that education makes all the difference in the world.

One other thing about this book that is special is the dedication. Last year, I lost a friend. She was my daughter-in-law's mother, Jane Clayton. Since Christina was seventeen years old, she, her mother, Jane, her father, Danny, and her brother, Daniel, have been part of my family. Of all my memories of Jane, there is this special one: At the kids' wedding rehearsal in Atlanta, she sat with my sister, Dannis, my son, Blayne, her husband, Danny, son, Daniel, daughter, Christina, my niece Maggie and me shooting down enemy aircraft in an arcade game. I remember her laughing as if she were a kid. She did have the most beautiful laugh.

Oh, what fun that was! Jane, laughing, with stars in her eyes.

This book is for you, Jane, so that your name will be remembered as long as the book stays in print anywhere in the world. Good night, my friend.

Thank you for reading *Invincible.* As always, I am your fan.

Love,

Diana Palmer

In Memoriam

For my friend Verna Jane Clayton; wife of Danny, sister of Nancy, mother of Christina and Daniel, grandmother of Selena Marie and Donovan Kyle.

Your smile burns bright in our memories

Where you will live on, forever young, forever loved.

Never forgotten.

It was a rainy Friday morning.

Carlie Blair, who was running late for her job as secretary to Jacobsville, Texas police chief Cash Grier, only had time for a piece of toast and a sip of coffee before she rushed out the door to persuade her ten-year-old red pickup truck to start. It had gone on grinding seemingly forever before it finally caught up and started.

Her father, a Methodist minister, was out of town on business for the day. So there was nobody to help her get it running. Luck was with her. It did, at least, start.

She envied her friend Michelle Godfrey, whose guardian and his sister had given her a Jaguar for Christmas. Michelle was away at college now, and she and Carlie still spoke on the phone, but they no longer shared rides to town and the cost of gas on a daily basis.

The old clunker ate gas like candy and Carlie's salary only

stretched so far. She wished she had more than a couple pairs of jeans, a few T-shirts, a coat and one good pair of shoes. It must be nice, she thought, not to have to count pennies. But her father was always optimistic about their status. *God loved the poor, because they gave away so much,* he was fond of saying. He was probably right.

Right now, though, her rain-wet jeans were uncomfortable, and she'd stepped in a mud puddle with her only pair of good shoes while she was knocking corrosion off the battery terminals with the hammer she kept under the front seat for that purpose. All this in January weather, which was wet and cold and miserable, even in South Texas.

Consequently, when she parked her car in the small lot next to the chief's office, she looked like a bedraggled rat. Her dark, short, wavy hair was curling like crazy, as it always did in a rainstorm. Her coat was soaked. Her green eyes, full of silent resignation, didn't smile as she opened the office door.

Her worst nightmare was standing just inside.

Carson.

He glared at her. He was so much taller than she that she had to look up at him. There was a lot to look at, although she tried not to show her interest.

He was all muscle, but it wasn't overly obvious. He had a rodeo rider's physique, lean and powerful. Like her, he wore jeans, but his were obviously designer ones, like those hand-tooled leather boots on his big feet and the elaborately scrolled leather holster in which he kept his .45 automatic. He was wearing a jacket that partially concealed the gun, but he was intimidating enough without it.

He was Lakota Sioux. He had jet-black hair that fell to his waist in back, although he wore it in a ponytail usually. He had large black eyes that seemed to see everything with one sweep of his head. He had high cheekbones and a light olive complexion. There were faint scars on the knuckles of his big hands. She noticed because he was holding a file in one of them.

Her file.

Well, really, the chief's file, that had been lying on her desk, waiting to be typed up. It referenced an attack on her father a few weeks earlier that had resulted in Carlie being stabbed. Involuntarily, her hand went to the scar that ran from her shoulder down to the beginning of her small breasts. She flushed when she saw where he was looking.

"Those are confidential files," she said shortly.

He looked around. "There was nobody here to tell me that," he said, his deep voice clear as a bell in the silent room.

She flushed at the implied criticism. "Damned truck wouldn't start and I got soaked trying to start it," she muttered. She slid her weather-beaten old purse under her desk, ran a hand through her wet hair, took off her ratty coat and hung it up before she sat down at her desk. "Did you need something?" she asked with crushing politeness. She even managed a smile. Sort of.

"I need to see the chief," he replied.

She frowned. "There's this thing called a door. He's got one," she said patiently. "You knock on it, and he comes out."

He gave her a look that could have stopped traffic.

"There's somebody in there with him," he said with equal patience. "I didn't want to interrupt."

"I see." She moved things around on her desk, muttering to herself.

"Bad sign."

She looked up. "Huh?"

"Talking to yourself."

She glared at him. It had been a bad morning altogether and he wasn't helping. "Don't listen, if it bothers you."

He gave her a long look and laughed hollowly. "Listen, kid, nothing about you bothers me. Or ever will."

There were the sounds of chairs scraping wood, as if the men in Cash's office had stood up and pushed back their seats. She figured it was safe to interrupt him.

Well, safer than listening to Mr. Original American here run her down.

She pushed the intercom button. "You have a visitor, sir," she announced.

There was a murmur. "Who is it?"

She looked at Carson. "The gentleman who starts fires with hand grenades," she said sweetly.

Carson stared at her with icy black eyes.

Cash's door opened, and there was Carlie's father, a man in a very expensive suit and Cash.

That explained why her father had left home so early. He was out of town, as he'd said he would be; out of Comanche Wells, where they lived, anyway. Not that Jacobsville was more than a five-minute drive from home.

"Carson," Cash said, nodding. "I think you know Reverend Blair and my brother, Garon?"

"Yes." Carson shook hands with them.

Carlie was doing mental shorthand. Garon Grier was senior special agent in charge of the Jacobsville branch of the FBI. He'd moved to Jacobsville some time ago, but the FBI branch office hadn't been here quite as long. Garon had been with the bureau for a number of years.

Carlie wondered what was going on that involved both the FBI and her father. But she knew that question would go unanswered. Her father was remarkably silent on issues that concerned law enforcement, although he knew quite a few people in that profession.

She recalled with a chill the telephone conversation she'd had recently with someone who called and said, "Tell your father he's next." She couldn't get anybody to tell her what they thought it meant. It was disturbing, like the news she'd overheard that the man who'd put a knife in her, trying to kill her father, had been poisoned and died.

Something big was going on, linked to that Wyoming murder and involving some politician who had ties to a drug cartel. But nobody told Carlie anything.

"WELL, I'LL BE OFF. I have a meeting in San Antonio," Reverend Blair said, taking his leave. He paused at Carlie's desk. "Don't do anything fancy for supper, okay?" he asked, smiling. "I may be very late."

"Okay, Dad." She grinned up at him.

He ruffled her hair and walked out.

Carson was watching the interplay with cynical eyes.

"Doesn't your dad ruffle your hair?" she asked sarcastically.

"No. He did lay a chair across it once." He averted his eyes at once, as if the comment had slipped out against his will and embarrassed him.

Carlie tried not to stare. What in the world sort of background did he come from? The violence struck a chord in her. She had secrets of her own from years past.

"Carson," Garon Grier said, pausing at the door. "We may need you at some point."

Carson nodded. "I'll be around."

"Thanks."

Garon waved at his brother, smiled at Carlie and let himself out the door.

"Something perking?" Carson asked Cash.

"Quite a lot, in fact. Carlie, hold my calls until I tell you," he instructed.

"Sure thing, Boss."

"Come on in." Cash went ahead into his office.

Carson paused by Carlie's desk and glared at her.

She glared back. "If you don't stop scowling at me, I'm going to ask the chief to frisk you for hand grenades," she muttered.

"Frisk me yourself," he dared softly.

The flush deepened, darkened.

His black eyes narrowed, because he knew innocence when he saw it; it was that rare in his world. "Clueless, aren't you?" he chided.

She lifted her chin and glared back. "My father is a minister," she said with quiet pride.

"Really?"

She frowned, cocking her head. "Excuse me?"

"Are you coming in or not?" Cash asked suddenly, and there was a bite in his voice.

Carson seemed faintly surprised. He followed Cash into the office. The door closed. There were words spoken in a harsh tone, followed by a pause and a suddenly apologetic voice.

Carlie paid little attention. Carson had upset her nerves. She wished her boss would find someone else to talk to. Her job had been wonderful and satisfying until Carson started hanging around the office all the time. Something was going on, something big. It involved local and federal law enforcement—she was fairly certain that the chief's brother didn't just happen by to visit—and somehow, it also involved her father.

She wondered if she could dig any information out of her parent if she went about it in the right way. She'd have to work on that.

Then she recalled that phone call that she'd told her father about, just recently. A male voice had said, simply, "Tell your father, he's next." It had been a chilling experience, one she'd forced to the back of her mind. Now she wondered if all the traffic through her boss's office involved her in some way, as well as her father. The man who'd tried to kill him had died, mysteriously poisoned.

She still wondered why anybody would attack a minister. That remark of Carson's made her curious. She'd said her father was a minister and he'd said, "Really?" in that sarcastic, cold tone of voice. Why?

"I'm a mushroom," she said to herself. "They keep me in the dark and feed me manure." She sighed and went back to work.

SHE WAS ON the phone with the sheriff's office when Carson left. He went by her desk with only a cursory glance at her, and it was, of all things, placid. Almost apologetic. She lowered her eyes and refused to even look at him.

Even if she'd found him irresistible—and she was trying not to—his reputation with women made her wary of him.

Sure, it was a new century, but Carlie was a small-town girl and raised religiously. She didn't share the casual attitude of many of her former classmates about physical passion.

She grimaced. It was hard to be a nice girl when people treated her like a disease on legs. In school, they'd made fun of her, whispered about her. One pretty, popular girl said that she didn't know what she was missing and that she should live it up.

Carlie just stared at her and smiled. She didn't say anything. Apparently the smile wore the other girl down because she shrugged, turned her back and walked off to whisper to the girls in her circle. They all looked at Carlie and laughed.

She was used to it. Her father said that adversity was like grit, it honed metal to a fine edge. She'd have liked to be honed a little less.

They were right about one thing; she really didn't know what she was missing. It seemed appropriate, because she'd read about sensations she was supposed to feel with men around, and she didn't feel any of them.

She chided herself silently. That was a lie. She felt them when she was close to Carson. She knew that he was aware of it, which made it worse. He laughed at her, just the way her classmates had laughed at her in school. She was the odd one out, the misfit. She had a reason for her ironclad morals. Many local people knew them, too. Episodes in her childhood had hardened her.

Well, people tended to be products of their upbringing. That was life. Unless she wanted to throw away her ideals and give up religion, she was pretty much settled in her beliefs. Maybe it wasn't so bad being a misfit. Her late grandfather had said that civilizations rested on the bedrock of faith and law and the arts. Some people had to be conventional to keep the mechanism going.

"What was that?" Sheriff Hayes's receptionist asked.

"Sorry." Carlie cleared her throat. She'd been on hold. "I was just mumbling to myself. What were you saying?"

The woman laughed and gave her the information the chief had asked for, about an upcoming criminal case.

SHE COOKED A light supper, just creamed chicken and rice, with green peas, and made a nice apple pie for dessert.

Her father came in, looking harassed. Then he saw the spread and grinned from ear to ear. "What a nice surprise!"

"I know, something light. But I was hungry," she added.

He made a face. "Shame. Telling lies."

She shrugged. "I went to church Sunday. God won't mind a little lie, in a good cause."

He smiled. "You know, some people have actually asked me how to talk to God."

"I just do it while I'm cooking, or working in the yard," Carlie said. "Just like I'm talking to you."

He laughed. "Me, too. But there are people who make hard work of it."

"Why were you in the chief's office today?" she asked suddenly

He paused in the act of putting a napkin in his lap. His expression went blank for an instant, then it came back to life. "He wanted me to talk to a prisoner for him," he said finally.

She raised both eyebrows.

"Sorry," he said, smoothing out the napkin. "Some things are confidential."

"Okay."

"Let's say grace," he added.

LATER, HE WATCHED the news while she cleaned up the kitchen. She sat down with him and watched a nature special for a while. Then she excused herself and went upstairs to read. She wasn't really interested in much television programming, except for history specials and anything about mining. She loved rocks.

She sat down on the side of her bed and thumbed through her bookshelf. Most titles were digital as well as physical these days, but she still loved the feel and smell of an actual book in her hands.

She pulled out a well-worn copy of a book on the Little Bighorn fight, one that was written by members of various tribes who'd actually been present. It irritated her that many of the soldiers had said there were no living witnesses to the battle. That was not true. There were plenty of them: Lakota, Cheyenne, Crow and a host of other men from different tribes who were at the battle and saw exactly what happened.

She smiled as she read about how many of them ended up in Buffalo Bill Cody's famous traveling Wild West show. They played before the crowned heads of Europe. They learned high society manners and how to drink tea from fancy china cups. They laughed among themselves at the irony of it. Sitting Bull himself worked for Cody for a time, before he was killed.

She loved most to read about Crazy Horse. Like Carson, he was Lakota, which white people referred to as Sioux. Crazy Horse was Oglala, which was one of the subclasses of the tribe. He was light-skinned and a great tactician. There was only one verified photograph of him, which was disputed by some, accepted by others. It showed a rather handsome man with pigtails, wearing a breastplate. There was also a sketch. He had led a war party against General Crook at the Battle of the Rosebud and won it. He led another party against Custer at the Little Bighorn.

Until his death, by treachery at the hands of a soldier, he was the most famous war leader of the Lakota.

Sitting Bull did not fight; he was not a warrior. He was a holy man who made medicine and had visions of a great battle that was won by the native tribes.

Crazy Horse fascinated Carlie. She bought book after book, looking for all she could find in his history.

She also had books about Alexander the Third, called the Great, who conquered most of the civilized world by the age of thirty. His ability as a strategist was unequaled in the ancient past. Hannibal, who fought the Romans under Scipio Africanus in the Second Punic War at Carthage, was another favorite. Scipio fascinated her, as well.

The ability of some leaders to inspire a small group of men to conquer much larger armies was what drew her to military history. It was the generals who led from the front, who ate and slept and suffered with their men, who won the greatest battles and the greatest honor.

She knew about battles because her secret vice was an online video game, "World of Warcraft." A number of people in Jacobsville and Comanche Wells played. She knew the gamer tags, the names in-game, of only a very few. Probably she'd partnered with some of them in raid groups. But mostly she ran battlegrounds, in player-versus-player matches, but only on weekends, when she had more free time.

Gaming took the place of dates she never got. Even if she'd been less moral, she rarely got asked on dates. She could be attractive when she tried, but she wasn't really pretty and she was painfully shy around people she didn't know. She'd only gone out a couple of times in high school, once with a boy who was getting even with his girlfriend by dating her—although she hadn't known until later—and another with a boy who'd hurt another girl badly and saw Carlie as an easy mark. He got a big surprise.

From time to time she thought about how nice it would be to marry and have children. She loved spending time in the baby section of department stores when she went to San Antonio with her father occasionally. She liked to look at knitted booties and lacy little dresses. Once a saleswoman had asked if she had children. She said no, she wasn't married. The saleswoman had laughed and asked what that had to do with it. It was a new world, indeed.

She put away her book on the Little Bighorn fight, and settled in with her new copy of a book on Alexander the Great. The phone rang. She got up, but she was hesitant to answer it. She recalled the threat from the unknown man and wondered if that was him.

She went to the staircase and hesitated. Her father had answered and was on the phone.

"Yes, I know," he said in a tone he'd never used with her. "If you think you can do better, you're welcome to try." He paused and a huge sigh left his chest. "Listen, she's all I've got in the world. I know I don't deserve her, but I will never let anyone harm her. This place may not look secure, but I assure you, it is…"

He leaned against the wall near the phone table, with the phone in his hand. He looked world-weary. "That's what I thought, too, at first," he said quietly. "I still have enemies. But it isn't me he's after. It's Carlie! It has to have something to do with the man she saw in Grier's office. I know that the man who killed Joey and masqueraded as a DEA agent is dead. But if he put out a contract before he died… Yes, that's what I'm telling you." He shook his head. "I know you don't have the funds. It's okay. I have plenty of people who owe me favors. I'll call in a few. Yes. I do appreciate your help. It's just…it's worrying me, that's all. Sure. I'll call you. Thanks." He hung up.

Carlie moved back into the shadows. Her father looked

like a stranger, like someone she'd never seen before. She wondered who he'd been speaking to, and if the conversation was about her. It sounded that way; he'd used her name. What was a contract? A contract to kill someone? She bit her lower lip. Something to do with the man she saw in the chief's office, the man she'd tried to describe for the artist, the DEA agent who wasn't an agent.

She frowned. But he was dead, her father had said. Then he'd mentioned that contract, that the man might have put it out before he died. Of course, if some unknown person had been paid in advance to kill her…

She swallowed down the fear. She could be killed by mistake, by a dead man. How ironic. Her father had said the house was safe. She wondered why he'd said that, what he knew. For the first time in her life, she wondered who her father really was.

SHE FIXED HIM a nice breakfast. While they were eating it she said, "Why do you think that man came to kill me?"

His coffee cup paused halfway to his mouth. "What?"

"The man with the knife."

"We agreed that he was after me, didn't we?" he said, avoiding her face.

She lifted her eyes and stared at him. "I work for the police. It's impossible not to learn a little something about law enforcement in the process. That man wasn't after you at all, was he? The man who was poisoned so he couldn't tell what he knew?"

He let out a breath and put the coffee cup down. "Well, Carlie, you're more perceptive than I gave you credit for."

He smiled faintly. "Must be my genes. Your mother, God rest her soul, didn't have that gift. She saw everything in black and white."

"Yes, she did." Talk of her mother made her sad. It had just been Carlie and Mary for a long time, until Mary got sick. Then Mary's mother, and her hophead boyfriend, had shown up and ransacked the place. Carlie had tried to stop them… She shivered.

It had been several days later, after the hospital visit and the arrests, when her father had come back to town, wearing khaki pants and shirt, and carrying a pistol.

There had been no money for doctors, but her father had taken charge and got Mary into treatment. Mary's mother and her boyfriend went to jail. Sadly, it had been hopeless from the start. Mary died within weeks. During those weeks, Carlie got to know her absent father. He became protective of her. She liked him very much. He was gone for a day after the funeral. When he came home, he seemed very different.

Carlie's father spoke to someone on the phone then, too, and when he hung up he'd made a decision. He took Carlie with him to Atlanta, where he enrolled in a seminary and became a Methodist minister. He said it was the hardest and the easiest thing he'd ever done, and that it was a good thing that God forgave people for horrible acts. She asked what they were. Her father said some things were best left buried in the past.

"We're still not sure he didn't come after me," her father said, interrupting her reverie.

"I heard you talking on the phone last night," she said.

He grimaced. "Bad timing on my part," he said, sighing.

"Very bad. So now I know. Tell me what's going on."

"That phone call you had came from a San Antonio number. We traced it, but it led to a throwaway phone," he replied. "That's bad news."

"Why?"

"Because a few people who use those phones are connected to the underworld in some fashion or other, to escape detection by the authorities. They use the phone once to connect with people who might be wiretapped, then they dispose of the phone. Drug lords buy them by the cartload," he added.

"Well, I didn't do anybody in over a drug deal, and the guy I gave the artist the description of died in Wyoming. So why is somebody still after me?" she concluded.

He smiled. "Smart. Very smart. The guy died. That's the bottom line. If he hired somebody to go after you, to keep you from recognizing him in a future lineup, and paid in advance, it's too late to call him off. Get the picture?"

"In living color," she said. She felt very adult, having her father give her the truth instead of a sweet lie to calm her.

"I have a couple of friends watching you," he said. "I don't think it's a big threat, but we'd be insane not to take it seriously, especially after what's already happened."

"That was weeks ago," she began.

"Yes, at the beginning of a long chain of growing evidence." He sipped coffee. "I still can't believe how many people's lives have been impacted by this man and whoever he was working for."

"You have some idea who his boss is...was?"

He nodded. “I can’t tell you, so don’t ask. I will say that several law enforcement agencies are involved.”

“I still don’t understand why you’re having meetings with my boss and that…that man Carson.”

He studied her flushed face. “I’ve heard about Carson’s attitude toward you. If he keeps it up, I’ll have a talk with him.”

“Don’t,” she asked softly. “With any luck, he won’t be around long. He doesn’t strike me as a man who likes small towns or staying in one place for any length of time.”

“You never know. He likes working for Cy Parks. And he has a few projects going with locals.”

She groaned.

“I can talk to him nicely.”

“Sure, Dad, and then he’ll accuse me of running to Daddy for protection.” She lifted her chin. “I can take whatever he can hand out.”

He smiled at her stubbornness. “Okay.”

She made a face. “He just doesn’t like me, that’s all. Maybe I remind him of someone he doesn’t care for.”

“That’s possible.” He stared into his coffee cup. “Or it could have something to do with asking him for a grenade to start a fire…”

“Aww, now, I wasn’t trying to start anything,” she protested.

He chuckled. “Sure.” He studied her face. “I just want to mention one thing,” he added gently. “He’s not housebroken. And he never will be. Just so you know.”

“I have never wanted to housebreak a wolf, I assure you.”

“There’s also his attitude about women. He makes no

secret of it." His face hardened. "He likens them to party favors. Disposable. You understand?"

"I understand. But honestly, that's not the sort of man I'd be seriously interested in. You don't have to worry."

"I do worry. You're not street-smart, pumpkin," he added, with the pet name that he almost never used. "You're unworldly. A man like that could be dangerous to you..."

She held up a hand. "I have weapons."

He blinked. "Excuse me?"

"If he starts showing any interest in me, I'll give him my most simpering smile and start talking about how I'd love to move in with him that very day and start having children at once." She wiggled her eyebrows. "Works like a charm. They actually leave skid marks..."

He threw back his head and laughed. "So that's what happened to the visiting police chief...?"

"He was very persistent. The chief offered to punt him through the door, but I had a better idea. It worked very nicely. Now, when he comes to see the chief, he doesn't even look my way."

"Just as well. He has a wife, God help her."

"What a nasty man."

"Exactly." He looked at his watch. "Well, I have a meeting with the church officials. We're working on an outreach program for the poor. Something I really want to do."

She smiled. "You know, you really are the nicest minister I know."

He bent and kissed her forehead before he left. "Thanks, sweetheart. Be sure to check your truck, okay?"

She laughed. "I always do. Don't worry."

He hesitated. He wanted to tell her that he did worry, and the whole reason why. But it was the wrong time.

She was already halfway in love with Carson. He knew things about the man that he'd been told in confidence. He couldn't repeat them. But if Carlie got too close to that prowling wolf, he'd leave scars that would cripple her for life. He had to prevent that, if he could. The thing was, he didn't know how. It was like seeing a wire break and being too far away to fix it.

He could talk to Carson, of course. But that would only make matters worse. He had to wait and hope that Carlie could hang on to her beliefs and ignore the man's practiced charm if he ever used it on her.

Carson seemed to hate her. But it was an act. He knew it, because it was an act he'd put on himself, with Carlie's late mother. Mary had been a saint. He'd tried to coax her into bed, but she'd refused him at every turn. Finally, in desperation, he'd proposed. She'd refused. She wasn't marrying a man because he couldn't have her any other way.

So he'd gone away. And come back. And tried the soft approach. It had backfired. He'd fallen in love for the first time in his life. Mary had tied him to her with strings of icy steel, and leaving her even for a few weeks at a time had been agonizing. He'd only lived to finish the mission and get home, get back to Mary.

But over the years, the missions had come closer together, taken longer, provoked lengthy absences. He'd tried to make sure Mary had enough money to cover her bills and incidentals, but one job had resulted in no pay and during that time, Mary had gotten sick. By the time he knew and came home, it was too late.

He blamed himself for that, and for a lot more. He'd thought an old enemy had targeted him and got Carlie by mistake. But it wasn't a mistake. Someone wanted Carlie dead, apparently because of a face she remembered. There might be another reason. Something they didn't know, something she didn't remember seeing. Even the death of the man hadn't stopped the threat.

But he was going to. Somehow.

Carlie loved the weekends. At work she was just plain old Carlie, dull and boring and not very pretty at all.

But in this video game, on her game server, she was Cadzminea, an Alliance night elf death knight, invincible and deadly with a two-handed great sword. She had top-level gear and a bad attitude, and she was known even in battlegrounds with players from multiple servers. She was a tank, an offensive player who protected less well-geared comrades. She loved it.

Above the sounds of battle, clashing swords and flashing spells thrown by magic-users, she heard her father's voice.

"Just a minute, Dad! I'm in a battleground!"

"Okay. Never mind."

There were footsteps coming up. She laughed as she heard them behind her. Odd, they sounded lighter than her father's....

"Sorry, we're almost through. We're taking out the enemy commander...."

She stopped while she fought, planting her guild's battle flag to increase her strength and pulling up her Army of the Dead spell. "Gosh, the heals in this battleground are great, I've hardly even needed to use a potion... Okay!" she laughed, as the panel came up displaying an Alliance win, that of her faction.

"Sorry about that..." She turned and looked up into a pair of liquid black eyes in a surprised face.

"A gamer," he said in a tone, for once, without sarcasm. "Put up your stats."

She was too startled not to obey. She left the battleground and brought up the character screen.

He shook his head. "Not bad. Why an NE?" he asked, the abbreviation for a night elf.

"They're beautiful," she blurted out.

He laughed deep in his throat. "So they are."

"How do you know about stats?"

He pulled out his iPhone and went to the game's remote app. He pulled up the Armory and showed her a character sheet.

"Level 90 Horde Tauren druid," she read, indicating that the player was from the Alliance's deadly counter faction, the Horde. "Arbiter." She frowned. "Arbiter?" She caught her breath. "He killed me five times in one battleground!" she exclaimed. "He stealthed up to me, hit me from behind, then he just...killed me. I couldn't even fight back."

"Don't you have a medallion that interrupts spells?"

"Yes, but it was on cooldown," she said, glowering. "And you know this guy?" she asked.

He put up the iPhone. "I am this guy."

She was stunned.

"It's a small world, isn't it?" he asked, studying her face.

Too small, she thought, but she didn't say it. She just nodded.

"Your father asked a couple of us to take turns doing a walk-around when he's not here. He had to go out, so I've got first watch."

She frowned. "A what?"

"We're going to patrol around the house."

"Carrying a Horde flag?" she asked, tongue-in-cheek.

He smiled with real amusement. "We'll be concealed. You won't even know we're on the place."

She was disconcerted. "What's going on?"

"Just a tip we got," he replied. "Nothing to worry about."

Her green eyes narrowed. "My father can pull that stunt. You can't. Give it to me straight."

His eyebrows arched.

"If it concerns me, I have the right to know. My father is overprotective. I love him, but it's not fair that I have to be kept in the dark. I'm not a mushroom."

"No. You're Alliance." He seemed really amused.

"Proudly Alliance," she muttered. "Darn the Horde!"

He smiled. "Better rune that two-hander before you fight me again," he advised, referring to a special weapons buff used only by death knights.

"It's brand-new. I haven't had time," she said defensively. "Don't change the subject."

"There may be an attempt. That's all we could find out."

"Why? The guy I recognized is dead!"

"We're pretty sure that he paid the contract out before he died," he replied. "And we don't know who has it. We tried backtracking known associates of the man who made the first attempt, the one who was poisoned awaiting trial. No luck whatsoever. But an informant needed a favor, so he gave up some information. Not much. There's more at stake than just your memory of a counterfeit DEA agent. Much more."

"And that's all I'm getting, right?"

He nodded.

She glared.

"So much frustration," he mused, studying her. "Why don't you go win a few battles for the Alliance? It might help."

"Not unless you're in one of them." Her eyes twinkled. "Better watch your back next time. I'm getting the hang of it."

He shrugged. "I don't want to live forever." He glanced around the room. It was Spartan. No lace anywhere. He eyed the title of a book on the desk next to her computer and frowned. "Hannibal?"

"Learn from the best, I always think."

He looked at her. He didn't look away.

Her eyes met his and she felt her body melting, tingling. There was a sudden ache in the middle of her body, a jolt of pure electricity. She couldn't even manage to look away.

"Wolves bite," he said in a soft, gruff whisper.

She flushed and dragged her eyes back to the computer.

Somebody sold her out. She wondered if it was the chief. She'd only called Carson a wolf to two people and her father would never have betrayed her.

He chuckled softly. "Be careful what you say when you think people aren't listening," he added. He turned and left her staring after him.

LATER, SHE ASKED her father if he'd ratted her out.

He chuckled. "No. But the house is bugged like a messy kitchen," he confessed. "Be careful what you say."

"Gee, thanks for telling me after I said all sorts of things about Carson," she murmured.

He laughed. "He's got a thick skin. It won't bother him."

She studied him quietly. "Why are they after me?"

He drew in a long breath. "There are some political maneuvers going on. You have a photographic memory. Maybe you saw someone other than the murder victim, and the man behind the plot is afraid you'll remember who it is."

"Shades of Dalton Kirk," she said, recalling that the Wyoming rancher had been warned by the woman who became his wife about a vision of him being attacked for something he didn't even remember he'd seen.

"Exactly."

She poured them second cups of coffee. "So I guess it's back to checking under the truck every time I drive it."

"Oh, that never stopped," her father said with a chuckle. "I've just been doing it for you."

She smiled at him. "That's my dad, looking out for me," she said with real affection.

His pale blue eyes were sad. "There was a long period of time when I didn't look out for anybody except myself," he said quietly. "Your mother wouldn't even let anybody tell me how sick she was until it was too late." He lowered his gaze to the coffee. "I made a lot of mistakes out of selfishness. I hope that someday I'll be able to make up for a little of it."

She sipped coffee. "You never talk about your life before you went to the seminary," she pointed out.

He smiled sadly. "I'm ashamed to."

"You were overseas a lot."

He nodded. "In a number of dangerous foreign places, where life is dirt cheap."

She pursed her lips and stared at him. "You know, Michelle's guardian, Gabriel Brandon, spent a lot of time overseas also."

He lifted an eyebrow and smiled placidly. "Are you fishing?"

She shrugged. But she didn't look away.

He finished his coffee. "Let's just say that I had connections that aren't obvious ones, and I made my living in a shadow world."

She frowned. "You aren't wanted in some country whose name I can't pronounce?"

He laughed. "Nothing like that."

"Okay."

He stood up. "But I do have enemies who know where I live. In a general sense. So it's smart to take precautions." He smiled gently. "I wasn't always a minister, pumpkin."

She was remembering Carson's sarcastic comment when

she'd mentioned that her father was a minister. She hadn't known that he was aware of things about her parent that she wasn't.

"I feel like a mushroom," she muttered.

He bent and kissed her hair. "Believe me, you're better off being one. See you later. I have some phone calls to make."

He locked himself in his study and she went to watch the news on television. It was mostly boring, the same rehashed subjects over and over again, interspersed with more commercials than she could stomach. She turned it off and went upstairs.

"No wonder people stopped watching television," she grumbled as she wandered back to her bedroom. "Why don't you just stop showing any programs and show wall-to-wall commercials, for heaven's sake!"

She pulled up her game and tried to load it when she noticed that the internet wasn't working.

Muttering, she went downstairs to reset the router, which usually solved the problem. Except the router was in the study, and her father was locked in there.

She started to knock, just as she heard her father's raised voice in a tone she'd rarely ever heard.

"I told you," he gritted, "I am not coming back! You can't say anything, threaten anything, that will make me change my mind. And don't you say one more word about my daughter's safety, or I will report you to the obvious people. I understand that," he continued, less belligerently. "Trust me when I say that nobody short of a ghost could get in here after dark. The line is secure and I've scrambled important conversations, like this one. I appreciate the tip, I really do. But I can handle this. I haven't forgotten anything you taught me." He laughed shortly. "Yes, I remember. They were good times."

There was another pause. "No. But we did find out who his enforcer is, and our local law enforcement people are keeping him under covert surveillance. That's right. No, I didn't realize there were two. When did he hire the other? Wait a minute—blond hair, one eye, South African accent?" He burst out laughing. "He hired Rourke as an enforcer?"

There was another pause. "Yes, please, tell him to come see me. I'd enjoy that. Like old times, yes. Okay. Thanks again. I'll be in touch."

Totally confused, Carlie softly retraced her steps, made a racket coming down the staircase and went directly to the study. She rapped on the door.

"Dad? The internet's out! Can you reset the router?"

There was the sound of a chair scraping the floor, but she never heard his footsteps. The door suddenly opened.

He pursed his lips and studied her flushed face. "Okay. How much did you hear?"

"Nothing, Mr. Gandalf, sir, I swear, except something about the end of the world," she paraphrased Sam from *Lord of the Rings.*

Her father laughed. "Well, it wasn't really anything you didn't already know."

"Who's Rourke?" she wondered.

"A man of many talents. You'll like him." He frowned.

"Just don't like him too much, okay? He has a way with women, and you're a little lamb."

She gave him a blithe look. "If I could get around Barry Mathers, I can get around Rourke."

Her father understood the reference. Barry, a classmate, had caused one of Carlie's friends a world of hurt by getting her into bed and bragging about it. The girl had been as innocent as Carlie. He wasn't even punished.

So then he'd bet his friends that he could get Carlie into bed. She heard about it from an acquaintance, led him around by the nose, and when he showed up at her house for the date, she had two girlfriends and their boyfriends all ready to go along. He was stunned. But he couldn't call off the date, or he'd have to face the razzing of his clique.

So he took all of them out to dinner and the movies, dutch treat, and delivered Carlie and the others back to her house where her friends' cars were parked.

She waited until the others left and she was certain that her father was in the living room before she spoke to Barry. She gave him such a tongue-lashing that he literally turned around and walked the other way every time he saw her after that. He never asked her out again. Of course, neither did anybody else, for the rest of her senior year.

Barry, on the other hand, was censured so much that his wealthy parents sent him to a school out of state. He died there soon afterward in a skiing accident.

"You had a hard time in school," her father said gently.

"No harder than most other people with principles do," she replied. "There are more of us than you might think."

"I reset the router," he added. "Go try your game."

"I promised to meet Robin for a quest," she said. "I'd hate to let him down."

Her father just smiled. They knew about Robin's situation. He was in love with a girl whose family hated his family. It was a feud that went back two generations, over a land deal. Even the principals didn't really remember what started it. But when Robin expressed interest in Lucy and tried to date her, the hidden daggers came out.

It was a tragic story in many ways. Two people in love who weren't even allowed to see each other because of their parents. They were grown now, but Lucy still lived at home and was terrified of her father. So even if Robin insisted, Lucy wouldn't go against her kin.

Robin worked in his dad's real estate office, where he wasn't harassed, and he was a whiz with figures. He was going to night classes, studying real estate up in San Antonio, where he hoped to learn enough to eventually become a full-fledged real estate broker. Carlie liked him. So did her father, who respected a parent's rights but also felt sympathy for young people denied the right to love whom they pleased.

CARLIE WENT ONLINE and loaded the game, then looked for Robin, who played a shaman in the virtual world. His was a healing spec, so it went well with Carlie's DK, who couldn't heal.

I have a problem, he whispered to her, a form of typed private communication in-game.

She typed, How can I help?

He made a big smiley face. I need a date for the Valentine's Day dance.

Should I ask why? she typed.

There was a smiley face. Lucy's going to the dance with some rich rancher her father knows from out of town. If you'll go with me, her dad won't suspect anything and I can at least dance with her.

She shook her head. One day the two of them were going to have to decide if the sneaking around was less traumatic than just getting together and daring their parents to say anything. But she just typed, I'll buy a dress.

There was a bigger smiley face. It's so nice to have a friend like you, he replied.

That works both ways.

LATER, SHE TOLD her father she had a date. He asked who, and she explained.

"You're both hiding, Carlie," he said, surprising her. His eyes narrowed. "You need to think about finding someone you can have a good relationship with, someone to marry and have children with. And Robin and Lucy need to stand up and behave like adults."

She smiled sadly. "Chance would be a fine thing," she replied. "You might not have noticed, but men aren't exactly beating a path to my door. And you know why."

"Young men look at what's outside," he said wisely. "When they're more mature, men look for what's inside.

You're just at the wrong period of your life. That will change."

She drew in a long breath. "You know, not everybody marries..."

He glared at her.

She held up both hands. "I'm not talking about moving in with somebody," she said hastily. "I mean, not everybody gets married. Look at Old Man Barlow, he never did."

"He never bathed," he pointed out.

She glowered at him. "Beside the point. How about the Miller brothers? They never married. Their sister was widowed and moved back in with them, and they're all single now. They seem perfectly happy."

He looked down his nose at her. "Who spends half her time in department stores, ogling baby booties and little gowns?"

She flushed and averted her eyes.

"Just what I thought," he added.

"Listen, there really aren't many communities in Texas smaller than Comanche Wells, or even Jacobsville. Most of the men my age are either married or living with somebody."

"I see your point."

"The others are having so much fun partying that they don't want to do either," she continued. "Come on, Dad, I like my life. I really do. I enjoy working for the chief and having lunch at Barbara's Café and playing my game at night and taking care of you." She gave him a close scrutiny. "You know, you might think about marrying somebody."

"Bite your tongue," he said shortly. "There was your mother. I don't want anybody else. Ever."

She stared at him with consternation. "She'd want you to be happy."

"I am happy," he insisted. "I'm married to my church, pumpkin. I love what I do now." He smiled. "You know, in the sixteenth century, all priests were expected to be single. It wasn't until Henry VIII changed the laws that they could even marry, and when his daughter Mary came to the throne, she threw out all the married priests. Then when her half sister Elizabeth became Queen, she permitted them to marry, but she didn't want married ministers preaching before her. She didn't approve of it, either."

"This is the twenty-first century," she pointed out. "And why are you hanging out with McKuen Kilraven?" she added, naming one of the federal agents who sometimes came to Jacobsville.

He laughed. "Does it show?"

"I don't know of anybody else who can hold forth for an hour on sixteenth-century British politics and never tell the same story twice."

"Guilty," he replied. "He was in your boss's office the last time I was there."

"When was that? I didn't see him."

"You were at lunch."

"Oh."

He didn't volunteer any more information.

"I need to go buy a new dress," she said. "I think I'll drive up to San Antonio after work, since it's Saturday and I get off at 1 p.m."

"Okay. I'll let you borrow the Cobra." He laughed at her astonished look. "I'm not sure your truck would make it even halfway to the city, pumpkin."

She just shook her head.

IT WAS A CONCESSION of some magnitude. Her father loved that car. He washed and waxed it by hand, bought things for it. She was only allowed to drive it on very special occasions, and usually only when she went to the big city.

San Antonio wasn't a huge city, but there was a lot to see. Carlie liked to stop by the Alamo and look at it, but El Mercado was her port of call. It had everything, including unique shops and music and restaurants. She usually spent half a day just walking around it. But today she was in a hurry.

She went from store to store, but she couldn't find exactly what she was looking for. She was ready to give up when she pulled, on impulse, into a small strip mall where a sale sign was out in front of a small boutique.

She found a bargain dress, just her size, in green velvet. It was ankle length, with a discreet rounded neckline and long sleeves. It fit like a glove, but it wasn't overly sensual. And it suited her. It was so beautiful that she carried it like a child as she walked to the counter to pay for it.

"That was the only size we got in this particular design," the saleslady told her as she packaged it on its hangar. "I wish it was my size," she added with a sigh. "You really are lucky."

Carlie laughed. "It's for a dance. I don't go out much."

"Me, either," the saleslady said. "My husband sits and

watches the Western Channel on satellite when he gets off work and then he goes to bed." She shook her head. "Not what I thought marriage would be like. But he's good to me and he doesn't cheat. I guess I'm lucky."

"I'd say you are."

CARLIE WAS IN the Jacobs County limits on a long, deserted stretch of road. The Cobra growled as if it had been on the leash too long and wanted off. Badly.

With a big grin on her face, Carlie floored the accelerator. "Okay, Big Red," she said, using her father's affectionate nickname for the car, "let's run!"

The engine cycled, seemed to hesitate, and then the car took off with a growl that would have done a hungry mountain lion proud.

"Woo-hoo!" she exclaimed.

She was going eighty, eighty-five, ninety, ninety-six and then one hundred. She felt an exhilaration she couldn't remember ever feeling before. The road was completely open up ahead, no traffic anywhere. Well, except for that car behind her...

Her heart skipped. At first she thought it was a police car, because she was exceeding the speed limit by double the posted signs. But then she realized that it wasn't a law enforcement car. It was a black sedan, and it was keeping pace with her.

She almost panicked. But she was close to Jacobsville, where she could get help if she needed it. Her father's admonition about checking the truck before she drove it made her heart skip. She knew he'd checked the car, but she hadn't counted on being followed. Someone was after her. She knew that her father's friends were watching her, but that was in Jacobsville.

Nobody was watching her now, and she was being chased. Her cell phone was in her purse on the floor by the passenger seat. She'd have to slow down or stop to get to it. She groaned. Lack of foresight. Why didn't she have it in the console?

Her heart was pumping faster as the car behind gained on her. What if it was the shadowy assassin come for a second try? What was she going to do? She couldn't outrun him, that was obvious, and when she slowed down, he'd catch her.

She saw the city-limit sign up ahead. She couldn't continue at this rate of speed. She'd kill someone at the next crossroads.

Groaning, she slowed down. The black sedan was right on top of her. She turned without a signal into the first side street and headed for the police station. If she was lucky, she just might make it.

Yes! The traffic light stayed green. She shot through it, pulled up in front of the station and jumped out just as the sedan pulled in front of her, braked and cut her off.

"You damned little lunatic, what the hell were you thinking!" Carson raged at her as he slammed out of the black sedan and confronted her. "I clocked you at a hundred miles an hour!"

"Oh, yeah? Well, you were going a hundred, too, because you were right on my bumper. And how was I supposed to know it was you?" she told him, red-faced with embarrassment.

"I called your cell phone half a dozen times, didn't you hear it ring?"

"I had it turned off. And it was on the floor in my purse," she explained.

He put his hands on his slim hips and glared at her. "You shouldn't be allowed out by yourself, and especially not in a car with that sort of horsepower!" he persisted. "I should have the chief arrest you!"

"Go ahead, I'll have him arrest you, too!" she yelled back.

Two patrol officers were standing on the sidelines, spellbound. The chief came out and stopped, just watching the two antagonists, who hadn't noticed their audience.

"What if you'd hit something lying in the middle of the road? You'd have gone straight off it and into a tree or a power pole, and you'd be dead!"

"Well, I didn't hit anything! I was scared because I saw a car following me. Who wouldn't be paranoid, with people watching you all the time and my father having secret phone calls…!"

"If you'd answered your damned cell phone, you'd have known who was following you!"

"It was in my purse and I was afraid to slow down and try to grab it out of my pocketbook!"

"Of all the stupid assignments I've ever had, this takes the prize," he muttered. "And why you had to go to San Antonio…?"

"I went to buy a dress for the Valentine's Day party!"

He gave her a cold smile. "Going alone, are we?"

"No, I'm not." She shot back. "I have a date!"

He looked oddly surprised. "Do you have to pay him when he takes you home?" he asked in a long, sarcastic drawl.

"I don't have to hire men to take me places!" she raged back. "And this man doesn't notch his bedpost and take in strays to have somebody to sleep with."

He took a quick step forward, and he looked dangerous. "That's enough," he snapped.

Carlie sucked in her breath and her face paled.

"It really is enough," Cash Grier said, interrupting them. He stepped between them and stared at Carson. "The time to tell somebody you're following them is not when you're actually in the car. Especially a nervous young woman whose life has been threatened."

Carson's jaw was set so firmly she wondered if his teeth would break. He was still glaring at Carlie.

"And you need to keep your phone within reach when you're driving," he told Carlie in a gentler tone and with a smile.

"Yes, sir," she said heavily. She let out a long sigh.

"She was doing a hundred miles an hour," Carson said angrily.

"If you could clock her, you had to be doing the same," Cash retorted. "You're both lucky that you weren't in the city limits at the time. Or that Hayes Carson or one of his deputies didn't catch you. Speeding fines are really painful."

"You'd know," Carson mused, relaxing a little as he glanced at the older man.

Cash glowered at him. "Well, I drive a Jaguar," he said defensively. "They don't like slow speeds."

"How many unpaid speeding tickets is it to date? Ten?" Carson persisted. "I hear you can't cross the county border up around Dallas. And you, a chief of police. Shame, shame."

Cash shrugged. "I sent the checks out yesterday," he informed the other man. "All ten."

"Threatening to put you under arrest, were they?"

"Only one of them," Cash chuckled. "And he was in Iraq with me, so he stretched the rules a bit."

"I have to get home," Carlie said. She was still shaking inside over the threat that turned out to be just Carson. And from Carson's sudden move toward her. Very few people knew what nightmares she endured from one very physical confrontation in the past.

"You keep under the speed limit, or I'm telling your father what you did to his car," Carson instructed.

"He wouldn't mind," she lied, glaring at him.

"Let's find out." He jerked out his cell phone and started punching in numbers.

"All right!" she surrendered, holding up both hands. "All right, I'll go under the speed limit." Her eyes narrowed. "I'm taking that sword to a rune forge tonight. So the next time you meet me on a battleground, Hordie, I'm going to wipe the ground with you."

He pursed his lips. "That would be a new experience for me, Alliance elf."

Cash groaned. "Not you, too," he said. "It's bad enough listening to Wofford Patterson brag about his weapons. He even has a dog named Hellscream. And every time Kilraven comes down here, he's got a new game he wants to tell me all about."

"You should play, too, Chief," Carlie said. She glanced at Carson. "It's a great way to work off frustration."

Carson raised an eyebrow. "I know a better one," he said with a mocking smile.

He might not mean what she thought he did. She flushed helplessly and looked away. "I'm leaving."

"Drive carefully. And buckle up," Cash told her.

"Yes, sir, Boss," she said, grinning.

She started the car, pulled it around and eased out of the parking lot.

She really hoped that her father wouldn't find out how she'd been driving his pet car. It would be like Carson to tell him, just for spite.

Odd, though, she thought, how angry he'd been that she'd taken such chances. It was almost as if he was concerned about her. She laughed to herself. Sure. He was nursing a secret yen for her that he couldn't control.

Not that he ever would ask her out or anything, but she had grave misgivings about him. He was known for his success with women, and she was soft where he was concerned. He could push her into something that he'd just brush off as insignificant, but her life would be shattered. She couldn't let her helpless interest in him grow. Not even a little. She had to remember that he had no real respect for women and he didn't seem capable of settling down with just one.

She pulled into her driveway and cut off the engine. It was a relief to be home. Just as she got out of the car she saw the black sedan drive by. He didn't stop or wave. He just kept going. Her heart jumped up into her throat.

In spite of all the yelling, he'd shepherded her home and she hadn't even noticed. She hated the warm feeling it gave her, knowing that.

3

CARLIE HAD HOPED that her father wouldn't hear about her adventure. But when she got inside the house, he was waiting for her, his arms crossed over his chest.

"He lied," she blurted out, blushing, the dress in its plastic bag hanging over one arm.

He blinked. "Excuse me?"

She hesitated. He might not know after all. She cocked her head. "Are you…angry about something?"

"Should I be?"

He made her feel guilty. She drew in a breath and moved toward him. "I was speeding. I'm sorry. Big Red can really run…"

"A hundred miles an hour," he said, nodding. "You need special training to drive at those speeds safely, and you don't have it," he added patiently.

"I didn't know it was Carson behind me," she said heavily. "I thought it might be whoever still has me targeted."

"I understand that. I gave him...well, a talking-to," he amended. "It won't happen again. But you keep your cell phone where you can get to it in a hurry, whatever you're driving. Okay?"

"Okay, Dad," she promised.

"Got the dress, did you?" he asked, and smiled.

"Yes! It's beautiful! Green velvet. I'll wear Mama's pearls with it, the ones you brought her from Japan when you first started dating."

He nodded. "They're very special. I bought them in Tokyo," he recalled, smiling. "She had the same skin tone that you inherited from her. Off-white pearls are just right for you."

She frowned. "You buy them for a skin color?"

"I always did. Pearls come in many colors, and many prices. Those are Mikimoto pearls. An armed guard stands in the room with them."

She lost a little color. "Maybe I should wear something else..."

"Nonsense. They need to be worn. That would be like getting a special dress and letting it hang in your closet for fear of spilling something on it. Life is what matters, child. Things are expendable."

"Most things," she agreed.

"I made supper, since I knew you were going to be late," he said.

Her eyebrows arched. "That was sweet of you, Dad," she said.

"It's just a macaroni and cheese casserole. Your mother taught me how to do it when we were first married. I never forgot."

"It's one of my favorite dishes. Let me hang up my dress and I'll be right down."

"Sure."

THE MEAL WAS DELICIOUS, even more so because she hadn't had to cook it. She noticed her father's somber expression.

"I'm really sorry about pushing Big Red," she began.

He leaned back in his chair. "It's not the car I was worried about." His pale eyes were narrow and thoughtful. "It might not be a bad idea to send you over to Eb Scott and let one of his guys teach you the finer points of defensive driving. Just in case."

Her heart jumped. "Dad, maybe there isn't a real threat," she said. "I mean, the guy who was afraid of what I remembered about him is dead."

He nodded. "Yes, but there are things going on that you don't know about."

"You were talking to somebody on the phone who wanted you to come back. Come back where?" she asked bluntly.

He grimaced. "I used to work for the feds. Sort of. It was a long time ago."

"Feds?" she repeated, trying to draw him out.

His chest rose and fell. "When you're young, you think you can do anything, be anything. You don't worry about consequences. You take the training and do the job. Nobody tells you that years down the line, you may have regrets." He studied her oval face. "I was away when your mother got sick. What happened to you, because nobody was at home, was my fault. I should have been there."

She glanced down. "They paid for it."

"Not enough," he said coldly, and his face was suddenly hard and merciless. "I don't wish harm to anyone as a rule, but when your grandmother left the world, I didn't shed a tear."

Carlie managed a smile. "Me, neither. I guess he's still around somewhere."

"No. He died in a prison riot last year."

"You didn't say," she faltered.

"I didn't know. My former boss and I were making connections. We looked for anyone dangerous who knew you in the past. I had someone do some checking. I only found out yesterday."

"It's a relief, sort of," she said heavily. She shook her head. "They were both crazy. She was the worst. My poor mother..."

He put his hand over hers and squeezed. "Mary was such a ray of light that nobody blamed her for what her mother did," he reminded her.

"I know, but people have long memories in small towns."

"You have your own spotless reputation," he said gently. "Don't worry about it."

"I guess you're right." She laughed. "Robin hired a limo for us, can you believe it?"

"I like Robin," he said. "I just wish he had more guts."

"Now, now, we can't all be real-life death knights with great swords."

"You and that game. You do need to get out more." He pursed his lips. "Maybe we need to organize some things for the young, single members of our church."

"All four of us?" she mused.

He rolled his eyes.

"I like my life," she declared. "Maybe it lacks excitement, but I'm happy. That should count for something, Dad."

He laughed softly. "Okay. I see your point."

THE CHIEF WAS UNHAPPY. He didn't come out and say so, but he was on a short fuse and it was difficult to get anything out of him past one-syllable words.

"Sir, what about the new patrolman's gear?" she asked gently. "You were supposed to give me a purchase order for it, weren't you?"

"New patrolman?" He frowned. "Oh, yes. Bartley. Okay. I'll do that today."

She bit her tongue so that she didn't remind him that he'd said the same thing the day before.

He caught her expression and laughed hollowly. "I know. I'm preoccupied. Want to know why?" He shoved a newspaper across his desk. "Read the headline."

It said, Matthew Helm to Fill Unexpired Term of U.S. Senator. She stared at Cash without understanding what he was upset about.

"There were three men in the running for the appointment," he said. "One was found by police in San Antonio, on the street, doped up by an apparent drug habit that nobody knew he had. A tip," he added. "The second withdrew from the nomination because his son was arrested for cocaine possession—a kid who'd never even used drugs, but apparently the glove compartment in his car was stuffed with the stuff. Another tip. The third contender, Helm, got the appointment."

"You think the others were set up," she began.

"Big-time," he replied. He glared at the headline. "If he wins the special election in May, we're in for some hard times in law enforcement. I can't prove it, but the prevailing theory is that Mr. Helm is in bed with Charro Mendez. Remember him?"

She nodded. "The enforcer who worked for the late El Ladrón," she said. "He was a cousin to the Fuentes brothers."

"The very same ones who used to run the distribution hub. He's now head of the drug cartel over the border in Cotillo. In fact, he's the mayor of that lovely little drug center."

"Oh, dear."

"I really wish somebody had furnished Carson with more than three hand grenades," he muttered.

"Shame!" she said.

He chuckled. "Okay. I'll get the purchase order filled out." He leaned forward. "Hell of a thing, to have a politician like this in Washington."

"He'll be a junior senator," she pointed out. "He won't have an important role in anything. He won't chair any important committees and he won't have powerful alliances."

"Yet."

"Surely, he won't win the special election," she ventured.

He looked at her. "Carlie, remember what I just told you about his rivals for the appointment?"

She whistled. "Oh, dear," she said again.

"Exactly."

The phone rang. She excused herself and went out to answer it.

CARSON WAS CONSPICUOUS by his absence for the next few days. Nobody said anything about him, but it was rumored that he was away on some job for Eb Scott. In the meantime, Carlie got her first look at the mysterious Rourke.

He stopped by her office during her lunch hour one day. He was wearing khakis with a sheepskin coat. He grinned at her where she sat at her desk eating hot soup out of a foam cup.

"Bad habit," he said, with a trace of a South African accent. "Eating on the job. You should be having that out of fine china in some exotic restaurant."

She was staring at the attractive man wearing an eye patch, with her spoon suspended halfway between the cup and her mouth. "Excuse me?" she faltered.

"An exotic restaurant," he repeated.

"Listen, the only exotic restaurant I know of is the Chinese place over on Madison, and I think their cook is from New York."

He chuckled. "It's the sentiment, you know, that counts."

"I'll take your word for it." She put down the cup. "How can I help you?"

"Is the boss in?" he asked.

She shook her head. "Sorry. He's at the exotic local café

having a thick hamburger and fries with a beautiful ex-motion picture star."

"Ah, the lovely Tippy," he chuckled. "Lucky man, to have a wife who's both kind and beautiful. The combination is rare."

"I'll say."

"So, okay if I leave a message?"

She pushed a pad and pen across the desk and smiled. "Be my guest."

He scribbled a few words and signed with a flourish.

She glanced at it. "You're Rourke?"

He nodded. His one pale brown eye twinkled. "I guess my reputation has preceded me?"

"Something like that," she said with a grin.

"I hope you were told it by your boss and not Carson," he said.

She shook her head. "Nobody told me. I overheard my dad talking about you on the telephone."

"Your dad?"

She nodded. "Reverend Jake Blair."

His face softened. "You're his daughter, then." He nodded. "It came as a shock to know he had a child, let me tell you. Not the sort of guy I ever associated with family."

"Why?" she asked, all innocence.

He saw that innocence and his face closed up. "I spoke out of turn, there."

"I know he did other things before he came home," she said. "I don't know what they were."

"I see."

In that instant, his own past seemed to scroll across his hard face, leaving scars that were visible for a few seconds.

"You need to go to one of those exotic restaurants and have something to cheer you up," she pointed out.

He stared at her for a moment and then chuckled. "How about going with me?" he teased.

She shook her head. "Sorry. I've been warned about you."

"How so?" he asked, and seemed really interested in her answer.

She grinned. "I'm not in your league, Mr. Rourke," she said. "Small-town girl, never been anywhere, never dated much…" He looked puzzled. She gave him her best star-struck expression. "I want to get married and have lots of kids," she said enthusiastically. "In fact, I'm free today after five…!"

He glowered at her. "Damn! And I've got a meeting at five." He snapped his fingers. "What a shame!"

"Just my luck. There, there, I'm sure you'll find someone else who can't wait to marry you," she added.

"No plans to marry, I'm afraid," he replied. Then he seemed to get it, all at once. His eyebrows arched. "Are you having me on?"

She blinked. "Am I having you on what?"

He stuffed his hands in his pockets. "I can't marry you," he said. "It's against my religion."

"Which religion would that be?"

"I'm not sure," he said. "I'll have to find one that prohibits marriage…" He burst out laughing.

She grinned.

"I get it. I'm a bit slow today. Must stem from missing breakfast." He shook his head. "Damned weird food you Yanks serve for breakfast, let me tell you. Grits? What the hell is a grit?"

"If you have to ask, you shouldn't eat one," she returned, laughing.

"I reckon." He smiled. "Well, it was nice meeting you, Ms. Blair."

"Miss," she said. "I don't run a company and I'm not planning to start my own business."

He blinked. "Come again?"

She frowned. "How can I come again if I haven't left?"

He moved closer to the desk. "Confound it, woman, I need a dictionary to figure out what you're saying."

"You can pin a rose on that," she agreed. "Are you from England?"

He glared at her. "I'm South African."

"Oh! The Boer Wars. You had a very famous general named Christiaan de Wet. He was a genius at guerilla warfare and was never captured by the British, although his brother, Piet, was."

He gaped at her.

She smiled shyly. "I collect famous generals. Sort of. I have books on famous campaigns. My favorites were American, of course, like General Francis Marion of South Carolina, the soldier they called the 'Swamp Fox' because he was so good at escaping from the British in the swamps during the Revolutionary War," she laughed. "Then there was Colonel John Singleton Mosby, the Gray Ghost of the Confederacy. I also like to read about Crazy Horse," she added shyly. "He was Oglala Lakota, one of the most able of the indigenous leaders. He fought General Crook's troops to a standstill at the Battle of the Rosebud."

He was still gaping.

"But my favorite is Alexander the Great. Of all the great military heroes, he was the most incredible strategist..."

"I don't believe it." He perched himself on the edge of her desk. "I know South Africans who couldn't tell you who de Wet was!"

She shrugged. "I used to spend a lot of time in the library. They had these old newspapers from the turn of the twentieth century. They were full of the Boer Wars and that famous Boer General de Wet," she laughed. "I almost missed class a couple of times because I was so entranced by the microfilm."

He laughed. "Actually, I'm distantly related to one of the de Wets, not really sure if it was Christiaan, though. My people have been in South Africa for three generations. They were originally Dutch, or so my mother said."

"Rourke is not really a Dutch name, is it?" she asked.

He sighed. "No. Her name was Skipper, her maiden name."

"Was your father Irish?"

His face closed up. That one brown eye looked glittery.

"Sorry," she said at once. "That was clumsy. I have things in my past that I don't like to think about, either."

He was surprised at her perception. "I don't speak of my father," he said gently. "Didn't mean to unsettle you."

"No problem," she said, and smiled. "We're sort of the sum total of the tragedies of our lives."

"Well put." He nodded thoughtfully. "I might reconsider about that marriage thing..."

"Sorry. My lunch hour's over."

"Damn."

She laughed.

He studied her with real interest. "There's this do, called a Valentine's Day dance, I think. If you need a partner...?"

"Thanks, but I have a date," she said.

"Just my luck, being at the end of the line, and all," he chuckled.

"If you go, I'll dance with you," she promised.

"Will you, now? In that case, I'll dust off my tux."

"Just one dance, though," she added. "I mean, we wouldn't want to get you gossiped about or anything."

"Got it." He winked and got to his feet. "If you'll pass that note along to the chief, I'll be grateful. See you around, I expect."

"I expect so," she replied.

WHAT A VERY strange man, she thought. He was charming. But she really didn't want to complicate her life. In his way, he seemed far more risky than even Carson, in a romantic sense.

When she got home, she mentioned his visit to her father.

"So now you know who Rourke is," he chuckled.

"He's very nice," she said. "But he's a sad sort of person."

"Rourke?" he asked, and seemed almost shocked.

"Yes. I mean, it doesn't show so much. But you can tell."

"Pumpkin, you really are perceptive."

"He said he'd take me to the Valentine's dance. That

was after he reconsidered the wedding, but I told him my lunch hour was over…"

"What?" he blurted out.

"Nothing to worry about, he said he wasn't free today anyway."

"Listen here, you can't marry Rourke," he said firmly.

"Well, not today, at least," she began.

"Not any day," came an angry voice from the general direction of the front door. Carson came in, scowling. "And what did I tell you about keeping that cell phone with you?" he added, pulling it out of his pocket. "You left it on your desk at work!"

She grimaced. "I didn't notice."

"Too busy flirting with Rourke, were you?" Carson added harshly.

"That is none of your business," she said pertly.

"It really isn't," her father interjected, staring at Carson until he backed down. "What's going on?" he added, changing the subject.

Carson looked worn. "Dead ends. Lots of them."

"Were you at least able to ascertain if it was poison?"

He nodded. "A particularly nasty one that took three days to do its work." He glanced at Carlie, who looked pale. "Should you be listening to this?" he asked.

"I work for the police," she pointed out. She swallowed. "Photos of dead people, killed in various ways, are part of the files I have to keep for court appearances by our men and women."

Carson frowned. He hadn't considered that her job would involve things like that. "I thought you just typed reports."

She drew in a breath. "I type reports, I file investigative material, photos, I keep track of court appearances, call people to remind them of meetings, and from time to time I function as a shoulder for people who have to deal with unthinkable things."

Carson knew what she was talking about. His best friend, years ago, had been a reservation policeman. He'd gone with the man on runs a time or two during college vacation. In the service, overseas, he'd seen worse things. He was surprised that Carlie, the innocent, was able to deal with that aspect of police work.

"It's a good job," she added. "And I have the best boss around."

"I have to agree," her father said with a gentle smile. "For a hard case, he does extremely well as a police chief." He sighed. "I do miss seeing Judd Dunn around."

"Who's Judd Dunn?" Carson asked.

"He was a Texas Ranger who served on the force with Cash," Jake said. "He quit to be assistant chief here when he and Christabel had twins. But he was offered a job as police chief over in Centerville. It's still Jacobs County, just several miles away. He took it for the benefits package. And, maybe, to compete with Cash," he chuckled.

"They tell a lot of stories about the chief," Carlie said.

"Most of them are true," Reverend Blair replied. "The man has had a phenomenal life. I don't think there's much he hasn't done."

Carson put Carlie's phone on the table beside her and glanced at his watch with a grimace. "I have to get going.

I'm still checking on the other thing," he added to Reverend Blair. "But I… Sorry."

Carson paused to take a call. "Yes, I know, I'm running late." He paused and smiled, gave Carlie a smug look. "It will be worth the wait. I like you in pink. Okay. See you in about thirty minutes. We'll make the curtain, I promise. Sure." He hung up. "I'm taking Lanette to see *The Firebird* in San Antonio. I have to go."

"Lanette?" Reverend Blair asked.

"She's a stewardess. I met her on the plane coming down with Dalton Kirk a few weeks ago." He paused. "There's still the matter of who sent a driver for him, you know. A man was holding a sign with his name on it. I tried to trace him, but I couldn't get any information."

"I'll mention it to Hayes," Reverend Blair said. "He's still hoping to find Joey's computer." Joey was the computer technician who'd been killed trying to recover files from Hayes's computer. The computer itself had disappeared, leading Hayes to reset all the department's sensitive information files and type most of his documentary evidence all over again.

Carson's expression was cold. "Joey didn't deserve to die like that. He was a sweet kid."

"I didn't know him," Reverend Blair said. "Eb said he was one of the finest techs he'd ever employed."

"One day," Carson said, "we'll find the person who killed him."

"Make sure you take a law enforcement officer with you if it's you who finds him," Reverend Blair said shortly.

"You're very young to end up in federal prison on a murder charge."

Carson smiled, but his eyes didn't. "I'm not as young as I look. And age has more to do with experience than years," he said, and for a minute, the sadness Carlie had seen on Rourke's face was duplicated on Carson's.

"True," Reverend Blair said quietly.

Carlie was fiddling with her phone, not looking at Carson. She'd heard about the stewardess from one of the sheriff's deputies, who'd heard it from Dalton Kirk. The woman was blonde and beautiful and all over Carson during the flight. It made Carlie sad, and she didn't want to be. She didn't want to care that he was going to a concert with the woman.

"Well, I'll be in touch." He glanced at Carlie. There was that smug, taunting smile again. And he was gone.

Her father looked at her with sympathy. "You can't let it matter," he said after a minute. "You know that."

She hesitated for a second. Then she nodded. "I'm going up. Need anything?"

He shook his head. He took her by the shoulders and kissed her forehead. "Life is hard."

"Oh, yes," she said, and tried to smile. "Night, Dad."

"Sleep well."

"You, too."

SHE PLUGGED IN her game and went looking for Robin to run some battlegrounds. It would keep her mind off what Carson was probably doing with that beautiful blonde stewardess. She saw her reflection in the computer screen and wished, not for the first time, that she had some claim to beauty and charm.

Robin was waiting for her in the Alliance capital city. They queued for a battleground and practiced with their weapons on the target dummies while they waited.

This is my life, she thought silently. A computer screen in a dark room. I'm almost twenty-three years old and nobody wants to marry me. Nobody even wants to date me. But I have bright ideals and I'm living the way I want to.

She made a face at her reflection. "Good girls never made history," she told it. Then she hesitated. Yes, they did. Joan of Arc was considered so holy that her men never approached her in any physical way. They followed her, a simple farm girl, into battle without hesitation. She was armed with nothing except her flag and her faith. She crowned a king and saved a nation. Even today, centuries later, people know who she was. Joan was a good girl.

Carlie smiled to herself. So, she thought. There's my comeback to that!

SHE WAS TYPING up a grisly report the next day. A man had been found on the town's railroad tracks. He was a vagabond, apparently. He was carrying no identification and wearing a nice suit. There wasn't a lot left of him. Carlie tried not to glance at the crime scene photos as she dealt with the report.

Carson came in, looking weary and out of sorts.

She stared at him. "Well, it wasn't you, after all," she said enigmatically.

He blinked. "Excuse me?"

"We found a man in a nice suit, carrying no identification. Just for a few minutes, we wondered if it was you," she said, alluding to his habit of going everywhere without ID.

"Tough luck," he returned. He frowned as he glanced at the crime scene photos. He lifted one and looked at it with no apparent reaction. He put it back down. His black eyes narrowed on her face as he tried to reconcile her apparent sweetness with the ability it took to process that information without throwing up.

"Something you needed?" she asked, still typing.

"I want to speak to Grier," he said.

She buzzed the chief and announced the visitor. She went back to her typing without giving Carson the benefit of even a glance. "You can go in," she said, nodding toward the chief's office door.

Carson stared at her without meaning to. She wasn't pretty. She had nothing going for her. She had ironclad ideals and a smart mouth and a body that wasn't going to send any man running toward her. Still, she had grit. She could do a job like that. It would be hard even on a toughened police officer, which she wasn't.

She looked up, finally, intimidated by the silence. He captured her eyes, held them, probed them. The look was intense, biting, sensual. She felt her heart racing. Her hands on the keyboard were cold as ice. She wanted to look away but she couldn't. It was like holding a live electric wire…

"Carson?" the chief called from his open office door.

Carson dragged his gaze away from Carlie. "Coming."

He didn't look at her again. Not even as he left the office scant minutes later. She didn't know whether to be glad or not. The look had kindled a hunger in her that she'd never known until he walked into her life. She knew the danger. But it was like a moth's attraction to the flames.

She forced her mind back on the job at hand and stuffed Carson, bad attitude and blonde and all, into a locked door in the back of her mind.

4

THINGS WERE HEATING UP. Reverend Blair went to San Antonio with Rourke. They seemed close, which fascinated Carlie.

Her dad didn't really have friends. He was a good minister, visiting the sick, officiating at weddings, leading the congregation on Sundays. But he stuck close to home. With Rourke, he was like another person, someone Carlie didn't know. Even the way they talked, in some sort of odd shorthand, stood out.

THE WEATHER WAS COLD. Carlie grimaced as she hung up the tattered coat, which was the only protection she had against the cold. In fact, she was worried about going to the dance with Robin because of the lack of a nice coat. The shoes she was going to wear with the green velvet dress were old and a little scuffed, but nobody would notice, she was sure. People in Jacobs County were kind.

She wondered if Carson might show up there. It was a hope and a worry because she knew it was going to hurt if she had to see him with that elegant, beautiful woman she'd heard about. The way he'd looked at her when he was talking to the woman on the phone was painful, too; his smug expression taunted her with his success with women. If she could keep that in mind, maybe she could avoid some heartbreak.

But her stubborn mind kept going back to that look she'd shared with Carson in her boss's office. It had seemed to her as if he was as powerless to stop it as she was. He hadn't seemed arrogant about the way she reacted to him, that once. But if she couldn't get a grip on her feelings, she knew tragedy would ensue. He was, as her father had said, not tamed or able to be tamed. It really would be like trying to live with a wolf.

On her lunch hour, she drove to the cemetery. She'd bought a small plastic bouquet of flowers to put on her mother's neat grave. A marble vase was built into the headstone, just above the BLAIR name. Underneath it, on one side, was the headstone they'd put for her mother. It just said Mary Carter Blair, with her birth date and the day of her death.

She squatted down and smoothed the gravel near the headstone. She took out the faded plastic poinsettia she'd decorated the grave with at Christmas and put the new, bright red flowers, in their small base, inside the marble vase and arranged them just so.

She patted her mother's tombstone. "It isn't Valentine's Day yet, Mama, but I thought I'd bring these along while I had time," she said, looking around to make sure nobody was nearby to hear her talking to the grave. "Dad's gone to San Antonio with this wild South African man. He's pretty neat." She patted the tombstone again. "I miss you so much, Mama," she said softly. "I wish I could show you my pretty dress and talk to you. Life is just so hard sometimes," she whispered, fighting tears.

Her mother had suffered for a long time before she finally let go. Carlie had nursed her at home, until that last hospital stay, taken care of her, just as her mother had taken care of her when she was a baby.

"I know you blamed yourself for what happened. It was never your fault. You couldn't help it that your mother was a…well, what she was." She drew in a breath. "Daddy says they're both gone now. I shouldn't be glad, but I am."

She brushed away a leaf that had fallen onto the tombstone. "Things aren't any better with me," she continued quietly. "There's a man I…well, I could care a lot about him. But he isn't like us. He's too different. Besides, he likes beautiful women." She laughed hollowly. "Beautiful women with perfect bodies." Her hand went involuntarily to her coat over her shoulder. "I'm never going to be pretty, and I'm a long way from perfect. One day, though, I might find somebody who'd like me just the way I am. You did. You weren't beautiful or perfect, and you were an angel, and Daddy married you. So there's still hope, right?"

She moved the flowers a little bit so they were more visible, then sat down. "Robin's taking me to the Valentine's Day dance. You remember Robin, I know. He's such a sweet man. I bought this beautiful green velvet dress to wear. And Robin's rented us a limo for the night. Can you imagine, me, riding around in a limousine?" She laughed out loud at the irony. "I don't even have a decent coat to wear over my pretty dress. But I'll be going in style."

She caressed her hand over the smooth marble. "It's hard, not having anybody to talk to," she said after a minute. "I only ever had one real girlfriend, and she moved away years ago. She's married and has kids, and she's happy. I hear from her at Christmas." She sighed. "I know you're around, Mama, even if I can't see you.

"I won't ever forget you," she whispered softly. "And I'll always love you. I'll be back to see you on Mother's Day, with some pretty pink roses, like the ones you used to grow."

She patted the tombstone again, fighting tears. "Well… bye, Mama."

She got to her feet, feeling old and sad. She picked up the faded flowers and carried them back to her truck. As she was putting them on the passenger's side floor, she noticed a note on the seat.

Keep the damned cell phone with you! It does no good sitting in the truck!

It was signed with a big capital *C*.

She glared at it, looking around. She didn't see anybody. But he'd been here, watching her. He'd seen her talking to her mother. Great. Something else for him to hold against her. She started to crumple up the note, but it was the first one he'd ever written her. She liked the way he wrote, very legible, elegant longhand. With a sigh, she folded it and stuck it in the glove compartment.

"Mental illness must be contagious," she muttered to herself. "Maybe I got it from Rourke."

She got in under the wheel and started the engine. It didn't occur to her until much later that it seemed to matter to Carson if something happened to her. Of course, it could have just been pride in his work that she wouldn't get killed on his shift. Still, it felt nice. Unless he'd seen her talking to Mary and thought she needed to be committed.

HER FATHER CAME in with Rourke that night just as she was taking the cornbread out of the oven. She'd made a big pot of homemade chili to go with it.

"What a delightful smell," Rourke said in the kitchen doorway.

She grinned. "Pull up a chair. All you need is some butter for the cornbread. I have real butter. Homemade chili to go with it. There's always plenty."

"By all means," Reverend Blair chuckled. "Carlie always makes extra, in case I bring someone home with me."

"Do you do that often?" Rourke asked.

"Every other day," the reverend confessed. "She never complains."

"He only brings hungry people who like the way I cook," she amended, and laughed. Her face, although she didn't realize it, was very pretty when she smiled.

Rourke studied her with real appreciation. If his heart hadn't been torn, he might have found her fascinating.

He looked around the stove and the cabinets.

"Did I forget something?" she asked.

"I'm looking to see if you cooked a grit."

She and her father both laughed.

"It isn't a grit, it's grits. They're made with corn," she pointed out.

He shook his head. "Foreign fare."

"Yes, well, I expect you know how to cook a springbok, but I'd have no idea," she said as she put the pot of chili on the table.

"And she knows about springboks!" Rourke groaned. He sat down and put his napkin in his lap. "She also knows the history of the Boer Wars," he said.

Her father shook his head. "She's a student of military history. A big fan of Hannibal," he confided.

"So am I. He was from Carthage. Africa," Rourke added.

There was silence while they ate. Rourke seemed fascinated with the simple meal.

"I've had cornbread before, but it's usually so dry that I can't eat it. My mother used to make it like this," he added quietly. "She was from the States. Maryland, I believe."

"How in the world did she end up in Africa?" Carlie exclaimed. She blushed. "I mean, if you don't mind my asking."

He put down his spoon. "I was very rude about my father. I'm sorry," he said, his brown eyes steady on her face. "You see, my birth certificate lists my mother's husband in that capacity. But a covert DNA profile tells a very different story." His face was hard. "I don't speak of it in company because it's painful, even now."

She was really blushing now. She didn't know what to say.

"But I wouldn't have hurt you deliberately just for asking an innocent question," Rourke continued gently. "You don't even know me."

She bit her lower lip. "Thanks," she said shyly.

"Now, if you'd been a *man*..." her father mused, emphasizing the last word.

Carlie looked at him inquisitively.

He exchanged a look with Rourke. "There was a bar in Nassau," her father said. "And a member of the group we were with made a sarcastic remark. Not to add that he did know Rourke, and he certainly knew better, but he'd had one too many Bahama mamas." He pursed his lips and studied Rourke's hard face. "I believe he made a very poetic dive into the swimming pool outside the bar."

"Deliberately?" Carlie asked.

"Well, if it had been deliberate, I don't think he'd have done it through the glass patio door," her father added.

Carlie sucked in a breath. She looked behind her.

"What are you looking for?" her father asked.

"Glass patio doors..."

Rourke chuckled. "It was a while back," he remarked. "I'm less hotheaded now."

"Lies," her father said. "Terrible lies."

"Watch it," Rourke cautioned, pointing his chili spoon at the reverend, "or I'll tell her about the Russian diplomat."

"Please do!" Carlie pleaded.

Her father glowered at Rourke. "It was a long time ago, in another life. Ministers don't hit people," he said firmly.

"Well, you weren't a minister then," Rourke teased, "and your embassy had to call in a lot of favors to keep you out of jail."

"What in the world did you people do in those days?" Carlie asked, shocked.

"Bad things," Reverend Blair said softly. "And it's time to change the subject."

"The things we don't know about our parents," Carlie mused, staring at her father.

"Some things are better not known," was the reply. "And isn't your chili getting cold, pumpkin?"

"Why do you call her 'pumpkin'?" Rourke wanted to know.

"Now that's a really long story…"

"And we can forget to tell it unless we want burned meat for a week," Carlie interjected.

The reverend just smiled.

HER FATHER WENT to answer a phone call while Carlie was clearing the dishes in the kitchen. Rourke sat at the kitchen table with a second cup of black coffee.

"You really don't know a lot about your dad, do you?" he asked her.

"Apparently not," she laughed, glancing at him with mischievous green eyes. "Do you take bribes? I can make almost any sort of pie or cake—"

"I don't like sweets," he interrupted. "And it's worth my life to tell you," he added with a laugh. "So don't ask."

She made a face and went back to the dishes in the sink.

"Don't you have a dishwasher?" he asked, surprised.

She shook her head. "Money is always tight. We get a little extra and there's a pregnant woman who can't afford a car seat, or an elderly man who needs dentures, or a child who needs glasses..." She smiled. "That's life."

He frowned. "You just give it away?"

She turned toward him, curious. "Well, can you take it with you when you go?" she asked.

He paused, sipping coffee.

"The Plains tribes had this philosophy," she began, "that the richest man in the village was the one who had the least because he gave it all away. It denoted a good character, which was far more important than wealth."

"I would ask why the interest in aboriginal culture," he began.

She turned, her hands around a soapy plate. "Oh, my best friend was briefly engaged to a Lakota man," she said. "We were juniors in high school. Her parents thought she was too young, and they made them wait a year."

"From your tone, I gather things didn't go well?"

She shook her head. She turned back to the sink to rinse the dish, aware of a pang in the region of her heart because the story hit close to home. "His parents talked him into breaking the engagement," she said. "He told her that his religion, his culture, everything was so different from hers that it would be almost impossible to make a life together. She'd have had to live on the reservation with him, and his parents already hated her. Then there was the problem of the children, because they would have been trapped between two cultures, belonging to neither."

"That's very sad," Rouke commented.

She turned to look at him, then lowered her eyes to the sink again. "I didn't realize how much difference there was, until I started reading about it." She smiled sadly. "Crazy Horse, Tashunka Witko in his own tongue—although that's translated different ways in English—was one of my favorite subjects. He was Oglala Lakota. He said that one could not sell the ground upon which the People—what the Lakota called themselves—walked." She glanced at him. "Things never mattered to them. Materialism isn't really compatible with attitudes like that."

"You're one of the least materialistic people I know, Carlie," her father said as he came back into the room. "And I'd still say it even if I wasn't related to you."

"Thanks, Dad," she said with a smile.

"I need to talk to you," he told Rourke. "Bring your coffee into the office. Carlie, that new science fiction movie you wanted to see is playing on the movie channel."

"It's not new, it's four months old," she laughed. "But you're right, I guess, it's new to me. I'll watch it later. I promised Robin I'd help run one of his little toons through a dungeon." She made a face. "I hate dungeons."

"Dungeons?" Rourke asked.

"She plays an online video game," her father explained, naming it.

"Oh, I see. You're Horde, too, huh?" Rourke teased.

She glared at him. "I'm Alliance. Proudly Alliance."

"Sorry," Rourke chuckled. "Everyone I know is in Horde."

She turned away. "It seems like it sometimes, doesn't it?" She sighed. She turned at the staircase and held up her hand as if it contained a sword. "For the Alliance!" she yelled, and took off running upstairs.

Her father and Rourke just laughed.

IT WAS FRIDAY. And not just any Friday. It was the Friday before the Saturday night when the Valentine's Day dance was being held at the Jacobsville Civic Center.

Carlie was all nerves. She was hoping that it would be warmer, so she could manage to go to the dance without wearing a coat, because she didn't have anything nice to go with her pretty dress. She had to search out a file for the chief, which she'd put in the wrong drawer, and then she hung up on a state senator by pushing the wrong button on her desk phone.

The chief just laughed after he'd returned the call. "Is it Robin that's got you in such a tizzy?" he teased.

She flushed. "Well, actually, it's the..."

Before she could finish the sentence and tell him it was her wardrobe that was the worry, the door opened and Carson came in. But he wasn't alone.

There was a beautiful blonde woman with him. She was wearing a black suit with a red silk blouse, a black coat with silver fur on the collar, and her purse was the same shade of deep red as the high-heeled shoes she was wearing. Her platinum-blond hair was pulled back into an elegant chignon. She had a flawless complexion, pale blue eyes, and skin like a peach. Carlie felt like a cactus plant by comparison.

But she managed a smile for the woman just the same.

The blonde looked at her with veiled amusement and abruptly looked toward the chief.

"Chief Grier, this is Lanette Harris," Carson said.

"So charmed to meet you," the blonde gushed in an accent that sounded even more Southern than Carlie's Texas accent. She held out a perfectly manicured hand. "I've heard so much about you!"

Cash shook her hand, but he didn't respond to her flirting tone. He just nodded. His eyes went to Carson, who was giving Carlie a vicious, smug little smile.

"What can I do for you?" he asked Carson.

Carson shrugged. "I was at a loose end. I wondered if you'd heard anything more from your contact?"

Cash shook his head. Just that. He didn't say a thing.

Carson actually looked uncomfortable. "Well, I guess we'll get going. We're having supper in San Antonio."

He was wearing a dark suit with a spotless white shirt and a blue pinstriped tie. His long hair was pulled back into a neat ponytail. He was immaculate. Carlie had to force herself not to look at him too closely.

"That desk is a mess! Don't you know how to file things away?" Lanette asked Carlie with studied humor, moving closer. Her perfume was cloying. "However do you find anything?"

"I know where everything is," Carlie replied pleasantly.

"Sorry," Lanette said when she saw Cash Grier's narrow look. "I can't abide clutter." She smiled flirtatiously.

"Don't let us keep you," Cash replied in a tone that sounded as icy as his expression looked.

"Yes. We'd better go." Carson moved to the door and opened it.

"Nice to have met you, Chief Grier," Lanette purred. "If you ever want a competent secretary, I might be persuaded to come out of retirement. I used to work for a law firm. And I know how to file."

Cash didn't reply.

"Lanette," Carson said shortly.

"I'm coming." She smiled again at Cash. "Bye now." She didn't even look at Carlie.

She went to the door and through it. Carlie didn't look up from her computer screen. She hoped she wasn't going to bite through her tongue. Only when she heard the door close did she lift her eyes again and looked through the window.

Carson was striding along beside the blonde and not with his usual smooth gait. He was almost stomping toward his black sedan.

Carlie started coughing and almost couldn't stop.

"You okay?" Cash asked with concern.

"Got…choked on the air, I guess," she laughed. She could barely stop. "Gosh, do you think she bathes in that perfume?"

"Go outside and take a break. I'll turn the AC on for a few minutes to clear the room," Cash said abruptly. "Go on."

She wasn't about to go out front and risk running into

Carson and his beautiful companion. "I'll just step out back," she managed, still coughing.

She got outside and leaned against the door, dragging in deep breaths until she was able to get her breath again. There must be something in that perfume that she was allergic to. Although, come to think of it, she'd almost choked sitting next to a woman in church the week before who'd been wearing a musky sort of perfume. She'd learned long ago that she could only manage the lightest of floral colognes, and not very often. Funny, her lungs giving her so much trouble over scent, and she didn't even smoke.

She went back inside after a couple of minutes. Cash was talking to two patrolmen who'd stopped by with a legal question about a traffic stop.

She went back to her desk and sat down.

"You should see your doctor," Cash said when the patrolmen went out.

She raised both eyebrows. "He's married."

He burst out laughing. "That's not what I meant, Carlie. I think you had a reaction to Ms. Harris's perfume."

"Too much perfume bothers me sometimes, it's just allergies." She shrugged. "I have a problem with pollen, too."

"Okay. If you say so."

"I'll get the files in better order," she offered.

"Don't let some outsider's comment worry you," he said curtly. "Women like that one tear holes in everything they touch."

"She was very beautiful."

"So are some snakes."

He turned and went back into his office. Carlie tried

not to mind that Carson's elegant girlfriend had treated her like dirt. She tried to pretend that it didn't bother her, that Carson hadn't brought her into the office deliberately to flaunt her.

If only I was beautiful, she thought to herself. I'd be twice as pretty as his friend there, and I'd have oodles of money and the best clothes and drive an expensive car. And I'd stick my nose up at him!

Fine words. Now, if she could only manage to forget the miserable afternoon. She was going to a dance, with a nice man. There might be an eligible man there who'd want to dance with her when he saw her pretty dress.

She smiled. It was a gorgeous dress, and she was going to look very nice. Even if she wasn't blonde.

THE LIMOUSINE WASN'T what she expected. It wasn't one of the long, elegant ones she'd seen in movies. It was just a sedan.

"Sorry," Robin said when they were underway, the glass partition raised between them and the driver. "I did order the stretch, but they only had one and somebody got there before I did. Some local guy, too, darn the luck."

"It's okay," she said, smiling. "I'm just happy I didn't have to bring my truck!"

He laughed. Then he frowned. "Carlie, why aren't you wearing a coat?" he asked. He moved quickly to turn up the heat. "It's freezing out!"

"I don't have a nice coat, Robin," she said, apologizing. "I didn't want to embarrass you by wearing something ratty..."

"Oh, for God's sake, Carlie," he muttered. "We've known each other since first grade. I don't care what the coat looks like, I just don't want you to get sick."

She smiled. "You really are the nicest man I know. Lucky Lucy!"

He laughed. "Well, at least she and I will get to dance together," he said, sighing. "You're so kind to do this for us." He shook his head. "I've tried everything I know to make her folks like me. They just can't get past who my grandfather was. Some grudge, huh?"

"I know." She searched his dark eyes. "You and Lucy should elope."

"Don't I wish." He grimaced. "When I get established in my own business, that's exactly what I have in mind. They're pushing Lucy at the guy who's bringing her tonight. He's old money from up around Fort Worth. She likes him but she doesn't want to marry him."

"They can't make her," she pointed out.

"No, they can't. She's as stubborn as I am."

THEY PULLED UP at the door to the civic center, just behind the stretch limousine that belonged to the same car service Robin had used.

"There's our car. At least, the car I wanted to order for us." He frowned. "Who is that?" he added.

Carlie didn't say, but she knew. It was Carson, resplendent in an immaculate dinner jacket. Getting out of the vehicle beside him was the blonde woman, in a saucy black gown that hugged every curve from shoulder to ankle, and left a lot of bare skin in between. Her breasts were almost completely uncovered except for a bit of fabric in strategic places, and her long skirt had a split so far up the thigh that you could almost see her panty line.

"Well, that's going to go over big in conservative Jacobsville," Robin muttered as the driver opened the backseat door for them. "A half-naked woman at a dance benefiting the local church orphanage."

"Maybe she'll get cold and put more clothes on," Carlie mused, only half-jokingly.

"Let's get you inside before you freeze," he added, taking her hand to pull her toward the building.

There was a crowd. Carlie spotted the chief and his beautiful wife, Tippy, over in a corner talking over glasses of punch. Rourke was standing with them. He looked oddly handsome in his formal attire. Tippy was exquisite in a pale green silk gown, decked out in emeralds and diamonds. Her long, red-gold hair was up in a French twist, secured with an emerald and diamond clasp. She looked like the world-class model she'd once been.

Close at hand was Lucy Tims, wearing a long blue gown with a rounded neckline, her black hair hanging down her back like a curtain. She was standing with a tall, lean man who seemed far more interested in talking to two of the local cattlemen than with his date.

She waved to Robin, said something to the tall man, who nodded, and made a beeline for Carlie and Robin.

"You made it!" Lucy enthused. "Oh, Carlie, bless you!" she added, hugging the other woman.

"You may call me Cupid," Carlie whispered into her ear, laughing.

"I certainly will. You don't know how grateful we are."

"Yes, she does because I told her all the way over here," Robin chuckled. "Shall we get some punch?"

"Great idea." Carlie looked down at the spotless green velvet dress. "On second thought, the punch is purple and I'm clumsy. I think I'll just look for a bottle of water!"

They both laughed as she left them.

Well, at least she didn't see Carson and his new appendage, she thought, grateful for small blessings. She walked down the table with a small plate, studying the various delicacies and grateful that food was provided. She'd been too nervous to eat anything.

She was trying to decide between cheese straws and bacon-wrapped sausages when she felt the plate taken from her hand.

She started to protest, but Carson had her by the hand and he was leading her out toward the dance floor.

"You...didn't ask," she blurted out.

He turned her into his arms and slid his fingers into hers. "I didn't have to," he said at her forehead.

Her heart was beating so hard that she knew he had to feel it. He had her wrapped up against him, so close that she could almost taste his skin. He was wearing just a hint of a very masculine cologne. His shirtfront was spotless. His black tie was ruffled. Just above her eyes she could see the smooth tan of his jaw.

He moved with such grace that she felt as if she had two left feet. She was stiff because it disturbed her to be so close to him. Her hand, entwined with his, was cold as ice. She could just barely get enough air to breathe.

"Your boyfriend's dancing with someone else," he observed.

She could have told him that she didn't have a boyfriend, that she was only helping play Cupid, but it wasn't her secret to tell.

"Will you relax?" he said at her ear, shaking her gently. "It's like dancing with a board."

She swallowed. "I was getting something to eat."

"The food will still be there when you go back."

She stopped protesting. But it was impossible to relax. She followed him mechanically, vaguely aware that the song they were playing was from the musical *South Pacific* and that the evening actually did seem enchanted. Now.

"Whose tombstone were you talking to?" he asked after a minute.

She cleared her throat. "Nobody was around."

"I was."

"You weren't supposed to be there."

He shrugged.

She drew in a steadying breath and stared at his shirt. "I took my mother a bouquet," she said after a minute. "I go by the cemetery and talk to her sometimes." She looked up belligerently. "I know it's not normal."

He searched her soft green eyes. "Normal is subjective. I used to talk to my mother, too, after she was gone."

"Oh." She glanced down again because it was like a jolt of lightning to look into those black eyes.

His fingers became caressing in between her own where they rested on top of his dinner jacket. "I was six when she died," he said.

"I was fourteen."

"How did she die?"

"Of cancer," she said on a long breath. "It took months. At least, until she went into hospital. Then it was so fast…" She hesitated. "How did your mother die?"

He didn't answer.

She groaned inside. She'd done it again. She couldn't seem to stop asking stupid questions…!

His hand contracted. "My father was drunk. She'd burned the bread. She tried to get away. I got in front of him with a chair. He took it away and laid it across my head. When I came to, it was all over."

She stopped dancing and looked up at him, her eyes wide and soft.

"She was very beautiful," he said quietly. "She sang to me when I was little."

"I'm so sorry," she said, and meant every word.

He smoothed his fingers over hers. "They took him away. There was a trial. One of her brothers was in prison, serving a life sentence for murder. He had the bad luck to be sent to the same cell block."

She studied his hard, lean face. She didn't say anything. She didn't have to. Her eyes said it for her.

The hand that was holding hers let go. It went to her face and traced the tear down to the corner of her full, soft mouth. It lingered there, the knuckle of his forefinger moving lazily over the pretty line of her lips.

She felt on fire. Her legs were like rubber. She could feel her heart beating. She knew he could, because his eyes suddenly went down to the discreet rounded neckline, and lower, watching the fabric jump with every beat of her heart, with her strained breathing.

Her whole body felt tight, swollen. She shivered just a little from the intensity of a feeling she'd never experienced before. She swallowed. Her mouth was so dry…

"You'd be a pushover, little girl," he whispered in a deep, gentle tone as he looked at her soft mouth. "It wouldn't even be a challenge."

"I…know," she managed in a broken tone.

His head bent. She felt his breath on her lips. She felt as if she were vibrating from the sensuous touch of his hand at her waist, pulling her close to the sudden, blunt hardness of his body.

He was burning. Hungry. Aching. On fire to touch her under that soft bodice, to feel her breasts under his lips. He wanted to push her down on the floor here, right here, and press himself full length against her and feel her wanting him. Her heartbeat was shaking them both. She was dying for him. He knew it. He could have her. She wouldn't even try to stop him. He could take her outside, into the night. He could feed on her soft mouth in the darkness, bend her to his will, back her up against the wall and…

"Carson!"

"CARSON!" THE STRIDENT voice came again.

The second time, Carson heard it. He steeled himself to look away from Carlie's rapt, shocked face and slowly let her move away from him.

He turned to Lanette. She was glaring at them.

"You promised me the first dance," she accused, pouting.

He managed to look unperturbed. "So I did. If you'll excuse me?" he asked Carlie without actually meeting her eyes.

She nodded. "Of course."

He took Lanette's hand and moved to the other side of the room.

Carlie was almost shaking. She went back to the buffet table mechanically and picked up another plate.

"Might better calm down a little before you try to eat," Rourke murmured. He took the plate away from her, just as Carson had, and pulled her onto the dance floor. "Just as well to escape before complications arise," he added with a chuckle. "You seem to be the subject of some heated disagreement."

She tossed a covert glance toward the other side of the room where Carson and his date appeared to be exchanging terse comments.

"I was just trying to get something to eat," she began.

He studied her. "That's a nice young man you came in with. Very polite. Odd, how he's ignoring you."

She looked up at him. "Private matter," she said.

"Ah. So many things are, yes?"

The way he said it amused her. She laughed.

"That's better," he replied, smiling. "You were looking a bit like the hangman's next victim."

She lowered her eyes to his shirt. It had ruffles, and crimson edging. He had a red carnation in the lapel of the jacket. "You're not quite conventional," she blurted out.

"Never," he agreed. "I like to buck the odds. Our friend over there is Mr. Conservative," he added. "He doesn't like the assumption of ownership, so you can figure the beautiful companion will be gone quite soon."

She tried not to look pleased.

He tilted her face up to his and he wasn't smiling. "That being said, let me give you some sound advice. He's living on heartache and looking for temporary relief. Do you get me?"

She bit her lip. She nodded.

"Good. You remember that. I've seen him walk on hearts

wearing hobnailed boots, and he enjoys it. He's getting even."

"But I haven't done anything to him," she began.

"Wrong assumption. He's paying back someone else. Don't ask," he said. "I'm not privy to his past. But I know the signs."

There was such bitterness in his voice that she just stared at him.

"Long story," he said finally. "And no, I won't share it. You just watch your step. Carson's big trouble for a little innocent like you."

"I'm the only one of my kind," she said a little sadly. "Everybody says I'm out of step with the world."

"Would you enjoy being used like a cocktail napkin and tossed in the bin after?" he asked bluntly.

She caught her breath at the imagery.

"I thought not." He drew her back into the dance. "That platinum-armored blond tank he's with doesn't care what she's asked to do if the price is right," he said with icy disdain. "She's for sale and she doesn't care who knows it."

"How do you know…?"

He looked down at her with weary cynicism. "This isn't my first walk round the park," he replied. "She's the sort to go on the attack if anything gets between her and something she wants."

"Well, he doesn't want me," she said, "but thanks for the warning."

He chuckled. "Not to worry, I'll be around."

"Thanks, Rourke."

"Stanton."

She pulled back and looked up at him with real interest. "Stanton?"

He smiled. "It's my first name. I only share it with friends."

She smiled back, shyly. "Thanks."

"And *Carlie?* Is it your name or a nickname?"

She looked around to make sure nobody was close enough to hear. "Carlotta," she whispered. "My mother thought it sounded elegant."

"Carlotta." He smiled gently. "It suits you."

"Just don't tell anyone," she pleaded.

"Your secret's safe with me," he promised.

She was remembering Lanette's nasty comment about her desk, right in front of her boss. She imagined the other woman was furious that she'd even danced with Carson. She just hoped there wouldn't be a price to pay.

APPARENTLY CARSON DIDN'T like possessive women, because Carlie had no sooner finished her small plate of canapés than he was back again. He stopped by the bandleader and made a request. Then he went straight to Carlie, took the punch out of her hand and led her to the dance floor.

"That's a tango," she protested. "I can't even do a two-step…!"

"I lead, you follow," he said quietly. He shot a look of pure malice at the blonde, who was standing across the room with an angry expression.

"You're getting even," she accused as the band began to play again.

"Count on it," he snarled.

He pulled her close and began to move with exquisite grace. He stopped abruptly, turned, and in a series of intricate steps, wound his legs around hers.

It shocked her that he was so easy to follow in such a hard dance. She laughed self-consciously. "This doesn't look like tangos in movies," she began.

"That's Hollywood," he mused. "This is how they do it in Argentina. People go to dance halls and do it with strangers. It's considered part of the culture. Strangers passing in the night."

"I see."

He pulled her close again, enjoying the soft feel of her slender young body in his arms. She smelled just faintly of roses. "Have you ever been to South America?"

"You're kidding, right?" She gasped as he pulled her suddenly closer and made a sharp turn, holding her so that she didn't stumble.

"Why would I be kidding?" he asked.

"I've never been any place in my life except San Antonio."

He frowned. "Never?"

"Never." She sighed. "I went up with Tommy Tyler once in his airplane when he bought it. It was one of those little Cessna planes. I threw up. I was so embarrassed that I never wanted to get on an airplane again."

He chuckled deeply. "I imagine he was unsettled, as well."

"He was so nice. That just made it worse. I apologized until we landed. He got somebody to come and clean it up. To his credit, he even offered me another ride. But I wouldn't go."

"Were you serious about him?"

"Oh, not that way. He was in his fifties, with grown children," she chuckled. "His wife and my mother were great friends."

"People around here are clannish."

"Yes. Most of us have been here for several generations. I had a teacher in grammar school who taught my grandfather and my mother."

He looked down at her curiously as he did another series of intricate steps, drawing her along with him. The close contact was very disturbing. He loved it. He glanced at the blonde, who was steaming. He enjoyed that. He didn't like possessive women.

Carlie followed his glance. "She'll be out for blood soon," she murmured.

"Which is none of your business." He said it gently, but his tone didn't invite comment.

She clenched her teeth and tried not to give away how hungry the contact was making her. She was astonished at how easy a partner he was. The tango was one of the hardest dances to master, she'd heard. She'd always wanted to try it, but she'd never had a date who could actually dance.

Carson could. He was light on his feet for such a big man, and very skilled. She didn't let herself think about how many partners he must have had to be so good on the dance floor. She drew in a quick breath. She was getting winded already. It irritated her that she couldn't run or even walk fast for long without needing to stop and catch her breath.

She'd never have admitted it to Carson. The feel of his body against hers was intoxicating. She felt his hand firm at her waist, his fingers curled around hers, as he led her around the dance floor.

She was vaguely aware that they were being watched by more people than just the angry blonde, and that the police chief and his wife had taken the dance floor with them.

Cash was a master at the tango. He and Tippy moved like one person. He danced closer to them, and winked. "You're outclassed, kid," he told Carson. "But not bad. Not bad at all."

Carson laughed. "Don't rest on your laurels. I'm practicing."

"I noticed," Cash said with a grin at Carlie, and he danced Tippy, who also smiled at them, to the other part of the dance floor.

Several other couples came out, trying to keep up with the two accomplished couples on the floor. Their attempts ranged from amusing to disastrous.

Carson's chest rose and fell with deep, soft laughter. "I think square dancing has a larger following in this vicinity than the tango," he pointed out.

"Well, not many men can dance. Even square-dance," she added shyly.

He slowed his movements, and held her even closer, his head bent to hers so that she could feel his breath, smell its minty tang, on her mouth. "My mother danced," he whispered. "She was like a fairy on her feet. She usually won the women's dances at powwows."

She looked up into liquid black eyes. "The Lakota have powwows?"

He nodded. "It's what we call them. The first in is the drum. Several men sit around it and play, but it's always called the drum. There are men's dances and women's dances. They're very old."

She nodded. "I went to a powwow up near San Antonio once," she recalled. "There were Comanche people there."

His fingers moved sensuously against hers. "I have Comanche cousins."

"Your people are clannish, too," she remarked.

"Very. Both sides."

"Both sides?"

"One of my great-great-grandmothers was blonde and blue-eyed," he said. "She married a Lakota man. He was a rather famous detective in Chicago at the turn of the twentieth century. He was at Wounded Knee. She nursed him back to health. Later, he was with Buffalo Bill's Wild West show for a time."

She wouldn't have mentioned it, but his skin was a light olive shade. She'd guessed that his blood was mixed.

"That must have been one interesting courtship," she said.

He chuckled. "So I'm told." He searched over her face. "Your father has Norwegian ancestors somewhere."

"Yes, from someplace with a name I can't even pronounce. I never met any of his people. He didn't come back here until I was thirteen..." Her voice trailed away. She didn't like thinking about that. "Mama had pictures of him, but I only saw him a few times when I was growing up. He'd stay for a day or two and go away again, and Mama would cry for weeks after."

He scowled. "Why didn't he stay with her?"

She stared at his shirtfront as the music began to wind down. "They argued once. I heard. He said that she trapped him into marrying her because I was on the way. I wouldn't speak to him after that when he came home. I never told him why. It wasn't until she was dying that he came home. He's…different now."

"That's what I've heard from other people who knew him. He seems to enjoy the life he has now."

"He says he has to do a lot of good to make up for the bad things he used to do," she replied. "He won't talk about them. At least, he wouldn't. Rourke had supper with us and he and Daddy talked about old times. It was fascinating."

"Rourke?"

She smiled. "He's really nice. He likes my cooking, too."

His hand on her waist contracted as if he were angry. "Rourke's more of a lobo wolf than I am. You'll break your heart on him."

She looked up at him with wide, shocked eyes. "What?"

He pulled her closer, bent her against his body in such a sensual way that she gasped. His head lowered until his mouth was almost touching hers as he twirled her around to the deepening throb of the music. "But better him than me, baby," he whispered at her soft mouth. "I don't do forever. Even a child on the way wouldn't change that."

She was barely hearing him. He'd called her "baby." No man had ever called her that, and certainly not in such a sexy, hungry sort of tone. She felt herself shiver as his hand smoothed up her rib cage, stopping just under her breast on the soft fabric. And she couldn't even protest.

She felt as if her body was going to explode from the tension he raised in it. She bit off a soft moan as she felt him drag her even closer, so that she was pressed against him from breasts to hips.

In all her life, she'd never felt a man become aroused, but he wanted her, and he couldn't hide it. She shivered again, her heart beating so hard that she thought it might break out of her chest.

"You...shouldn't," she choked.

His cheek rasped against hers. "You'd be the sweetest honey I ever had," he breathed at her ear. "I'd go so hard into you that you'd go up like a rocket."

She moaned and hid her face, shocked, embarrassed...excited. Her nails bit into his jacket. Her body moved against his helplessly as his long leg moved in and out between hers as the dance slowly wound down.

He arched her against him as it ended, positioning her so that her head was down and leaning back, his mouth poised just over hers.

She held on for dear life. Her eyes were locked into his, imprisoned, helpless. He pulled her up with exquisite slowness, held her against him while people clapped. Neither of them noticed.

He let her go, his cheeks ruddy, as if he were angry and unsettled by what had happened. He had to recite math problems in his mind to force his body to relax before he let her go. She wouldn't realize what was going on, but that blonde would see it immediately.

"You dance well," he said stiffly. "All you need is practice."

She swallowed. "Thanks. You're…amazing."

His eyes, narrow and wise, searched hers. "You have no idea how amazing, in the right circumstances," he whispered huskily, his eyes falling to her mouth. "And if you're very lucky, you won't find out."

She felt her heart shaking her. She knew he must be able to feel it, too. She could barely get her breath. Funny, it felt as if air could get in but couldn't get back out. She coughed slightly.

He frowned. "What's wrong?"

"Perfume," she faltered. "It bothers me sometimes."

He arched an eyebrow. "I don't wear perfume."

"Not you," she muttered. "Other women."

He sniffed the air and smiled. "Florals, musk, woodsy tones," he said. His eyes smoothed over her face. "You smell of roses."

"I love roses," she told him.

"Do you?"

She nodded. "I grow them at home. Antique roses. My mother used to plant them."

"My mother was an herbalist," he replied. "She could cure anything."

"The music has stopped," the blonde pointed out coldly.

Carlie and Carson turned and looked at her blankly.

"And I'd like some punch, if you please?" Lanette added icily.

Carson let Carlie go. He hadn't realized that the music

had stopped, or that he and Carlie were standing so close together…alone on the dance floor.

"I'll be back in a minute," he told Lanette. He let go of Carlie's hand and moved toward the restrooms.

Carlie, left alone with the overperfumed blond wildcat, braced herself for what she knew to expect.

"WELL, THAT WAS an exhibition if I ever saw one!" Her pale blue eyes were like ice. "Don't you get any ideas about Carson, you little hick secretary. He's mine. Hands off. Do you understand me?"

Carlie just stared at her with equally cold green eyes. She was still shaking inside from Carson's sensual dance and the things he'd said to her. But she wasn't going to let the other woman cow her. "That's his choice."

"Well, he's not choosing you. I'm not kidding," the other woman persisted. She smiled coldly. "You think you're something, don't you?" She looked Carlie up and down. "Did your dress come from some bargain basement up in San Antonio?" she asked sarcastically. "Marked down 75 percent, perhaps?" she added and laughed when Carlie blushed. "And those shoes. My God, they must be ten years old! I'm surprised he wasn't embarrassed to be seen dancing with you in that dress…!"

"Got yours at a consignment sale, darling?" came a soft, purring voice from beside Carlie.

Tippy Grier moved closer, cradling a cup of punch in her hands. She looked elegant in her green silk gown, dripping diamonds and emeralds. She smiled at the blonde. "That particular dress was in a collection of only five gowns. I recognize it because I know the designer," she added, watching the blonde's eyes widen. "It isn't to my taste," she added, "because I don't sell myself."

"How dare you…I was on the runway!" Lanette almost spat at her, reddening.

"Honey, the only runway you've been on is at the airport," Tippy drawled. She looked down. "Those shoes are two seasons out of date, too, but I suppose you thought nobody would notice." She pursed her bow lips in a mock pout. "Shame."

Lanette's hands were clenched at her sides.

"Run along now, kitty cat," Tippy dismissed her. "Your saucer of cream's waiting outside the door." She smiled. "Do have a lovely evening."

Lanette was almost sputtering. She turned and went storming off toward Carson, who was just returning. She ran into his arms, making a big production of crying, wiping at her eyes, and gesturing toward Tippy and Carlie. The look Carson gave Carlie was livid before he took Lanette's arm and walked her toward the front door.

"WOW," CARLIE SAID to Tippy. She shook her head. "You're just incredible! I didn't even have a comeback."

Tippy laughed. It sounded like silver bells. Her reddish-gold hair burned like fire in the lights from overhead. Her green eyes, lighter than Carlie's, twinkled. "I've seen her kind in modeling. They think they're so superior." Her smile was mischievous. "When I was new to the runway, there was this terrible woman from upstate New York who made fun of everything from my big feet to my accent. I cried a lot. Then I got tough." She pursed her lips. "You know, if you time it just right, you can trip someone on the runway and make it look like a terrible accident!"

"You wicked woman," Carlie gasped, laughing.

"She really did have it coming." She shook her head. "I almost felt sorry for her. She lost her contract with the designer. She didn't work for six months. When she finally got another job, she was a different person." Her green eyes glittered. "I hate people like that woman. I know what it is to be poor."

"Thanks," Carlie said. "I couldn't think of a thing to say. It is a sale dress, and my shoes are really old."

"Carlie, you look lovely," Tippy told her solemnly. "It doesn't matter how much the dress cost if it flatters you. And it does." She smiled. "I hope she tells Carson what I said to her."

"If she does, he might have something to say to you."

Tippy laughed again. "He can take it up with my husband," she replied, and raised her cup of punch to her lips.

"HOW WAS THE DANCE?" Reverend Blair asked when Carlie came in the front door.

"It was very nice," she said.

He moved closer, his eyes probing. "What happened?"

She drew in a breath. "Carson danced with me and his girlfriend got really angry. She said some really unpleasant things to me."

His pale blue eyes took on a glitter. "Perhaps I should speak to her."

She smiled. "Tippy Grier spoke to her."

"Say no more. I've heard about Mrs. Grier's temper."

"She was eloquent," Carlie said. She shook her head. "And she never said a single bad word the whole time."

"Good for her. You don't have to use bad words to express yourself. Well, unless you're trying to start a lawnmower," he amended.

She pursed her lips. "Daddy, you think 'horsefeathers' is a bad word."

He frowned. "It is!"

She laughed. "Well, I did enjoy the dancing. Rourke is really light on his feet."

"Yes." He gave her a concerned look.

She waved a hand at him. "No way I'd take on that South African wildcat," she said. "I have a good head on my shoulders."

He seemed relieved.

"I'm going on up. You sleep well, Daddy."

"You, too, pumpkin," he replied with a smile.

SHE WAS HALF-ASLEEP when her cell phone rang. She picked it up and punched the button. "Hello?" she asked drowsily.

There was a pause. "It will come when you least expect it," came an odd-sounding masculine voice. "And your father won't walk away." The connection was broken.

"Right." She turned off the phone and closed her eyes. She'd remember to tell her father in the morning, but the last threat about her father had never materialized, nor had any threat against herself. She was beginning to think that it was a campaign of terror. If so, it wasn't going to work. She refused to live her life afraid.

But she did say an extra prayer at church the next day. Just to be on the safe side.

HER FATHER WASN'T at the breakfast table Monday morning. She had a cup of coffee and two pieces of toast and paused to check the truck over before she started it. She wasn't afraid, but caution wasn't too high a price to pay for safety.

She got into the office, put her coat away and shoved her purse under the desk. She pushed her hair back. It was a damp morning, so her naturally wavy hair was curling like crazy because of the humidity.

She turned the mail out of its bag onto the desk. She'd stopped by the post office, as she did every morning on her way to work. There was a lot of it to go through before the chief came in. She made coffee and shared it with one of the patrolmen. He went out, leaving the office empty.

She sat down at her desk and picked up a letter opener. She'd just started on the first letter when the door opened and a cold wind came in.

Carson was furious. His black eyes were snapping like flames. He stopped in front of the desk.

"What the hell did you say to Lanette Saturday night?" he demanded.

She blinked. "I didn't—"

"She was so upset she couldn't even talk," he said angrily. "She cried all the way home. Then she phoned me this morning, still in tears, and said she was having to go to the doctor for anxiety meds because of the upset."

"I didn't say anything to her," she repeated.

His eyes narrowed. "Don't get ideas."

"Excuse me?"

"It was only two dances," he said in a mocking tone. "Not a marriage proposal. I've told you before, you're not the sort of woman who appeals to me. In any way."

She stood up. "Thank God."

He just stared at her. He didn't speak.

"Your girlfriend was showing more skin than a bikini model," she pointed out. "Obviously that's the sort of woman you like, one who advertises everything she's got in the front window, right? You know why you like her? Because she's temporary. She's a throwaway. She's not the sort of woman who'd want anything to do with a permanent relationship or children..."

His face went hard. His black eyes glittered. "That's enough."

She bit her lip. "You're right, it's none of my business. But just for the record," she added angrily, "you're the sort of man I'd run from as fast as my legs would carry me. You think you're irresistible? You, with your notched bedpost and years of one-night stands? God only knows what sorts of diseases you've exposed yourself to...!"

The insult put a fire under him. He started toward her with blood in his eye, bent on intimidation. The movement was quick, threatening, dangerous. The shock of it took her stumbling backward toward the wall. On the way, she grabbed a chair and held it, trembling, legs out, toward him while she cursed herself for her stupid runaway tongue.

He stopped suddenly. He realized, belatedly, that she was afraid of him. Her face was chalk-white. The chair she'd suspended in midair was shaking, like her slender young body. She was gasping for breath. Wheezing. Coughing.

He frowned.

"Don't…!" she choked, swallowing, coughing again.

The door opened. "What in the hell…?"

"Stay with her," Carson said curtly, running past Cash. He made a dash to his car, grabbed his medical kit and burst back in the door just as Cash was taking the chair from Carlie and putting her firmly down in it.

"Grab her driver's license," he ordered Cash as he unzipped the kit. He pulled a cell phone out of his slacks. "Who's her doctor?"

"Lou Coltrain," Cash replied.

Carlie couldn't speak. She couldn't even breathe.

She heard Carson talking to someone on the other end of the phone. She heard her boss relaying statistics. Why did they need her weight? She couldn't breathe. It felt as if the air was stuck inside her lungs and couldn't get out. She heard a weird whistling sound. Was that her?

Carson tore open packages. He swabbed the bend of her elbow and pulled up a liquid from a small bottle into a syringe. He squirted out a drop.

"This may hurt. I'm sorry." He drove the needle into her arm. His face was like stone. He was almost as pale as she was.

Her breathing began to ease, just a little. Tears sprung from her eyes and ran, hot, down her cheeks.

"Call the emergency room," Carson told Cash. "Tell them I'm bringing her in. She needs to be checked by a physician."

"All right," Cash said tightly. "Then we'll have a talk."

Carson nodded curtly. He handed Carlie her purse, picked her up in his arms and carried her out the door.

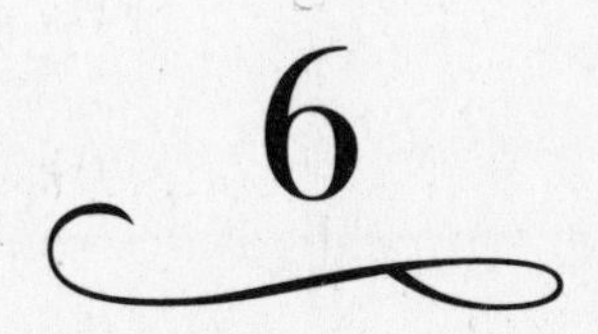

OUTSIDE, A PATROL car was waiting, its lights flashing like mad.

"Chief said for me to lead you to the emergency room," the patrolman called to Carson.

"Thanks," he said. He put Carlie in the passenger seat, strapped her in and threw himself behind the steering wheel.

He ran two red lights, right behind the police car. It was only a short drive to the hospital, but he wanted to get Carlie there as quickly as he could. Her color was still bad, although she was breathing a little easier.

"Damn…you," she cursed, sobbing.

"Yes," he rasped. He glanced at her as he pulled up at the emergency entrance. "God, I'm sorry!"

He got out, unfastened her seat belt and carried her right

past the waiting gurney with its attendant, past the clerk, back into a waiting room, trailing irritated people.

"Dr. Coltrain is ready for her, we called ahead," he said over his shoulder.

"Is that Carlie?" the clerk exclaimed. "Is she all right?"

"Not really," Carson said in a rough tone. He carried her into a treatment room. Seconds later, a blonde woman in a white lab coat came in, a stethoscope around her neck.

"Are you the one who called me from her office?" she asked, glancing at Carson. "You said that she was upset and having trouble breathing."

"Yes," Carson said quietly. "I'd bet my left arm on asthma."

"Asthma?" Dr. Lou Coltrain frowned at him.

She turned to Carlie, who was still gasping. "Epinephrine. You said on the phone that you were giving her epinephrine."

"Yes," Carson replied tersely. He reminded her of the dosage. "I checked her weight on her driver's license first."

She nodded. "Fran, bring me an inhaler," she said to a nurse nearby. She gave the name brand and the dosage. "Hurry."

"Yes, Doctor," the woman said, and went to get it.

Lou examined Carlie, aware that she was glaring at the man who'd brought her in. He had his hands shoved deep in his pockets and he looked as if somebody had cut the life out of him. She didn't have to guess what had prompted Carlie's attack. Guilt was written all over him.

"She has no history of asthma," Lou said.

"Allergies to perfume, difficulty breathing after exertion, coughing fits," Carson said.

Lou frowned as she glanced at him. "Sporadic?"

"Very. Difficult to diagnose without proper equipment. I'd recommend an allergist."

"Yes. So would I."

She finished her examination. Fran was back with the inhaler. Lou instructed her in its use and waited until she'd taken several puffs.

"You're lucky that you had no underlying heart conditions, like a sinus node issue," Lou said as she watched Carlie suck in the meds. "Epinephrine can kill someone with a serious arrhythmia." She glanced at Carson. "You knew that."

He nodded. His face was solemn, still. He didn't add anything to the nod.

"One more puff, and then I want you to lie there and rest. I'll be back to check on you in a minute. Feeling better?" Lou asked Carlie, and smiled as she smoothed the ruffled wavy dark hair.

"Much. Thanks, Lou."

Lou turned to Carson. "Can I speak with you?"

He glanced at Carlie. She averted her eyes. He sighed and followed Lou into an empty treatment room nearby.

Lou turned, pinning him with pale eyes. "You know too much for a layman."

"Field medic in the military," he replied.

She pursed her lips. "Try again."

He drew in a breath. She was quick. Nobody else had ever questioned his skills. "I finished medical school and got my degree. I'd have gone into an internship after, but I quit."

"I thought so. Why did you quit?"

His face closed up. "Personal issues. Serious ones. I went off the deep end for a few years."

"I think you're still there," Lou replied. "Off the deep end, I mean." She jerked her head toward Carlie. "What do you know about her?"

"A hell of a lot more than I thought I did, after the past few minutes," he said flatly. "We had an argument. My fault. I'm hotheaded and I was…frustrated. I started toward her…" He held up a hand when she looked ready to explode. "I've never hit a woman in my life," he interrupted, his black eyes flashing. "My father beat my mother to death in a drunken fit. He went to prison and he was killed by one of her relatives who was serving life on a murder charge. I know more about violence than you have time to hear."

Her face relaxed, just a little. "I'm sorry."

"I would never have struck her. I just went closer." He drew in a breath and leaned back against the block wall, his arms crossed over his chest, his eyes sad. "She backed away and picked up a chair to hold me at bay. That's when I noticed that she was barely able to breathe. I frightened her. I don't know why. Unless there's some violence in her past that I'm not aware of."

"There is," Lou said quietly. "But I don't discuss patients." She smiled to soften the words.

"I understand."

"You reacted very quickly. You may have saved her life."

She studied him from across the cubicle. "You also treated Sheriff Hayes Carson when you rescued him and Minette, across the border. You know, doctors are getting thin on the ground. Except for specialists, there's just me and Copper," she added, referring to her husband, also a physician, "and Micah Steele."

His face tautened. "I'm doing a job I like."

"Really?"

He averted his eyes.

"I'm no psychologist," she said after a minute, "but even I can see through the anger. You're hiding, inside yourself."

"Don't we all do that?" he asked.

"To some extent, yes." She smiled. "I'll stop. I just hate to see waste. You surely don't want to spend the rest of your life feeding people to crocodiles?" she added.

He groaned. "Does everybody know everything in this town?"

"Pretty much," she agreed. "We don't have secrets from each other. We're family," she explained. "We come from all backgrounds, all cultures, all religions. But there are so few of us in Jacobsville and Comanche Wells that we think of ourselves as just one big family."

"Not what I connected with small towns," he confessed. "And I don't share my secrets."

"You never carry ID with you," she began. "You work for Cy Parks, but Eb Scott sends you on assignments periodically. You have a very bad reputation for being a womanizer. You don't drink or smoke, you keep to yourself, and you and Rourke are friends."

"Damn," he muttered.

"See?" she added smugly. "Family."

He shouldered away from the wall. "Not for long. I'm moving on soon."

"Because of Carlie." She laughed softly.

He glared at her. "Because I don't stay in one place long. Ever."

She crossed her arms with a sigh. "You can't run away from the past," she said gently. "It's portable. No matter how far you go, it travels with you. Until you come to grips with it, face what you're running away from, you'll never be satisfied."

"Well, if it catches up with me, it had better be wearing track shoes," he replied. He stood erect. "I need to get Carlie home."

"She's more fragile than she looks," Lou said surprisingly. "Try not to hurt her too much."

He didn't say a word. He just walked by her.

CARLIE REFUSED TO be carried. She walked out the front door beside him, slowly, although her breathing was easier.

"I have to go to the pharmacy," she began.

"I'll drive you. Don't argue," he said heavily. "It's the least I can do."

She shrugged. "Okay. Thanks."

She got in and fastened her seat belt so that he wouldn't have to do it for her. She didn't want him any closer than necessary. He affected her too much, and her nerves were raw after what had happened.

HE DROVE HER to the pharmacy and went inside with her. Bonnie, at the counter, smiled at Carlie.

"How's it going?" she asked as Carlie handed her the prescription. She read it and grimaced. "Oh. I see how it's going."

"Can you fill it while I wait?" Carlie asked in a subdued tone.

"Sure. Let me see if we have this in stock." She went to talk to the pharmacist Nancy, who waved and smiled. Bonnie gave Carlie a thumbs-up and went to fill the order.

One of the other clerks, a new girl, who was returning from lunch, stopped by Carson and smiled. "Can I help you?" she asked in a very sweet tone.

He didn't even look at her. "I'm with her." He nodded toward Carlie.

"Oh. Okay." She gave him a hopeful look. He didn't even glance her way.

She went on to the pharmacy, smiling at Carlie.

Carlie was breathing much better, but the experience had shaken her badly. She hated showing weakness in front of the enemy. Because that's what Carson was, however much she tried to convince herself otherwise.

Filling the prescription didn't take long. Bonnie motioned her to the counter and smiled as Carlie handed her a debit card.

"Directions are on the box," Bonnie said. "I hope you feel better."

"Me, too." Carlie sighed. "Asthma. Bummer. I never even guessed I had it. Dr. Lou's sending me to an allergist, too."

"It will probably be Dr. Heinrich," Bonnie said. "He comes here every Friday to see patients. He's from San Antonio. It will save you that long drive." She looked at Carlie over her glasses as she finished ringing up the purchase, returned the card and handed Carlie the medicine in its white bag. "Especially after you were doing a hundred on the straightaway in your dad's Cobra," she added with pursed lips.

Carlie flushed. "Don't you start."

"I like you," Bonnie replied. "And I hate funerals."

"Same here!" Nancy called across the counter.

"Okay. I'll drive like an old lady," she muttered.

"Mrs. Allen is an old lady, and she pushes that Jaguar of hers over a hundred and twenty when the sheriff's deputies aren't looking," Nancy reminded her.

"I'll drive like a conventional old lady," Carlie corrected.

"Senior citizen," Bonnie whispered. "It's more politically correct!"

Carlie laughed, for the first time since the ordeal began.

THEY WERE BACK in the car. Carlie glanced at Carson, who still looked like a locked and boarded-up house. "Thanks for taking me to the pharmacy," she began.

He ignored her. He wasn't driving toward her house. He went down the highway until he spotted a roadside park by the Jacobs River. He stopped at a convenience store and parked the car.

"Come on," he said gently, helping her out.

"Where are we going?" she asked.

"Lunch." He led the way inside. She picked out a packaged ham and cheese sandwich, a bag of chips, and a soft drink. He got a roast beef sandwich and a soft drink. He paid for all of it and led her behind the store to a picnic area beside the river, complete with concrete table and benches.

The sound of the river, even in winter, was soothing. It was February, and her ratty old coat felt good, but she could have taken it off. It was warmer in the sun.

They ate in silence for several minutes. She liked being outside. When she was at home, she did all the yard work, planted a garden, tended flowers, raked leaves, did all the things she could to keep her out of the house. She loved the seasons, the rain and the rare snowfall. She was an outdoor girl at heart.

When they finished eating, he took the waste paper and put it in a container. There was a recycling bin for the soft drink cans, and he put them in it.

She started toward the car, but he caught her hand gently in his and led her down to the river. He leaned against a tree, still holding her hand.

"Your Dr. Coltrain said that I'm hiding from the past. She's right." He drew in a long breath. "I was married."

Carlie caught her breath. His hand tightened around her fingers.

"She was younger than me. Pretty, bright, full of fun. She teased me and provoked me. I loved her more than my life. We grew up together on the Wapiti Ridge Sioux Reservation in South Dakota. Our people had known each other for generations. She was several grades behind me, but we were always friends. I was in my final year of…graduate school—" he didn't want to say "medical school" "—when we went to a dance together and fell in love. Her parents thought she was too young, but we wouldn't listen. We were married by the local priest."

He hesitated, then went on. "It was a long commute for me, and expensive because I had to fly there. And I had to stay in the dorm during the week. I had a scholarship, or I could never have managed it. My people were poor." He watched the river, his eyes sad and quiet. "She got tired of staying in the little house all alone. She liked to party. She thought I was a real stick-in-the-mud because I didn't drink or smoke." He laughed hollowly. "I guess she understood the drinking part because my father was a drunkard. Everybody on the rez knew about him."

She swallowed. "They say that alcoholism is a problem in some Native American cultures…"

"My father was white," he said, and his voice was cold as ice. "He sold seed and fertilizer for a living. He met my mother at a feed store when he was restocking there. He flattered her, took her places, bought her flowers. She was crazy about him. They got married and he moved onto the rez to live with her. She didn't know he was an alcoholic until she was pregnant with me. He started beating her then, when he lost his temper." His eyes closed. "When I was six, and he was beating my mother, I tried to block him with a kitchen chair. He picked it up and laid it across my head. When I came to, she was lying on the floor, still and quiet, and he was gone. I ran for help. It was too late."

She held her breath, listening. He'd told her some of this before, but not in such detail. She could only imagine the terror he'd felt.

"He went to prison and I went to live with my mother's uncles, aunts and cousins in a small community on the rez. One of my uncles was a reservation cop. He formally adopted me in a tribal ceremony, so I call him Dad, even though he isn't really. He's great with livestock. He and my other relatives were good to me, but they were poor and we didn't have much. I wanted more. I knew the only way to get out was to get an education. So I studied like crazy. I worked at anything I could get paid for, on ranches, in stores, on the land, and I saved every penny. When I graduated from high school, I was second in my class. I got scholarships and commuted back and forth. I graduated with honors and went on to grad school. But then, suddenly, there was Jessie. I couldn't really afford to get married, but I was conventional in those days. My people were religious." He let go of Carlie's hand and folded his arms across his broad chest. His eyes had a lost, faraway look. "Things were good the first two years. But we were drifting apart. I still had a long way to go to a profession and I was away a good deal of the time. There was a man on the rez who wanted her. He bought her stuff, took her to dances, while I was at school or working after classes to help pay for the tuition. I came home one weekend, just after finals, and she was gone. She'd moved in with him."

He drew in a breath. "I tried to get her to come home, but she said she loved him and she was carrying his child. She wasn't coming back. I was sick at heart, but I couldn't force her to leave him. I went back to school and gave up the house. No reason to keep renting it just for weekends, anyway."

"I was getting ready for the graduation exercises when one of my cousins came to see me at school. Another relative back home told him that she'd lied. The child she was carrying was mine. The man she was living with couldn't have children. And worse, he was beating her. She'd just come back from the hospital. He'd beaten her so badly that she had a concussion."

His face hardened. "So I went home. I had a beat-up old car parked in Rapid City that would hardly make the trips back and forth from my house to the airport, and there were heavy floods, but I made it home. I went to see her. I told her that I knew about the child and that if she wouldn't come back to me, I'd have her boyfriend put in jail for beating her. She looked ancient," he said, his face twisting. "What she'd endured was written all over her. But she loved him, she told me. She was very sorry, but she loved him. I could see the child when it came, but she wasn't leaving him, even if I refused to give her a divorce."

He swallowed. "He drove up. We exchanged words. He said no way was she leaving him. He grabbed her by the hand and dragged her out to his car. I tried to stop him, but he was a big guy and I had no combat skills at the time. He wiped the floor with me. He threw her into his car and took off. I picked myself up, got in my own car and chased after him."

He shook his head. "I don't know what I thought I could do. She wanted to stay with him and he wasn't going to give her up. But I knew if she stayed he'd kill her one day, just as my father had killed my mother. And my child would die with her.

"He speeded up and so did I. His car was all over the road." His eyes closed. "If I'd had any sense, I'd have stopped, right then, but I didn't. He went onto a bridge that was unsafe. There was even a sign, but he didn't pay it any attention." He looked away, hesitated. "The bridge collapsed. They fell down in the car, into the river below. It was deep and in full flood." His eyes closed. He shuddered. "They found the bodies almost two days later. If they'd been found sooner, the child might have lived." He bit his lower lip. "It was a boy…"

"I'm so sorry," she whispered. Her eyes were wet. "So sorry."

He turned, pulled her to him and held her. Just held her. Rocked her. "I've never spoken of it, except once. Dalton Kirk's wife, in Wyoming, sat at a table with me and told me all about it, and she'd never met me or heard anything about me. It was a shock."

"I heard about her." She savored the feel of his jacket. It was leather, but soft and warm from his body, fringed and beaded. She'd never seen anything so beautiful. She closed her eyes. He'd frightened her earlier. Now she began to understand him, just a little.

He smoothed over her dark, wavy hair. "I would never have hit you," he whispered at her ear. "I know too much about brutality and its result."

"You move so quickly," she faltered.

"And for all the wrong reasons sometimes." He sighed. "Dalton Kirk's wife told me that my wife's boyfriend was drinking at the time. I didn't really notice, but if you drink something like vodka, others may not be able to smell it on your breath. She said that was why he went off the bridge, not because of me. I checked the police report. She was right. But it didn't help much. Nothing does. I still feel like a murderer."

"It isn't fair, to blame yourself for something like that." She drew back and looked up at him. "You aren't a person of faith."

"No," he said stiffly. "I don't believe in anything anymore."

"I believe that things happen the way they're meant to," she said softly. "That sometimes God uses people to say things or do things that hurt us, so that we learn lessons from it. My dad says that we should always remember that events in our lives have a purpose. It's all lessons. We learn from adversity."

He searched her green eyes quietly. "You're such an innocent, Carlie," he said gently, and her heart leaped because it was the first time he'd ever called her by name. "You know nothing about the world, about life."

"And you know everything," she murmured with a flash of laughter.

"I do." He traced a line down her cheek. "We're total opposites."

"What happened," she asked. "After?"

He looked over her head. "I went to my own graduation, alone, and enlisted in the military the same week. I learned how to fight, how to kill. I took the most dangerous assignments I could find. For a long time, I avoided women like the plague. Then it became second nature to take what was offered and walk away." That wasn't quite true, but he'd shared enough secrets for one day. "I never got serious about anyone again. I met Cy Parks overseas. He and his group were doing a stint as private contractors for the military, teaching tactics to locals. I fell in with them and came back here to work for Cy and, occasionally, for Eb Scott. It's an interesting life. Dangerous. Unpredictable."

"Sort of like you," Carlie mused.

He looked down into her eyes. "Sort of like me," he agreed.

She drew in a breath. It was much easier to do that now.

"I am truly sorry for what happened this morning," he said, searching her eyes. "I had no right to frighten you."

"You're scary when you lose your temper," she replied.

"Sheltered little violet, under a stair," he said softly.

"Not so much," she replied. "It just seems that way." Her own eyes were sad and quiet.

"You know my secrets. Tell me yours."

She swallowed. "When I was thirteen, my mother was diagnosed with cancer. She was in and out of hospitals for a year. During one of those times, her mother showed up." Her face hardened. "My grandmother was a pig, and that's putting it mildly. She had a reputation locally for sleeping with anything in pants. She had a boyfriend with her, a man who used drugs and supplied them to her. I had the misfortune to come home while they were ransacking my mother's bedroom, looking for things they could sell. I'd hidden Mama's expensive pearls that Daddy brought her from Japan, just in case, but they were trashing the house. I tried to stop them."

She shivered.

He pulled her closer. “Keep talking,” he said over her head.

Her small hand clenched on his jacket. “Her boyfriend picked up a beer bottle and started hitting me with it.” She shivered again. “He kept on and on and on until I was on the floor. I fought until I was so numb that I just gave up.” She laughed. “You think you can fight back, that you can save yourself in a desperate situation. But that’s not how it works. You feel such…despair, such hopelessness. After a while, it seems more sensible to just lie down and die…”

“Go on.”

“Our next-door neighbor heard me scream and called the police. They got there just in time to keep him from killing me. As it was, I had a concussion and broken ribs. I spent several days in the hospital. They took my grandmother and her boyfriend to jail. She testified against him and got off, but our police chief—one of the ones before Cash Grier—had a nice talk with her and she left town very quickly. She didn’t even apologize or come to see me. I heard later that she died from a drug overdose. He was killed in a prison riot just recently.” She shook her head. “I’ve been terrified of violent behavior ever since.”

“I can see why.”

“One of our patrolmen brought a man in handcuffs in the office once to ask the chief a question. The man grabbed a nightstick off the counter and came at me with it. I fainted.” She sighed. “The chief turned that man upside down, they said, and shook him like a rat until he dropped the nightstick. Then he threw him into the patrol car and told the officer to get him to the county detention center right then. He took me to the emergency room himself. I had to tell him why I fainted." She shrugged. "He isn't what he seems, is he?" she asked, looking up. "I mean, criminals are terrified of him. Even some local men say he's dangerous. But he was like a big brother with me. He still is."

"I respect him more than any other man I know, with the possible exception of Cy Parks."

"Mr. Parks is pretty scary, too," she added.

He smiled. "Not when you get to know him. He's had a hard life. Really hard."

"I know a little about him. It's a sad story. But he and his wife seem to be very happy."

"They are."

She searched his serious eyes. "I didn't say anything to your...date," she said quietly. "She was making fun of my dress and my old shoes." She lowered her eyes. "I didn't have a comeback. It was a bargain dress, and my shoes are really old. I didn't wear a coat because this is the only one I have—" she fingered the frayed collar "—and I didn't want to embarrass Robin by showing up in it."

He was very still. "She said that you insulted her."

"Tippy Grier did," she replied. She tried not to smile at the memory. "She was eloquent. She said that my dress looked nice on me and it didn't matter where it came from."

He let out a long breath. "Damn."

"It's all right. You didn't know."

His hand smoothed over her dark hair as he stared down at the river below. For a minute, there was only the sound of the water running heavily over the rocks. "She didn't mention Tippy."

"I just stood there," she said. "I guess she was mad that I danced with you."

His hand caught her hair at her nape and turned her face up to his. Black eyes captured hers and held them. "She was mad that I wanted you," he said curtly.

"Wa…wanted me?" She hesitated.

He let out a rough breath. "God in heaven, can't you even tell when a man wants you?" He burst out.

"Well, I don't know a lot about men," she stammered.

His hand slid down her back and plastered her hips to his. His smile was smug and worldly as he let her feel the sudden hardness of his body. "Now you do."

She flushed and pulled away from him. "Stop that."

He actually laughed. "My God," he said heavily. "I'm dying and you're running for cover." He shook his head. "Just my luck."

She swallowed. It was embarrassing. She tried to draw away completely but he held her, gently but firmly.

"Doesn't your friend Robin ever touch you?" he asked sarcastically. "Or are you having a cerebral relationship with him?"

She wasn't about to admit the truth to him. Robin felt like protection right now, and she needed some.

"He reads poetry to me," she choked. Actually, he wrote poetry about Lucy and read it to Carlie, but that was beside the point.

"Does he now?" He brushed his nose against hers and began to quote. "When I am dead, and above me bright April shakes out her rain-drenched hair, though you should lean above me broken-hearted, I shall not care. I shall have peace, as leafy trees are peaceful when rain bends down the bough; and I shall be more silent and cold-hearted than you are now," he whispered deeply, reciting lines from a poem called "I Shall Not Care," by Sara Teasdale. "It was written in 1919," he added. "Long before either of us was born."

Her heart jumped, stopped and ran away. His voice was like velvet, deep and sexy and overwhelmingly sensual. Her nails curled against the soft leather of his jacket.

"Yes, I read poetry," he whispered, his mouth hovering just above hers. "That was one of my favorites. I learned it by heart just before Jessie died."

Her mouth felt swollen. Her whole body felt swollen. "D...did you?" she asked in a voice that wasn't quite steady.

His lips brushed like a whisper over hers. "Are you sure you don't know what desire is, Carlie?" he whispered huskily.

She was almost moaning. His mouth teased hers, without coming to rest on it. His body was close, warm, powerful. She felt the heat of it all the way down. She couldn't get her breath, and this time it wasn't because of the asthma. She knew he could feel her heartbeat. She could hear it.

"Your father is going to kill me," he said roughly.

"For...what?"

"For this." And his mouth went down against hers, hard enough to bruise, hard enough to possess.

7

CARLIE WAS DYING. Her whole body was pressing toward Carson's, pleading for something she didn't quite understand. She shivered as his mouth pressed harder against hers, insistent, parting her lips so that he could possess them.

Her arms reached up, around his neck. He lifted her, riveted her body to his, as the kiss went on and on and on. She moaned under his mouth, shivering, wanting something more, something to end the torment, to ease the tension that seemed bent on pulling her young body apart.

"Carlie," he whispered roughly as his fingers tightened in her hair and he paused to catch his breath. "This is not going to end well," he rasped.

She looked up at him, breathless, wordless, shivering with needs she hadn't even known she could feel.

"Oh, what the hell," he muttered. "I'm damned already!"

He kissed her as if he'd never felt a woman's mouth under

his own, as if he'd never felt desire, never known hunger. He kissed her with utter desperation. She was an innocent. He couldn't have her. He wasn't going to marry her, and he couldn't seduce her. It was one hell of a dead end. But he couldn't stop kissing her.

Her mouth was soft and warm and sweetly innocent, accepting his, submitting, but not really responding. It occurred to him somewhere in the middle of it that she didn't even know how to kiss.

He lifted his mouth and searched her wide, soft, dreamy eyes. "You don't even know how," he whispered huskily.

Her lips were as swollen as her body. "Know how to what?" she began dazedly.

The sound of a car horn intruded just as he started to bend his head to her again. She jumped. He caught his breath and moved back from her just as Cash Grier got out of his patrol car and started down to the river where they were standing, now apart from each other.

"Dum dum de dum dum de dum da da de dum," Carson hummed Gounod's "Funeral March of a Marionette" as Cash approached. He smiled wryly, through the piercing agony of his unsatisfied need.

Carlie chuckled.

"Your father was concerned," Cash told Carlie. "He asked me to look for you."

"I'm okay," Carlie said, trying to disguise the signs that she'd been violently kissed. She pushed back her disheveled hair. "He bought me lunch." She nodded at Carson.

"Did you have it tested for various poisons first?" Cash asked blandly.

She laughed again.

"I was apologizing," Carson said heavily. "I jumped on her for something she didn't even do."

"Which was?" Cash asked, and he wasn't smiling.

"Lanette said that Carlie insulted her and made her cry," he returned.

"That wasn't Carlie. That was my wife." Cash smiled coldly. "I understand that she was eloquent."

"Quite," Carlie confirmed.

"Your friend has a rap sheet," he told Carson. He smiled again. This time it was even colder.

Carson scowled. "A rap sheet?"

"It appears that she wasn't always a stewardess. In fact, I don't know how she got to be accepted in that type of job. Probably her lawyer helped her out more than once," he said.

"What was she arrested for?" Carson asked.

"Assault with a deadly weapon. A smart lawyer got her off by pleading temporary insanity, acting in a fit of jealousy." He pursed his lips, enjoying Carson's discomfiture. "She went after another woman with a knife. Accused her of trying to steal her boyfriend."

Carson didn't show it, but he felt uneasy. Lanette had made some threats about Carlie, and he hadn't taken them seriously.

Carlie's face fell at the realization that the blonde might be more dangerous than she'd realized already.

"I'd watch my back if I were you," Carson told Carlie somberly. "The rest of us will help. It seems you've got more trouble than we realized."

"There was another phone call the other night, too," she said, suddenly recalling the cryptic message. It was a male voice. He said to tell Dad he was coming soon. It didn't make sense."

"A male voice?" Cash asked at once.

"Yes." She frowned. "Odd-sounding voice. If I ever heard it again, I think I'd remember it. Why is somebody after Dad?"

"I don't know," Cash said tersely.

"Rourke and I are trying to dig that out," Carson said abruptly. "We have contacts in, shall we say, unusual places."

"So do I," Cash reminded him. "But mine were a dead end."

"One of my cousins is a U.S. senator," Carson said, surprisingly. "He's using some of his own sources for me."

"A senator." Cash grinned. "Not bad."

"Well, not quite in the same class with having a vice president or a state attorney general for a relative," Carson retorted, smiling back.

Cash shrugged. "We all have our little secrets." He glanced at Carlie, who'd reddened when he said "secrets." His eyes narrowed. "You told him?"

She nodded.

He looked at Carson and the smile was gone. "I'll tell you once. Don't ever do that again."

"I can promise you that I never will."

Cash jerked his head in a nod.

Carson glanced at Carlie. "I tried to take him once, in a fight." He grimaced. "It wasn't pretty."

"I was a master trainer in Tae Kwon Do," Cash explained. "Black belt."

Carson rubbed one arm. "Very black."

Cash laughed.

"I was going to take her home, but we hadn't had lunch," Carson explained.

"Or dessert," Carlie mused.

Carson glanced at her with warm, hungry eyes. "Oh, yes, we had dessert."

She blushed further, and he laughed.

"Come on," Cash told them. "It isn't wise to be out in the woods alone with crazy people on the loose."

"Did somebody escape from jail?"

"Nothing like that," Cash said. "I was remembering Carlie's phone call and your girlfriend's rap sheet."

"Oh." Carson didn't say another word. He helped Carlie into the passenger seat of his car and made sure her seat belt was fastened before he closed the door.

Cash drew him over to the patrol car, and he was somber. "You need to do something about that temper."

"I had anger management classes," Carson said quietly. "They helped, for a while." He shook his head. "It's the past. I can't deal with it. I can't live with what I did. I'm at war with myself and the world."

Cash put a heavy hand on the younger man's shoulder. He knew about Carson's past. The two were close. "I'll tell you again that it was her time. Nothing could have stopped it. Somewhere inside, you know that. You just won't accept it. Until you do, you're a walking time bomb."

"I would never hurt her," he assured Cash, nodding toward the car. "I've never hit a woman."

"The threat of force is as bad as the actual thing," Cash replied. "She hasn't gotten over what happened to her, either. We carry the past around like extra luggage, and it gets heavy from time to time."

"You'd know," Carson said gently.

Cash nodded. "I've killed men. I have to live with it. It's not easy, even now."

"For me, either." He shoved his hands into his pockets. "I didn't realize Lanette had started the trouble. She was so upset that it really got to me. She's just someone to take around. Something pretty to show off." He shrugged. "Maybe a little more than that. But nothing permanent."

"Your past in that respect isn't going to win you points with certain people around here," Cash said.

"I'm just beginning to realize that. When I was in Wyoming, Dalton Kirk's wife told me that my past was going to have a terrible impact on my future, that it was going to stand between me and something I want desperately."

"It wouldn't matter so much if you didn't flaunt it, son," Cash replied.

Carson drew in a breath. "I don't know why I taunt her," he said, and they both knew he meant Carlie. "She's a kind, generous woman. Innocent and sweet."

"Something to keep in mind," Cash added. "You'd walk away and forget about it. She'd throw herself off a cliff. You know what I'm talking about."

Carson seemed to pale. "Nothing so drastic..."

"You don't know anything about people of faith, do

you?" he asked. "I didn't, until I came here and had to face living my life with what I'd done hanging over me like a cloud. I came to faith kicking and screaming, but it gave me the first peace I've ever known. Until that happened, I didn't understand the mindset of people like Carlie." His face tautened. "I'm not joking. Her faith teaches her that people get married, then they become intimate, then children come along. It doesn't matter if you agree, if you disagree, if you think she's living in prehistoric times. That's how she thinks."

"It's radical," Carson began. "She's totally out of step with the times. Everybody does it—"

"She doesn't," Cash interrupted. "And everybody around here knows it. It's why she doesn't date. Her grandmother was the town joke. She had sex with a department store manager in a closet and they got caught. He was married with three kids. She thought it was hilarious when his wife left him. In fact, that's why she did it. She was angry at the woman for making a remark about her morals."

"Good grief," Carson exclaimed.

"She was caught with men in back rooms, in parked cars, even once in a long-haul truck in the front seat at a truck stop with people walking by." He shook his head. "It was before I came here, but I heard about it. Carlie's mother was a saint, an absolutely good woman, who had to live with her mother's reputation. Carlie's had to live it down, as well. It's why she won't play around."

"I didn't realize that people knew about it."

"We know everything," Cash said simply. "If you don't care about gossip, it doesn't affect you. But Carlie's always going to care. And if something happens to her, it will show like a neon sign. Everybody will know. She won't be able to hide it or live with it in a small community like this."

"I get your point." He grimaced. "Life is never easy. I don't want to make it even harder for her," he added, glancing toward Carlie, who was watching them curiously.

"No." Cash studied the younger man. "The world is full of women like your pretty blonde, and they work for scale. Don't try to class Carlie with them." He smiled coldly. "Or you'll have more trouble than you can handle. You do not want to make an enemy of Reverend Blair."

"I do have some idea about her father's past," Carson confessed.

"No, you don't," Cash replied. "Just take my word that you don't ever want to see him lose his temper. And you work on controlling yours."

"I'm reformed." Carson took his hands out of his pockets. "I suppose we all have memories that torment us."

"Count on it. Just try not to make more bad ones for Carlie."

"I'll drive her home." He hesitated. "Is her father there?"

Cash nodded.

Carson sighed. "There are a few unmarked places on me," he commented wryly. "I guess I can handle some more. Time to face the music."

Cash laughed. "Well, you've got guts, I'll give you that."

"Not going to arrest me?" he added.

"Not this time," Cash said.

"Just as well. You can't prove I'm me."

"Why in the hell don't you carry identification?" Cash

asked. "Don't you realize that if you were ever injured, nobody would know anything about you, right down to your weight or your medical history?"

Carson smiled wryly. "When I was doing wet work overseas, it would have been fatal to carry any. I just got into the habit of leaving it behind."

"I know, but you're not in the same line of work now," Cash said.

"Certain of that, are you?" he asked with a vague smile.

"Yes."

Carson made a face. "All right," he said after a minute. "I'll think about it."

"Good man."

Carson went around the car and got in under the steering wheel. Cash drove off as Carson was starting up the car.

"Look in the glove compartment and hand me my wallet, will you?" he asked Carlie.

She rummaged around through the papers and produced it. "Do you have a last name?" she wondered aloud.

"Look at the license."

Curious, she opened the wallet. His driver's license read "Carson Allen Farwalker."

She handed it to him. He shoved it into his jacket while they were at a stoplight.

"No comment?" he asked.

"I'd be embarrassed," she replied softly.

He laughed. "On the morning I was born, a man came into our small rural community, walking. It was driving snow, almost a blizzard. He said he'd come from Rapid City, all the way on foot in his mukluks and heavy coat, hitching rides, to see a sick friend who lived near us. It was a far walk. So my mother named me Far Walker." He glanced at her. "Our names don't translate well into English sometimes, but this one did." His face tautened. "I refused to take my father's name, even as a child. So I was known on the rez as Far Walker. When I got my first driver's license, that's what I put on it, Anglicized into one word. It's my legal name now."

"It suits you," she said. "You walk like an outdoorsman."

He smiled.

"I read about how native people get their names. We tend to distort them. Like Crazy Horse. That wasn't his Lakota name, but it was what he was called by Wasichu—by white people," she said, and then flushed. She hadn't meant to give away her interest in his culture.

"Well," he said and chuckled. "Hannibal and Crazy Horse. You have wide interests. Do you know his Lakota name?" he added.

"Yes. It was Tashunka Witko." She laughed. "Although I've seen that spelled about four different ways."

"And do you know what it really means, in my tongue?" he asked.

She grinned. "'His horse is crazy,'" she replied. "I read somewhere that the day he was born, a man on a restless horse rode by and his people named him Crazy Horse."

"Close enough." He smiled gently as he met her eyes. "You're an eternal student, aren't you?"

"Oh, yes. I might have gone to college, but I didn't make high grades and we were always poor. I take free classes on the internet, though, sometimes. When I'm not grinding Horde into the ground," she added without looking at him.

"Runed that sword, did you? We'll find out how well it works on the next battleground we fight."

"I can't wait," she said smugly. "I've been practicing." She glanced at him. "What's a mukluk?"

"Heavy boots that come up to the knee, made of fur. I have some at home. I bought them in Alaska. They're made with beaver fur, with wolf fur trim and beadwork."

"Your jacket is beautiful," she remarked, glancing at it. "I've never even seen one that looks like that before."

"You never will. A cousin made it for me." He smiled. "He makes these from scratch, right down to the elk he hunts for them. He eats the meat and cures the hides. Not the wolves, however. It's illegal to kill them in the States, so he buys the fur from traders in Canada."

"I saw this movie with Steven Seagal, about Alaska. He was on a talk show wearing a jacket a lot like yours. He said the native people he worked with on the movie made it for him."

"Not a bad martial artist. I like Chuck Norris best, however, for that spinning heel kick. The chief does one just like it. Ask him sometime how he learned it," he teased.

"I already know," she laughed. "He says it's his claim to fame locally."

"Feeling better?"

She nodded. "I never dreamed it was asthma," she said heavily. She frowned and glanced at him. "But you knew right away," she said. "You even knew what to give me…"

“I was a field medic in the army,” he said easily. “Emergencies were my specialty.”

“You must have been very good at it,” she said.

“I did what the job called for.”

He pulled up in front of her house. Reverend Blair was waiting on the porch, wearing a leather bomber jacket and a black scowl.

He came down the steps and opened Carlie’s door. He hugged her close. “You okay?” he asked tersely.

“I’m fine. Honest. I just overreacted.”

He didn’t reply. He was glaring at Carson, who came around the car to join them.

“It was my fault,” Carson said bluntly. “I accused her of something she didn’t do and I was overly aggressive.”

The reverend seemed to relax, just a little. “You take it on the chin, don’t you?” he asked half-admiringly.

“Always.” He sighed. “If you want to hit me, I’ll just stand here. I deserve it.”

The reverend cocked his head. His blue eyes were glittery and dangerous, hinting at the man he might once have been.

“He treated me in the office, took me to the emergency room, then the pharmacy and bought me lunch after,” Carlie said.

The reverend lifted an eyebrow and glanced at Carson. “Treated her?”

“I was a field medic in the army,” Carson replied. “I recognized the symptoms. But if you’re thinking I acted without a doctor’s orders, you’re wrong. I had her doctor on the phone before I opened my medical kit.”

The reverend relaxed even more. "Okay."

"I was more aggressive than I meant to be, but I would never have raised a hand to her," he added. "Violence is very rarely the answer to any problem."

"Rarely?"

Carson shrugged. "Well, there was this guy over in South America, in Carrera. Rourke and I sort of fed him to a crocodile."

The reverend glowered at him. "You're not helping your case."

"The guy cut up a young woman with his knife and left her scarred for life," Carson added. His black eyes glittered. "He bragged about it."

"I see."

"It was an act of mercy, anyway," Carson added doggedly. "The crocodile was plainly starving."

Reverend Blair couldn't suppress a laugh, although he tried. "I begin to see why you get along so well with Grier."

"Why, does he feed people to reptiles, too?"

"He's done things most men never dream of," the reverend said solemnly. "Lived when he should have died. He took lives, but he saved them, as well. A hard man with a hard past." The man's pale blue eyes pinned Carson's. "Like you."

Carson scowled. "How do you know anything about me?"

"You might be surprised," was the bland reply. He shook a finger at Carson. "You stop upsetting my daughter."

"Yes, sir," he said on a sigh.

"I'd invite you to supper but she might have some poisonous mushrooms concealed in the cupboard."

"I won't poison him," Carlie promised. She smiled. "You can come to supper if you like. I'll make beef Stroganoff."

Carson looked torn, as if he really wanted to do it. "Sorry," he said. "I promised to take Lanette out to eat. I need to talk to her."

"That's okay," Carlie said, hiding the pain it caused her to hear that. "Rain check."

"Count on it," he said softly, and his eyes said more than his lips did. "You okay?"

She nodded. "I'll be fine."

"I'm really sorry," he said again.

"Stop apologizing, will you? You'll hurt your image," she said, grinning.

"I'll see you."

She nodded. He nodded to the reverend, got in the car and left.

"I HAVE TO see an allergist," Carlie said miserably. "Asthma, can you believe it? I couldn't get my breath, I felt like I was suffocating. Carson knew what it was, and what to do for it. He was amazing."

"He needs to work on his self-control," her father said tersely, sipping coffee while she dished up pound cake for dessert.

For just an instant she thought of Carson out of control at the river, hungry for her, and she flushed. Then she realized that he was talking about another sort of self-control.

The reverend wasn't slow. He had a good idea why she was blushing.

"Carlie," he said gently, "he goes through women like hungry people go through food."

"I know that, Dad."

"He isn't a person of faith. He works in a profession that thrives on the lack of it, in fact, and he's in almost constant danger." He hesitated. "What I'm trying to say is that he isn't going to settle down in a small town and become a family man."

"I know that, too," she replied. She put his cake down in front of him on the table and refilled his coffee cup.

"Knowing and walking away are two different things," he said curtly. "Your mother was like you, sweet and innocent, out of touch with the real world. I hurt her very badly because we married for the wrong reasons. I wasn't ready. Before I knew it, I was a father." He looked down at the uneaten cake. "I felt trapped, hog-tied, and I resented it. I made her pay for it." His lips made a grim line. "I stayed away, out of that resentment. She didn't deserve the life I gave her."

She was shocked to hear him say such things. She knew that they'd had to get married. She'd heard him say it. But even so, she'd thought her parents married for love, that her father was away because he was making a living for them.

He didn't seem to notice Carlie's surprise. He wasn't looking at her. "I didn't know she was sick. One of my friends had a cousin here, who told him, and he told me that she was in the hospital. I got back just after her mother and her drug-crazed boyfriend did a number on you." His teeth ground together. "That was when I realized what a mess I'd made of all our lives. I walked away from the old life that same day and never looked back. I only wish I'd been where I was supposed to be so that you'd have been spared what happened to you."

"You're the one who's always saying that things happen to test us," she reminded him.

"I guess I am. But for someone who'd never hurt anybody in her life, you paid a high price," he added.

"Mama said that if she'd been a different sort of person, you would have been happy with her," she recalled. "She said her way of thinking ruined your life." She frowned. "I didn't understand what that meant at the time. But I think I'm beginning to." She did, because Carson was the same sort of person her father must have been.

"No. I ruined hers," he said. "I knew I couldn't settle down. I let my heart rule my head." He smiled sadly. "You see, pumpkin, despite how it must sound, I really loved your mother. Loved her desperately. But I loved my way of life, too, loved being on my own, working in a profession that gave me so much freedom. I was greedy and tried to have it all. In the process, I lost your mother. I will never get over what happened to her because of me. If I'd been here, taking care of her…"

"She would still have died," Carlie finished for him. "It was an aggressive cancer. They tried chemo and radiation, but it only made her sicker. Nothing you could have done would have stopped that, or changed a thing."

He studied her soft eyes. "You always make excuses for

me." He shook his head. "Now you're making them for the wild man from South Dakota."

"He's wild for a reason," she said quietly.

"And you're not sharing it, right?"

"I'm not," she agreed. "It's his business."

"Nice to know you can keep a secret."

"For all the good it does me. You won't share any of yours," she pointed out.

"Why give you nightmares over a past I can't change?" he asked philosophically. He glanced at his watch and grimaced. "I'm late for a prayer meeting. You'll be okay here, right? Got the inhaler Lou prescribed?"

She pulled it out of her pocket and showed it to him.

"Okay." He shook his head. "I should have recognized the symptoms. My father had it."

"Your father? I never met him."

"He was dead by the time I married your mother," he said. He smiled. "You'd have liked him. He was a career officer in the navy, a chief petty officer."

"Wow."

"I've got photographs of him somewhere. I'll have to look them up."

"What was your mother like?"

"Fire," he chuckled. "She left trails of fire behind her when she lost her temper. She had red hair and an attitude. Tippy Grier reminds me of her, except that my mother wasn't really beautiful. She was a clerk in a hotel until she retired. She died of a stroke." He shook his head. "Dad was never the same after. He only outlived her by about two years."

"I'm sorry."

"Me, too."

"Mama said my grandfather was a kind man. He died when she was very small. He worked for the sheriff's department. His wife was my crazy grandmother who couldn't control herself."

"I remember Mary speaking of him." He cocked his head. "Your family goes back generations in this community. I envy you that continuity. My folks moved a lot, since Dad was in the service. I've lived everywhere."

"And I've never been anywhere," she mused. "Except to San Antonio."

"Next time you go there, I'm driving," he said flatly.

She made a face at him.

"I'll be home soon."

"Please be careful. Check your car before you start it."

"Cash and Carson told me about the phone call," he replied. "Apparently I'm the target."

"I don't know why," she said. "I was the one who could identify the man who was killed in Wyoming. You never saw him."

"Pumpkin, you're not the only one with enemies," he said softly.

"Would this be connected with that past you won't tell me about?"

"Dead right." He bent and kissed her forehead. "Keep the door locked."

"I will. Drive safely."

He chuckled as he went out the door.

Carlie cleaned up the kitchen, played her video game with Robin for an hour and went to bed. Her dreams were vivid and vaguely embarrassing. And of Carson.

8

ROURKE WAS SITTING with a worried politician in one of the best restaurants in San Antonio. Unknown to the man, Rourke was working with the feds. Rourke had managed to wiggle himself into the man's employ.

This particular politician, Matthew Helm, had been named the acting U.S. senator, and was hoping to be elected to a full term at the special election in a few months. Rourke was equally determined to find a way to connect him with the murder of a local assistant district attorney. All the evidence had been destroyed. But there were other ways to prove collusion.

Rourke had been in touch with Lieutenant Rick Marquez of the San Antonio Police Department and was keeping him informed through Cash Grier. This politician had also been responsible for the attempt on Dalton Kirk's life, and the one on Carlie Blair's father—or Carlie herself—the intended victim had never been determined—in Jacobsville.

His murdering henchman, Richard Martin, had been killed in Wyoming, but the man's evil deeds persisted. Word was that before he'd died, he'd hired someone to kill Carlie. Nobody knew who had the contract.

Rourke was hoping against hope that this man might provide answers to many questions. But Helm was secretive. So far he hadn't said one incriminating word. Rourke would have known. He was wearing a wire, courtesy of Rick Marquez.

"There are too many loose ends," Matthew Helm said after a minute. He glanced at his other enforcer, Fred Baldwin, and glared at him. "You take care of that problem up in Wyoming?"

"Oh, yes, sir," the big, brawny man assured him. "You can stop worrying."

"I always worry." Helm then glared at Rourke. "What have you found out about my competition for the job?"

"Both men are clean as a whistle," Rourke replied easily. "No past issues we can use against them."

Helm smiled secretly. "So far," he murmured.

"You thinking of planting some?" Rourke asked conversationally.

Helm just stared at him. "What the hell does that mean?"

"Just a comment."

"Well, keep your comments to yourself," Helm said angrily. "I don't fix elections, in case you wondered."

"Sorry. I'm new here," Rourke apologized.

"Too new," Helm said suspiciously. "I can't dig out any information on you. Any at all."

"I'm from South Africa, what do you expect?" he added.

"Well, that last name you gave, Stanton," Helm began, "is a dead end."

"I like to keep my past in the past," Rourke returned. "I'm a wanted man in some places."

"Is that it?" Helm studied him for a long moment. "Then maybe you're not as suspicious as you seem, huh?" He snickered. "Just don't expect instant trust. I don't trust anybody."

"That's a good way to be," Rourke agreed.

Helm drew in a long breath. "Well, we need to get back to the office and work up some more ads and a few handouts for the campaign office. Not much time to bring this all together."

"Okay, boss," Rourke said. "I'll see you there." He got up, nodded to both men, paid for his coffee and pie, and left.

Helm studied his other enforcer. "I don't trust him," he told the man. "You keep a close eye on him, hire extra men if you have to. See where he goes, who he associates with. I don't want any complications."

"Yes, Boss."

"And start checking out our sources. We'll need some more drugs planted. I can't afford competition for the job," he added. His face firmed. "You don't share that information with Rourke, got it? You don't tell him anything unless you clear it with me."

"I got it, Boss."

"You destroyed the watch, right?"

The other man nodded vigorously. "Oh, yeah, Boss, I smashed it into bits and tossed it into a trash bin."

"Good. Good."

The other man was hoping his uneasiness didn't show. He couldn't destroy the watch, he just couldn't. It was the most beautiful timepiece he'd ever seen, and it played that song he liked.

Fred Baldwin had envied Richard Martin, wearing that watch that cost as much as a sports car. He'd tried to borrow it once, but Martin had looked at him like he was a worm.

Well, Martin was dead now, and Baldwin had the watch. It was warm against his fingers, warm in his pocket where he kept it. He'd set the alarm so it wouldn't go off accidentally. Nobody was crazy enough to throw away a watch that cost so much money! Who knew, one day he might be desperate enough to pawn it. A man had to live, after all, and what Mr. Helm paid him was barely enough to afford his keep. His criminal record made him vulnerable. He couldn't get another job and Mr. Helm warned him that if he even tried to leave, he'd make sure Fred never worked again. It wasn't a threat. It was a promise. Fred knew better than to try to quit, although he hated the job.

Of course, that watch had a history, and Fred knew it. He might be desperate enough one day to talk to somebody in law enforcement about it. The watch could tie Mr. Helm to a murder. So, no, Fred wasn't about to throw it away. That didn't mean he didn't have to keep it hidden, of course. And he did.

ROURKE STOPPED BY Carlie's house that evening to talk to Reverend Blair. He was amused that Helm's men had tried to follow him. He'd had Carson take his car to San Antonio and park it at a bar. The trackers were sitting out in the parking lot in the freezing cold, waiting for Rourke to come out. He laughed. It was going to be a long night for them.

"Well, you look happy," Carlie remarked when she let him in.

"I've discovered that misdirection is one of my greater talents," he mused, grinning. "Got any more of that wonderful cornbread?"

She shook her head. "But I just took a nice enchilada casserole out of the oven, and I have sour cream and tortilla chips to top it with," she said.

"Be still my heart," Rourke enthused. "Listen, are you sure you wouldn't like to marry me tomorrow?"

"Sorry," she said, "I'm having my truck waxed."

"Ah, well," he sighed in mock sorrow.

"Stop trying to marry my daughter," Jake Blair muttered, his ice-blue eyes penetrating, as Rourke joined him at the kitchen table. "You are definitely not son-in-law material."

"Spoilsport," Rourke told him. "It's hard to find a nice woman who can also cook and play video games."

"You don't play video games," Jake pointed out.

"A lot you know! The police chief is teaching me."

"Cash Grier?" Carlie exclaimed. "My boss doesn't play."

"Apparently that's why he thinks it's a good idea if he does the teaching. His young brother-in-law has forced him into it," he laughed, "because he can't get any friends to play with him. Cash is always up for anything new and exciting."

Jake shook his head. "I just don't get it. Running around a cartoon world on dragons and fighting people with two-handed swords. It's…medieval."

"Teaches combat skills, strategy, social interaction and how to deal with trolls," Carlie retorted, pouring coffee for all of them.

"Trolls?" Rourke asked. "Those great Norwegian things…?"

"Internet trolls," she clarified with a glower. "People who start fights and stand back and watch. They're really a pain sometimes, especially if somebody new to the game makes the mistake of asking for help on trade chat." She started laughing.

"What's so funny?" her father asked.

"Well, this guy wanted a mage port—that's a portal they can make to the major cities. He didn't know what class could do ports, so he asked if anybody could send him to the capital. This warlock comes on and offers to port him for fifty gold." She was laughing heartily. "Warlocks can't port, you see. They can summon, but that's a whole other thing." She shook her head. "I've spent months wondering how that came out."

"Probably about like the death knight your boss told me about, who offered to heal for a dungeon group," Rourke replied, tongue-in-cheek.

Carlie looked shocked. "DKs can't heal!"

"I'm sure the dungeon group knows that now," he quipped, and he was rakishly handsome when he smiled.

"I guess I'm missing a lot," Jake Blair said.

"You should come and play with us," Carlie said.

He shook his head. "I'm too old to play, pumpkin."

"You're kidding, right? One of the best raid leaders on our server is seventy-three years old."

His eyebrows arched. "Say what?"

"Not only that, there's a whole guild that plays from a nursing home."

"I met them," Rourke said. "Cash and I were in a dungeon with several of them. Along with a ten-year-old Paladin who kicked butt, and a sixty-eight-year-old grandmother who was almost able to kill the big boss single-handed."

"I suppose my whole concept of gaming is wrong," Jake laughed. "I had no idea so many age groups played together."

"That's what makes it so much fun," Carlie replied. "You meet people from all over the world in-game, and you learn that even total strangers can work together with a little patience."

"Maybe I'll get online one of these days and try it," Jake conceded.

"That would be great, Dad!" Carlie exclaimed. "You can be in our guild. Robin and I have one of our own," she explained. "We'll gear you and teach you."

"Maybe in the summer, when things are a little less hectic," Jake suggested.

"Oh. The building committee again," Carlie recalled.

"One group wants brick. The other wants wood. We have a carpenter in our congregation who wants the contract and doesn't understand that it has to be bid. The choir wants a loft, but the organist doesn't like heights. Some people don't want carpet, others think padded benches are a total sellout… Why are you laughing?" he asked, because Rourke was almost rolling on the floor.

"Church," Rourke choked. "It's where people get along and never argue…?"

"Not in my town," Reverend Blair said, sighing. He smiled. "We'll get it together. And we argue nicely." He frowned. "Except for Old Man Barlow. He uses some pretty colorful language."

"I only used one colorful word," Carlie remarked as she served up the casserole, "and he—" she pointed at her father "—grounded me for a month and took away my library card."

He shrugged. "It was a very bad word." He glowered at her. "And Robin should never have taught it to you without explaining what it meant!"

"Robin got in trouble, too," she told Rourke. "But his parents took away his computer for two weeks." She shook her head. "I thought withdrawal was going to kill him."

"He uses drugs?" Rourke asked curiously.

"No, withdrawal from the video game we play together," she chuckled. She glanced at her father. "So I had to do battlegrounds in pugs for those two weeks. It was awful."

"What's a pug?" Reverend Blair asked.

"A pickup group," Rourke replied. "Cash taught me." He glared. "There was a tank in the last one that had a real attitude problem. Cash had him for lunch."

"Our police chief is awesome when he gets going," Carlie laughed. "We had one guy up for speeding, and when he came in to pay the ticket he was almost shaking. He just wanted to give me the fine and get out before he had to see the chief. He said he'd never speed in our town again!"

"What did Cash do?" Jake asked.

"I asked. He didn't really do anything. He just glared at the man while he wrote out the ticket."

"I know that glare." Rourke shook his head. "Having been on the receiving end of it, I can tell you truly that I'd rather he hit me."

"No, you wouldn't," Carlie mused. "I wasn't working for him then, but I heard about it. He and Judd Dunn were briefly interested in the same woman, Christabel, who eventually married Judd. But it came to blows in the chief's office at lunch one day. They said it was such a close match that both men came out with matching bruises and cuts, and nobody declared victory. You see, the chief taught Judd Dunn to fight Tae Kwon Do–style."

"Wasn't he going to teach you and Michelle Godfrey how to do that?" Jake asked suddenly.

"He was, but it was sort of embarrassing, if you recall, Dad," she replied. She glanced at Rourke, who was watching her curiously. "I tripped over my own feet, slid under another student, knocked him into another student on the mat, and they had to go to the emergency room for pulled tendons." She grimaced. "I was too ashamed to try it again, and Michelle wouldn't go without me. The chief wanted us to try again, but I'm just too clumsy for martial arts."

Rourke's eyes twinkled. "I can sympathize. On my first foray into martial arts, I put my instructor through a window."

"What?" she exclaimed.

"We were standing near it. He threw a kick, I caught his foot and flipped him. The momentum took him right into a backward summersault, right out the window. Fortunately for him it was a low one, raised, and very close to the ground."

"Well!" she laughed.

"I've improved since then." He shared an amused look with Jake.

"Shall we say grace?" Jake replied, bowing his head.

"YOU DIDN'T TELL me that it was the police chief's wife, not Carlie, who insulted you," Carson said as they shared coffee during intermission at the theater in San Antonio.

Lanette looked at him under her long lashes. "I was very upset," she remarked. "Perhaps I was confused. Honestly, that girl is so naïve. And she isn't even pretty! I don't understand why you were dancing with her in the first place!"

He studied her covertly. She was getting more possessive by the day, and she was full of questions about Carlie. It bothered him. He kept thinking of her rap sheet, too.

"Several of us are watching her," he said after a minute. "There was an attempt on her father's life, and she was injured. We think there may be another one."

"On a minister?" she exclaimed, laughing loudly. "Who'd want to kill a preacher?"

His black eyes narrowed. "I don't recall telling you that her father was a man of the cloth," he said.

Her face was blank for just an instant and then she smiled prettily. "I was asking about her at the dance. Someone told me who her father was."

"I see."

"She's just a backward little hick," she muttered irritably. "Let's talk about something else. Are we going to see the symphony Friday night? I bought a new dress, specially!"

He was thoughtful. He didn't like the way Lanette had started to assume that he was always available to take her out. She was beautiful to look at, to show off in public. The poor reservation kid in him enjoyed the envious looks he got from other men when he escorted his striking blonde companion in the evenings. But she was shallow and mean-spirited. He forgave a lot because she eased the ache in him that Carlie provoked.

Funny thing, though. Although he enjoyed the physical aspects of their relationship, he couldn't quite manage to go all the way with his gorgeous blonde. It unsettled him, and irritated and insulted her, but expensive presents seemed to pacify her.

He didn't understand his reticence. Lanette was eager and accomplished, but her talents were wasted on him. Deep down, he knew why. It didn't help the situation. Carlie was never going to fall into bed with him. And if she did, her father would kill him and Cash Grier would help.

"I'll be very happy when you're finished with this dumb assignment and you don't have to be around that little hick," Lanette was saying. She brushed back her long, thick, blond hair.

"People in Jacobs County are very protective of her," was all he said.

"She's probably not even in trouble," she muttered. "I expect people are just overreacting because of that attack on her father. For goodness sake, maybe whoever's after her isn't even after her, maybe it's her father!" She glanced at him. "Isn't that what you said about that knife attack, that he was trying to kill her father and she tried to stop him?"

"That's what they said."

She shook her head. "Well, it was a really stupid job," she murmured. "Imagine a man going to the victim's house in the middle of the day, in broad daylight, and attacking a minister in his own house!"

Carson frowned as he listened. "I didn't know it was in broad daylight."

"Everybody knows," she said quickly. "They were even talking about it at that silly dance you took me to."

"Oh."

She glanced away, smiling to herself. "They also said that the man who tried to kill the preacher ended up dead himself."

"Yes, poisoned. A very nasty, slow poison. Something the late Mr. Martin was quite well-known for in intelligence circles."

"I hate poison," she said under her breath. "So unpredictable."

"Have you been poisoning people, then?" he mused.

She laughed. "No. I like to watch true crime shows on television. I know all about poisons and stuff." She moved very close to him. "Not to worry, handsome, I'd never want to hurt you!" she added, and lifted her arms toward his neck.

He raised an eyebrow and stepped back.

"Oh, you and your hang-ups," she muttered. "What's wrong with a hug in public?"

"It would take too long to tell you," he said, not offering the information that in his culture, such public displays were considered taboo by the elders.

"All right," she said with mock despair. "Are we going to the theater Friday?"

"Yes," he said. It would keep his mind off Carlie.

"Wonderful!" She smiled secretly to herself. "I'm sure we'll have a lovely time." She paused. "That mad South African man you know, he isn't coming to the theater, is he?"

"Rourke?" He laughed to himself. "Not likely on a Friday night."

"Why not on a Friday?" she asked.

He almost bit his tongue. Rourke played poker with Cash Grier. He didn't dare let that slip, just in case Lanette knew anyone who had contact with Matthew Helm. "Rourke drinks on weekends," he lied.

"I see." She thought for a minute. "What about your friend the police chief?" she asked, laughing. "I'll bet he takes that prissy wife of his to the theater."

"Not on a Friday night," he chuckled. "The police chief and several other men get together at the chief's house and play poker after supper."

"Exciting game, poker. Especially the strip kind," she purred.

He sighed. "I don't gamble. Sorry."

"Your loss, sweetie," she said with pursed red lips. "Your loss."

FRIDAY NIGHT, REVEREND BLAIR had a call from a visitor to the community who was staying in a local motel outside town.

"I just want to die," the man wailed. Jake couldn't quite place the accent, but it definitely wasn't local. "I hate my life! They said you were a kind man who would try to help people. They gave me your number, here at this motel—" he named it "—so I said I'd call you. Before I did it, you know. Will God forgive me for killing myself? I got some rat poison…"

"Wait," Jake Blair said softly. "Just wait. I'll come to see you. We'll talk."

"You'd come all this way, just to talk to me?" The man sounded shocked.

"I know the motel you mentioned you were staying at," Jake said. "It's just a few minutes from here. I'll be on my way in a jiffy. What's your room number?"

The man told him. "Thank you. Thank you!" he sobbed. "I just don't want to live no more!" He hung up.

"Pumpkin, I have to go out," he informed his daughter as he shrugged into his bomber jacket. "I've been contacted by a suicidal man in a motel. I'm going to try and talk him down before he does something desperate."

She smiled. "That's my dad, saving the world."

He shrugged. "Trying to, anyway. You stay inside and keep the doors locked," he added. "And keep that cell phone close, you hear me?"

"I'll put it in my pocket, I swear."

"Good girl." He kissed her forehead. "Don't wait up. This may take a while."

"Good luck," she called after him.

He waved at her, left and closed the door behind him.

Carlie finished cleaning up the kitchen and went upstairs to play her game. On the kitchen table, forgotten, was the cell phone she'd promised to keep with her. The only other phone in the house was a fixed one, in her father's office…

"GOODNESS, COFFEE JUST goes right through me," Lanette whispered into Carson's ear. "Be right back."

He just nodded, aware of irritated glances from other theatergoers nearby. He wasn't really thrilled with the play. It was modern and witty, but not his sort of entertainment at all, despite the evident skill of the actors.

His mind went back to Carlie on the riverbank, standing so close that he could feel every soft line of her body, kissing him so hungrily that his mind spun like a top. Carlie, who was as innocent as a newborn, completely clueless about the hungers that drove men.

He wanted her until he couldn't sleep for wanting her. And he knew he could never have her. He wasn't going to settle down, as Cash Grier had, with a wife and child and a job in a small town. He liked adventure, excitement. He wasn't willing to give those up for some sort of middle-class dream life in a cottage or a condo, mowing the grass on weekends. The thought of it turned his stomach.

He brushed away a spec on his immaculate trousers and frowned. He didn't understand why Carlie appealed to his senses so strongly. She wasn't really pretty, although her mouth was soft and beautiful and tasted as sweet as honey. Her body was slender and she was small-breasted. But she had long, elegant legs and her waist was tiny. He could feel her small breasts swelling against his hard chest when he kissed her, feel the tips biting into his flesh even through layers of fabric.

He groaned silently. His adventures with women had always been with beautiful, practiced, elegant women. He'd never been with an innocent. And he wasn't about to break that record now, he assured himself firmly.

He'd been vulnerable with Carlie because he felt guilty about sending her to the hospital when he lost his temper. That was all. It was a physical reaction, prompted only by guilt. He was never going to forgive himself for frightening her like that. Her white face haunted him still. He'd only moved closer to make his point, it hadn't been a true aggression. But it must have seemed that way to a young girl who'd been beaten, and then later stabbed by an assassin.

But he hadn't hurt her at the dance, when they'd moved together like one person, when he'd felt the hunger so deeply that he could have laid her down on the dance floor right then. What the hell was he going to do? It was impossible. Impossible!

While he was brooding, Lanette returned. She slid her hand into his and just smiled at him, without saying a word. He glanced at her. She really was beautiful. He'd never seen a woman who was quite this exquisite. If it hadn't been for her attitude, and her other flaws, she might have seemed the perfect woman. That made it all the more inexplicable that he couldn't force himself to sleep with her; not even to relieve the ache Carlie gave him.

CARLIE WAS FIGHTING two Horde in the battleground. Sadly, neither of them was Carson. She flailed away with her two-handed sword, pulled out her minions, used every trick she could think of to vanquish them, but they killed her. She grimaced. She had the best gear honor points could buy, but there were these things called conquest points that only came from doing arenas. Carlie couldn't do arena. She was too slow and too clumsy.

So there were people far better geared than she was. Which was just an excuse, because the playing field was level in battlegrounds, regardless of how good your armor was.

The painful truth was that there were a lot of players who were much better at it than Carlie was. She comforted herself with the knowledge that there was always somebody better at the game, and eventually everybody got killed once or twice during a battle. She was just glad that she didn't have to do it in real life.

"Ah, well," she said, and sighed.

She resurrected at the battleground cemetery, got on her mount and rode back off to war. Before she got to either her home base or the enemy's, the end screen came up. The Alliance had lost to the Horde. But it had been an epic battle, the sort that you really didn't mind losing so much because it was fought by great players on both sides.

"Next time," she told the screen. "Next time, we'll own you, Hordies!"

She was about to queue for the battleground again when she heard a knock at the door downstairs.

She logged out of her character, although not out of the

game, mildly irritated by the interruption, and went down the staircase. She wondered if maybe her father had forgotten to take his house key with him. He was so forgetful sometimes, it was funny. Twice now, he'd had to wake Carlie up when he came back from a committee meeting that lasted longer than expected, or when he returned from visiting and comforting congregation members at hospitals.

She peered through the safety window and frowned. There was a big man in a suit outside. He looked uneasy.

"Is there something you want?" she asked through the door.

"Yeah," he said after a minute. "I need help."

"What sort of help?" she answered.

He paused for a minute. He looked through the small window at the suspicious young woman who was obviously not about to open that door to a man she didn't know.

He thought for a minute. He was slow when it came to improvisation. Maybe he could fool her if he was smart. Yeah. Smart. Who would she open the door for?

"I, uh, came to tell you about your dad," he called through the door. "There's been an accident. I was passing by and stopped. He asked me to come and get you and drive you to the hospital where they're taking him."

"Dad's been in a wreck?" she exclaimed. "Why didn't the police come?"

What did she mean? Did police notify people about wrecks here? He supposed they did. He'd done that once, long ago. He paused.

"Well, they were coming, but I told them your dad wanted me to bring you, and they said it was okay."

She still hesitated. Perhaps it was one of the new patrolmen, and her father had been impatient about getting word to her. A kind stranger might have been imposed upon to fetch Carlie.

"He's hurt pretty bad, Miss," he called again. "We should go."

She couldn't bear to think of her father injured. She had to go to him. She grabbed her coat off the rack near the door. Her pocketbook was upstairs, but she couldn't think why she'd need it. Her father would have money in his wallet and a house key.

"Okay, I'm coming," she said, and opened the door.

He smiled. "I'll take you to him," he promised.

She closed and locked the door behind her. Too late, she remembered her cell phone lying on the kitchen table.

"Have you got a cell phone?" she asked abruptly.

"Yeah, I got one," he said, leading the way to his late model sedan. "Why?"

"In case we have to call somebody," she explained.

"You can call anybody you like, Miss," he said. "Just get right in."

She bent down to slide into the open passenger side when she felt a cloth pressed against her mouth and pressure behind it. She took a breath. The whole world went black.

THE BIG MAN cuffed her hands together behind her before he slid her onto the backseat. She was breathing sort of funny, so he didn't gag her. He hoped that would be okay with the boss. After all, where they were going, nobody was likely to hear her.

Before he got into the car, he dropped a piece of paper on the ground deliberately. Then he got in the car, started it and drove away.

9

Reverend Jake Blair knocked at the motel door, but there was no answer. He immediately thought the worst, that the man had actually attempted suicide before his arrival. He might be inside, fatally wounded.

He ran to the motel office, explained the situation, showed his ID and pleaded with the man to open the door.

The manager ran with him to the room, slid home the key and threw open the door.

"Is this some sort of joke?" the manager asked.

Jake shook his head. "He phoned me at home and begged me to come and speak with him. He said that someone locally had recommended that he call me and gave him the number. He said he was suicidal, that he was going to take poison." He turned to the man. "Did you rent this room tonight?"

"Yes. To some big guy with a Northern accent," he replied. "He didn't have any luggage, though, and he didn't look suicidal to me." He glowered. "He just left without paying the bill or handing back the key," he muttered.

"Isn't that the key?" Jake asked, nodding toward the bedside table.

It was. There was a fifty-dollar bill under it.

"Well," the manager chuckled drily. "A man with a sense of honor, at least. Sort of."

"Sort of." Jake shook his head. "I can't imagine why he'd fake something like this." Then he remembered. Carson had a date. Rourke was playing poker with Cash Grier. Jake was here. Carlie was alone. At home.

He bit off a bad word, chided himself for the slip and ran for his car. On the way he dialed Carlie's cell phone, but there was no answer. He was referred to her voice mail. He'd told her to keep that phone with her. She never remembered. He dialed the home phone. The answering machine picked up after four rings. Now, that was unusual. Carlie would hear it, even if she was playing, and she'd pick it up before the message finished playing.

He was very concerned. He wasn't certain that someone was after him because of his past, despite the threatening phone call Carlie had taken. The man with the knife went for Carlie deliberately, it had seemed to Jake. He groaned as he pictured it, recalled her pain and terror. She'd had so much misery in her short life, so much violence. He hated what she'd gone through. Some of it was his fault.

He burned rubber getting home. He ran up the porch steps, put his key in the lock and went in like a storming army. But the house was empty. Carlie's computer was still on. And, although she'd logged out temporarily, her character screen was still up and the game was still running. That meant she'd been interrupted while she was playing. He checked every room. In the kitchen he found her cell phone, lying on the table.

He backtracked out the front door and, with a flashlight in addition to the porch light, searched around. He noticed tire tracks that weren't his. He also noted a piece of paper. It was a rough drawing, a map of sorts. It was a clue that the police would want undisturbed. He had no idea what the map depicted. But he knew what to do at once. He pulled out his cell phone and called Cash Grier.

"I HAD TO call Hayes," Cash apologized when he was on the scene. "You don't live in the city limits."

"That's okay." Jake clapped him on the back. "You're forgiven."

"Don't worry. Hayes has an investigator who dines out on forensics. He even has membership in several professional societies that do nothing else except discuss new techniques. Zack's good at his job."

"Okay." Jake shoved his hands into his pockets. He felt as if it was the end of the world. "I should have realized it was a ruse. Why didn't I think?"

"We'll find her," Cash promised.

"I know that. It's what condition we'll find her in that concerns me," Jake said tautly.

"I don't think they'll harm her," Cash said. "They want something. Maybe it's you."

"They can have me, if they'll let my daughter go," he rasped.

"I phoned my brother," Cash added. "It's a kidnapping. That makes it a federal crime. He'll be over as soon as he gets dressed."

Cash's brother, Garon Grier, was the senior special agent at the Jacobsville FBI office. He was formerly with the FBI's Hostage Rescue Team, and one of the best people to call in on the case. But Jake was concerned that the police presence might cause the kidnapper to panic and kill Carlie in order to get away.

"Where's Rourke?" Jake asked. "Was he playing poker with you?"

"He was, but he had a call from the politician he's supposedly the enforcer for," came the reply. "It seems the other enforcer was indisposed and he needed Rourke to run an errand for him."

"Interesting timing," Jake said.

Cash knew that. He could only imagine how he'd feel if it was his little girl, his Tris, who was missing. He drew in a breath and patted Jake on the back. "Don't worry," he said again. "It's going to be all right."

"Yes," Jake said and managed a smile. "I know that."

JAKE BLAIR EXCUSED himself in the early hours of the morning by saying that he had to visit a sick member of his congregation at the hospital. He left his cell phone number with Cash and asked him to please call if there was any word from the kidnapper.

He went inside and put on jeans and a pair of high-topped moccasins with no soles and his bomber jacket, along with a concealed knife in a scabbard, a .45 magnum in a Velcro holster and a pair of handcuffs.

With his equipment carefully hidden under the roomy bomber jacket, he waved to local law enforcement and spun out of the yard in the Cobra.

Unknown to the others, he'd had time to process the crude drawing on that map. He didn't for a moment think it had been dropped accidentally. No, this was a setup. They wanted Jake to come after Carlie. Which meant that, in his opinion, Jake was the real target.

He assumed that someone in his past was out to get him. He didn't know why. But there were plenty of reasons. His former life had been one of violence. He'd never expected that he would ever revisit it. Until now. His old skills were still sharp. Nobody was hurting Carlie. And as the Good Book said, God helps those who help themselves.

Probably, he amended, God didn't mean with guns. But then, he rationalized, they hadn't had guns in Biblical days, either. He was winging it. He wouldn't kill anybody. Unless it came to a choice between that and watching Carlie die. He couldn't do that. He couldn't live with it.

He followed the highway to a dirt road leading off to a deserted area with just the beginnings of scrubland, with cactus and sand. He parked the car, got out, checked his weapon, stuck it back in the holster and belted it around his waist. He strapped the bottom of the holster to his thigh with the Velcro tabs. He pulled out his knife in its sheath from under the jacket and fixed it on the other side of the belt buckle. Then he started off, with uncanny stealth, down the road.

CARLIE REGAINED CONSCIOUSNESS slowly. Her mind felt as if it was encased in molasses. She couldn't imagine why she was so sluggish, or why it was so hard to breathe.

She tried to move and realized, quite suddenly, that it was because her hands were tied behind her. She was lying on her side on a makeshift pallet. A big, worried man was standing nearby, wearing a business suit and a big gun. He wasn't holding it on her. It was on his belt, inside his open jacket.

"You okay?" he asked. "You was breathing awful jerky-like."

"I'm okay." She tried to take small breaths. She was scared to death, but she was trying not to let it show. "What am I doing here?" She swallowed. "Are you going to kill me?"

"No!" he said, and looked shocked. "Look, I don't do women. Ever." He blinked. "Well, there was one, once, but she shot me first." He flushed a little.

He was the oddest sort of kidnapper she'd ever seen. He was as big as a house and he seemed oddly sympathetic for a man who meant her harm.

"Then why did you bring me here? You said my father was hurt…!" she remembered, almost hysterical.

"Not yet," he said. "We had to get him out of the house so we could get to you," he explained. "It takes time to do these things right, you know. First we get you. Then he comes out here, all alone, and we get him. Real easy."

"Why do you want my father?" she asked, relieved that her dad was all right, but nervous because the man was making threats.

"Not me," he said with a shrug. "Somebody else."

"Why?"

"Lady, I don't know," he muttered. "Nobody tells me nothing. They just say go do something and I go do it. I don't get paid to ask questions."

"Please don't hurt my dad," she said plaintively.

He made a face. "Look, I'm not going to do anything to him," he promised. "Honest. I don't kill people for money. I just had to get him out here. There's two guys outside… they'll do it."

Her heart jumped up into her throat. Her father would be lured here because she was under threat. He'd walk right up to the door and they'd kill him. She felt sick all over. "Couldn't you stop them?" she asked. "Don't you have a father? Would you like to see that done to him?"

His face closed up. "Yeah, I had a father. He put me in the hospital twice. I wouldn't care if somebody did it to him. No way."

Her eyes were soft with sadness. "I'm so sorry," she said gently.

He looked uncomfortable. "Maybe you should try to sleep, huh?"

"My wrists hurt."

"I can do something about that." He went around behind her and fiddled with the handcuffs. They were less tight. "So funny, I got kicked off the force five years ago, and here I am using cuffs again," he mused.

"The force?"

"I was a cop. I knocked this guy down a staircase. Big guy, like me. He was trying to kill his kid. They said I used excessive force. There was a review and all, but I got canned anyway." He didn't add that it was really because he'd ruffled his partner's feathers when he wouldn't take bribes or kickbacks. That was sort of blowing his own horn. He'd been set up, but that was ancient history now. The bad thing was that it had given Mr. Helm a stick to hit him with, because he'd been honest about losing his job. He hadn't known at the time that Mr. Helm was even more crooked than his old partner.

"I work for the police chief, here," she said. "He'd use excessive force with a guy who was trying to kill his kid, too, but nobody would fire him for it."

He moved back around in front of her. He smiled faintly. He had dark eyes and a broad face with scars all over it. He had thick black wavy hair. He was an odd sort of gangster, she thought.

"Maybe he knows the right people," he told her. "I didn't."

She studied him curiously. "You aren't from Texas," she said.

He shrugged. "From Italy, way back," he said.

Her eyes widened. "Are you in the Mafia?" she asked.

He burst out laughing. He had perfect white teeth. "If I was, they'd kill me for telling people about it."

"Oh. I get it."

"Your wrists okay now? That feel better?"

"Yes. Thanks." She made a face. "What did you do to me?"

"Chloroform," he said. "Put it on a handkerchief, see, and it works quick."

She drew in another breath. Her chest felt tight.

"You ain't breathing good," he remarked, frowning.

"I have asthma."

"You got something to use for it?"

"Sure. It's back at my house. Want to take me there to pick it up?" she asked. She wasn't really afraid of him. Odd, because he looked frightening.

He smiled back. "Not really, no. I'd get fired."

"Not a bad idea, you could do something honest for a living before your bosses get you locked up for life," she returned.

He seemed disturbed by that. He checked his watch. It was an oddly expensive-looking one, she thought. He'd said they didn't pay well, but if he could afford a timepiece like that, perhaps he'd just been joking about his salary.

He drew in a long breath. "I have to make a phone call," he said. "You just stay there and be quiet so I don't have to gag you, okay?"

"I can't let them kill my father," she said. "If I hear him coming, I'm going to warn him."

"You're an honest kid, ain't you?" he asked admiringly. "Okay. I'll try not to make it too tight, so you can breathe."

He took out a clean handkerchief and rolled it up, tied it around her mouth. "That okay?" he asked.

She groaned.

"Come on, don't make me feel no worse than I do.

You're just a kid. I wouldn't hurt you. Not even if they told me to."

She made a face under the gag. Reluctantly, she nodded.

"Okay. I won't be long."

She heard him go to the door. Just as he started to open it, she thought she must be hallucinating, because she heard a chiming rock song. It went away almost at once, followed by a mild curse. The door opened and closed. She heard voices outside.

What could she possibly do that would save her father? She squirmed her way to the edge of the bed and wiggled so that her feet made it to the floor. She was still a little dizzy, but she managed to get to her feet.

She moved to the door and listened. She heard distant voices. She looked around. The room had no windows. There was a pallet on the floor, nothing else. There wasn't even a table, much less anything she could try to use to untie herself.

Well, she could at least listen and try to hear her father's voice. She might be able to warn him before they shot him. She groaned inwardly. It was going to be on her conscience forever if he died because she'd opened the door to a stranger. When she recalled what the big man had told her, it was so obviously a ruse that she couldn't imagine why she hadn't questioned his story. He'd said her father was hurt. After that, her brain had gone into panic mode. That was why she'd agreed to leave with him.

But it was going to make a really lousy epitaph for her father. If she was lucky, the FBI would involve itself because it was a kidnapping. There was also her boss, who'd come looking for her. Maybe Carson would, too. Her heart jumped. Sure he would. He was probably up in San Antonio with that gorgeous blonde, out on a date. He wouldn't even know she was missing and probably wouldn't mind unless somebody asked him to help find her. That made her even more depressed.

But how would they ever find her in time to save her father? She hoped he had no idea where to find her, that they hadn't left some sort of clue that would lead him here. But there were armed guards at the door, and they were waiting for him, her kidnapper had said. That meant they had to have left some clue to help him find this place.

She closed her eyes and began to pray silently, the last hope of the doomed…

CARSON HAD JUST walked back into his apartment, after insistently leaving Lanette at hers, when his cell phone went off.

He locked himself in and answered it, tired and out of sorts. "Carson," he said shortly.

"It's Cash. I thought you might want to know that we've had some developments down here."

He grimaced as he went into the kitchen to make coffee. "Somebody confessed to trying to off the preacher?"

There was a pause. "Someone's kidnapped Carlie…"

"What the hell! Who? When?"

Cash wanted to tell him to calm down, but he had some idea about Carson's feelings for the woman, so he bit his tongue. "We don't know who. Her father was hoaxed into going to a motel to counsel a suicidal man, who conveniently disappeared before he showed up. Rourke and I were playing poker. We had no idea Carlie was going to be home alone. Somehow she was lured out. Her father said that he found her telephone on the kitchen table and her purse upstairs."

"That damned phone..."

"I know, she's always forgetting it," Cash replied heavily. "It seems that Carlie was the target all along. There was one clue, a crude drawing of a building in the area, but nobody knows where it is. The map isn't very helpful."

"Where's her father?"

"Funny thing," Cash mused. "He says he has to visit a sick member of his congregation at the hospital. The timing strikes me as a bit odd."

"I'll be there in fifteen minutes."

"You won't help her if you die on the way."

"Thanks for the tip." He hung up.

"JAKE BLAIR'S ONLY been gone a few minutes," Cash told Carson when he arrived.

Carson glanced past him. "Crime scene guys at work already, I gather."

"Yes."

Carson went inside and looked at the map lying on the table in a protective cover. It had already been dusted for prints—none found—and cataloged in position. He also saw Carlie's cell phone.

"May I?" he asked.

"It's been dusted. Only prints are hers," Zack, Sheriff Hayes Carson's chief investigator, told him with a smile.

"We checked her calls, too. Nothing." He went back to work.

Carson's fingers smoothed over the phone absently. It might have been one of the last things she touched. It was comforting, in some odd way. He thought of her being held, terrified, maybe smothering because the asthma would be worsened by the fear and confusion. His face mirrored his own fear.

He stuck the phone in his pocket absentmindedly as he studied the map once more. His black eyes narrowed. The drawing was amateurish, but he recognized two features on that map because they were on the way to Cy Parks's ranch. He drove the road almost every day. There was a ranch house that had burned down some time back, leaving only a ramshackle barn standing. It had to be where they had Carlie.

He was careful not to let his recognition show, because if the gangbusters here went shoving in, they'd probably shock the kidnappers into killing her quickly so they could escape. He couldn't risk that.

"Any idea where this place is?" he asked Cash with a convincing frown.

"Not a clue," Cash said tautly, "and I've been here for years."

"It's a pretty bad map," Carson replied.

"Yes."

"You said her father just left?" Carson asked in a low voice, incredulous. "His daughter's been kidnapped, and he's visiting the sick?"

Cash motioned him aside, away from his brother and

the sheriff's department. "He was carrying a .45 magnum in his belt. Nicely hidden, but I got a glimpse of it." He pursed his lips. "Can you still track?"

"Not on pavement," he returned.

"He drives a red Cobra," he pointed out. "Not the easiest ride to conceal. And this is a small community."

"I'll have a look around."

"I'd go with you, but I can't leave." He hesitated. "Don't try to sneak up on him," he advised tersely, lowering his voice. "He's a minister now, but you don't ever lose survival instincts."

"What do you know that I don't?" Carson asked.

"Things I can't tell. Go find him."

"I'll do my best." He glanced past Cash at the other law enforcement people. "Why aren't they looking?"

"Forensics first, then action," Cash explained. His face hardened. "I know. I never really got the hang of it, either." His dark eyes met Carson's. "Her father knows where she is, I'm sure of it. Find him, you find her. Try to keep them both alive."

Carson nodded. He turned and went out the door.

JAKE SLOWED AS he neared the turnoff that led, eventually, to Cy Parks's ranch. Carlie, if the map was accurate, was being held at an old cattle ranch. The ranch house was long since burned down and deserted, but there was a barn still standing. He got around to the back of the building without being detected and observed two men standing guard in front of the door.

They were obviously armed, judging from the bulges

under their cheap jackets. Apparently whoever hired them didn't pay much.

Jake had spent years perfecting his craft as a mercenary. He could move in shadow, in light, in snow or sleet, without leaving a trace of himself. He was going to have to take down two men at once. He would also have to do it with exquisite care, so as not to alert what might be a third man inside the structure holding Carlie.

It would seem impossible to survive a frontal assault against armed men. He only smiled.

He was able to get very close before he moved out into the open with both arms up. He approached the men who belatedly drew their weapons and pointed them at him. The element of surprise had confused them just enough, he hoped.

"Stop there," one of them said.

He kept walking until he was close to them.

"I said stop!" the other threatened.

"Here?" Jake asked, looking down at his feet. "Next to this snake?"

They looked down at his feet immediately. Big mistake. He ducked under them, hit one in the diaphragm to momentarily paralyze him while he put pressure to the carotid artery of the other man and watched him go down, unconscious. The second one, with his gun drawn, bent over, was easy to knock out with the .45.

Very quiet. Very precise. Not a sound came after. And he hadn't had to kill them. He drew out two lengths of rawhide from his bomber jacket and got busy trussing up the gunmen.

He knew he'd have to work fast. If someone had Carlie at gunpoint inside, they might have heard the men ordering him to stop. It was a long shot, though. He wasn't that close to the barn.

He secured them by their thumbs, on their bellies with their hands behind them, and moved quickly toward the shed.

On the way, he had company, quite suddenly, but not from ambush. The man, moving quickly, seemed to deliberately make a sound. He'd been warned, Jake thought and smiled. He turned to the newcomer with the knife still in his hand. When he recognized the man, he slid it quickly into its sheath.

The action wasn't lost on Carson, who was remembering what Cash had told him about this enigmatic man.

"Good thing you came with a little noise," the minister said softly. His glittering blue eyes were those of a different person altogether. "I wouldn't have hesitated, under the circumstances."

Carson stared at him with open curiosity. "I've never seen an action carried out more efficiently."

"Son, you haven't seen anything yet," Jake told him. "You get behind me. And you don't move unless I tell you to. Got it?"

Carson just nodded.

They got to the door. Jake pulled a device out of his pocket and pressed it to the old wood. His jaw tautened.

He drew back and kicked the door in, an action that is much easier in movies with balsa wood props than in real life with real wood. It flung back on its hinges. Jake had the automatic leveled before it even moved, and he walked in professionally, checking corners and dark places on his way to an inner room.

Carlie was, fortunately, on her feet about a yard away from the door her father had just broken down. She cried out through the gag as she saw him.

"Dear God," Jake whispered, holstering the gun as he ran to her. "Honey, are you okay?"

"Dad!" she managed through the gag. She hugged him with her cuffed hands around his neck, sobbing. She was breathing roughly.

Carson dug an inhaler out of his pocket and handed it to her while he took off the gag. "Two puffs, separated," he instructed. He touched her hair. "What did they do to you?" he asked angrily.

"Nothing," she choked. "I mean, he brought me in here and tied me up, but he promised he wouldn't hurt me and he didn't. Except for keeping me tied up all night, I mean," she stammered between puffs of the inhaler. "Thanks," she told Carson. "I forgot mine."

"And your damned phone," Carson muttered, digging it out of his jacket pocket. He handed it to her.

"They had armed men at the door," she exclaimed, gaping at her father. "He said the idea of taking me was to lure you here. He wasn't going to hurt you. But he said the two men, they were going to do it! They were supposed to kill you…!"

He shrugged. "They're not a threat anymore, pumpkin." He pulled a tool from his pocket and very efficiently unlocked her cuffs, touching only the chain. He turned to

Carson. “You wouldn’t happen to have an evidence bag on you?” he mused.

Carson pursed his lips, produced one from his jacket pocket and handed it to Jake. “I had a feeling,” he replied.

Carlie watched her father slide the cuffs, gently and still without touching the parts that had locked her wrists, into the evidence bag. He laid them on the table and took a quick shot with his smartphone’s camera. “Just in case,” he told them.

“Someday, you have to tell me about your past,” Carlie said.

“I don’t, pumpkin. There are things that should never be spoken of.” He smoothed over her hair. “Let’s get out of here.”

“I couldn’t agree more,” she said.

Carson took her arm. “Can you walk?” he asked softly, his eyes darker with concern.

“Sure,” she said, moving a little stiffly. “I’m fine. Honest.” It delighted her that he’d come with her father to rescue her. She hadn’t expected it. She imagined his girlfriend was livid.

Her father led the way out. He had the automatic in his hand and he didn’t apologize or explain why.

Carson let him lead, Carlie moving stiffly at his side.

The two previously armed men were still lying on the ground where Jake had left them. “Did one of these guys kidnap you?” her father asked.

She was staring almost openmouthed at them. Two automatic weapons lay in the dirt near them. They weren’t moving. But they were certainly vocal.

"No," she said. "I didn't see these ones. Just the man who tied me up."

"You'll pay for this!" one of the captives raged.

"Damned straight!" the other one agreed. "The boss will get you!"

"Well, not if he's as efficient as you two," Jake replied blithely. "And I expect you're going to have a little trouble with the feds. Kidnapping is a felony."

"Hey, we didn't kidnap nobody! We was just guarding her!" the small man protested.

"Yeah. Just guarding her. So she didn't get hurt or nothing," the other man agreed.

As he spoke, several cars came into view along the road. Two of them had flashing blue lights.

Jake turned to Carson with a sigh. They'd figured out the map and now he was going to be in the soup for jumping the gun and leaving them out of the loop. He just shook his head. "You can bring Carlie to visit me in the local jail tonight. I hope they have somebody who can cook."

For the first time, Carson grinned.

BUT JAKE WASN'T ARRESTED. Cash Grier had already briefed his brother, who was in charge of the operation. A man with Jake's background couldn't convincingly be excluded from a mission that involved saving his child from kidnappers. So no charges were pressed. It would have been unlikely anyway, since Jake knew one of the top men at the agency and several government cabinet members, as well. Carlie hadn't known that, until she overheard her dad talking to Garon Grier.

"How did you get past the men with guns?" Carlie asked Carson while she was being checked out at the emergency room. Her father had insisted that Carson take her there, just in case, while he tried to explain his part in her liberation.

"I didn't," he mused. "Your father took them down." He shook his head. "I never saw it coming, and I was watching."

She signed herself out, smiled at the clerk and followed Carson out the front door. "My father is a mystery."

"He's very accomplished," he remarked.

"I noticed."

He stopped at his car and turned to her on the passenger side. "Are you sure you're all right?" he asked.

"Don't you start," she muttered. "I'm fine. Just a little bruised."

He caught her face in his big, warm hands and tilted it up to his eyes. "I thought they might kill you," he said with involuntary concern.

"And you'd miss killing me in battlegrounds online?" she asked, trying to lighten the tension, which was growing exponentially.

"Yes. I'd miss that. And other…things," he whispered as he bent and kissed her with a tenderness that was overwhelming. Then, just as suddenly, he whipped her body completely against his and kissed her with almost bruising intensity. He jerked his mouth away before she could even respond. "Next time, if there is a next time, don't open the door to anybody you don't know!"

"He said Daddy was in a wreck," she faltered. The kiss had shaken her.

"Next time, call Daddy and see if he answers," he retorted.

She searched his angry eyes. "Okay," she whispered softly.

"And for the last time, keep that damned cell phone with you!"

She nodded. "Okay," she said again, without an argument.

The tenderness in her face, the soft, involuntary hunger, the unexpected obedience almost brought him to his knees.

He'd been out of his mind when he'd heard she'd been taken; he couldn't rest until he'd got to her. After Cash had called him, he'd gone crazy on the way down from San Antonio as his mind haunted him with all the things that could have happened to her. The thought of a world without Carlie was frightening to him. He was only just beginning to realize what an impact she had on him. He didn't like it, either.

He fought for self-control. People were walking around nearby, going to and from cars. He let her go and moved away. He felt as if he were vibrating with feeling. "I need to get you home," he said stiffly.

"Okay," she said.

He helped her inside the car, started it and drove her home. He didn't say a word the whole way.

When he let her out at the front door, she ran to her father and hugged him tightly.

"I'm okay," she promised.

He smoothed her hair, looking over her head at Carson. "Thanks."

Carson shrugged. "No problem. Lock her in a closet and lose the key, will you?" he added, not completely facetiously.

Jake chuckled. "She'd just bang on the door until I let her out," he said, giving her an affectionate smile.

"Where's local law enforcement?" Carson asked.

"Packed up all the vital clues and left. They were just a little late backtracking the kidnapper to a lonely barn over near your boss's house," Jake said with biting criticism.

"You did that quite neatly yourself," Carson replied. "I'm reliably informed that local law enforcement followed you there after being tipped off."

"Did you tip them off?" Jake asked with a knowing smile.

Carson sighed. "Yes. I didn't want to have to bury both of you."

Jake became less hostile. "Carson," he said softly, "I wasn't always a minister. I can handle myself."

"And now I know that." Carson managed a smile, glanced at Carlie with painfully mixed feelings and left.

LATER, IN THE corner table at the local café, Carson cornered Rourke. "Okay, let's have it," he demanded.

"Have what?" Rourke asked with a smile.

"That mild-mannered minister—" he meant Jake Blair "—took down two armed men with a speed I've never seen in my life. I didn't even hear him walk toward them, and I was out of my car and heading that way at the time."

"Oh, Jake was always something special," Rourke replied with a smile of remembrance. "He could move so silently that the enemy never knew he was around. They called him "Snake," because he could get in and out of places that an army couldn't. He had a rare talent with a knife. Sort of like you," he added, indicating the big bowie knife that Carson was never without. "He'd go in, do every fourth man in a camp, get out without even being heard. The next morning, when the enemy awoke, there would be pandemonium." He hesitated. "Don't you ever tell her," he added coldly, "or you'll find out a few more things about the reverend Blair."

"I never would," Carson assured. "There are things in my past just as unsavory."

Rourke nodded. "His specialty was covert assassination, but he didn't work with a spotter or use a sniper kit. He went in alone, with just a knife, at night." He shook his head. "We tried one night to hear him leave. None of us, not even those with sensitive hearing, could ever spot him. The government begged him to come back when he left for the seminary. He told them he was through with the old life and he was never doing it again. Carlie's his life, now. Her, and his church." He glanced at Carson. "He says she's the only reason he didn't commit suicide after her mother died. You know, I don't really understand religion, but I guess it has its place."

"I guess it does," Carson replied thoughtfully.

"How was your date?" Rourke asked.

Carson made a face. "Tedious."

"She's a looker."

Carson stared at him with cool, cynical eyes. "They all look alike, smell alike, sound alike," he said. "And they don't last long. I don't like possession."

Rourke toyed with his coffee cup. "I don't, either," he said slowly, thinking of Tat. The last he'd heard, she went into a small, war-torn African nation, named Ngawa in Swahili, for a species of civet cat found there, to cover the agony of the survivors. She wouldn't answer his phone calls. She wouldn't return his messages. She might as well have vanished off the face of the earth. He had…feelings for her, that he could never, ever express. He, like Carson, had placated the ache with other women. Nothing did much good.

Carson finished his coffee. "I have to get back up to San Antonio. I may have an offer soon."

Rourke studied him. "Tired of working for Cy?"

Carson's lips made a thin line. "Tired of aching for something I can never have."

"Boy, do I understand that feeling," Rourke said tersely.

Carson laughed, but it had a hollow sound.

He was supposed to take Lanette dancing tonight. He wasn't looking forward to it, but he'd given his word, so he'd go. The job offer would involve travel to some South American nation for a covert op with some ex-military people, on the QT. They needed a field medic, and Carson's reputation had gotten around.

It was a good job, paid well, and it would get him away from Carlie. Suddenly that had become of earthshaking importance. He didn't want to pursue that line of thought, so he called Lanette before he left Jacobsville and told her he'd pick her up at six.

10

Carlie described the kidnapper to Zack the next day, with her boss and the FBI special agent in charge, Garon Grier, listening in Cash's office.

"He sounded just like one of those gangsters in the old black-and-white movies," she said. "He was big as a house and a little clumsy. He was kind to me. He didn't say a thing out of the way or even threaten me."

"Except by kidnapping you," Garon Grier mused.

"Well, yes, there was that," she agreed. "But he didn't hurt me. He said he was supposed to take me out there to lure my dad to come get me. I suppose that meant they wanted to get him out of town to someplace deserted. I was so scared," she recalled. "I managed to get to my feet, to the door. I listened really hard, so if I heard Dad's voice, I might have time to warn him."

"You weren't afraid for yourself?" Cash asked.

"Not really. He didn't want to hurt me. I was just afraid for Dad. He's absentminded and he forgets things, like his house keys," she said with a smile. Then the smile faded. "But he took down these two huge guys. They had guns, too." She frowned worriedly. "I don't know how he did it. He even kicked in the door! I only just managed to get out of the way in time! And Dad had a gun..."

"He didn't use it," Cash reminded her.

"No. Of course not." She rubbed her wrists. "The kidnapper apologized for the handcuffs. He knew how to loosen them. He said he was a cop once. He knocked a man down a staircase for roughing up a child and they fired him." She looked up. They were all staring at her.

"What else did he say?" Garon asked. He was taking notes on his cell phone.

"I asked why he wanted my dad hurt and he said his bosses didn't pay him to ask questions," she recalled. She was going to add that he was wearing an expensive watch, and about that funny chiming sound she thought she'd heard, but she wasn't certain that she hadn't been confused by the chloroform the kidnapper had used on her. No use making wild statements. She needed to stick to the facts.

"That's not much to go on, but it's more than we had," Garon said a few minutes later. "Thanks, Carlie."

"You're very welcome." She got up. "I'll just get the mail caught up," she told her boss, rolling her eyes. "I expect that will last me a few hours.."

Cash chuckled. "No doubt. Hey," he added when she reached the door. She turned. "I'm glad you're okay, kid," he said gently.

She grinned. "Me, too, Chief. Where would you ever get another secretary who didn't hide in the closet every time you lost your temper?"

She went out before he could come back with a reply.

"ISN'T THIS LOVELY?" Lanette asked Carson as they did a lazy two-step on the dance floor.

"Lovely," he said without feeling it.

"You're very distracted tonight," she said. She moved a little away so that he could see how nicely her red sequined cocktail dress suited her, exposing most of her breasts and a lot of her thigh in a side split. Her exquisite hair was put up in a nice French twist with a jeweled clasp that matched the dress and her shoes. She looked beautiful and very expensive. He wondered vaguely how she managed to afford clothes like that on a stewardess salary. And she never seemed to go on any trips.

"Do you work?" he asked, curious.

"I work very hard," she said. She smiled secretively. "I was a stewardess, but I have a new job now.. I work in…personnel," she concluded. "For a big corporation."

"I see."

"What do you do?" she asked.

He smiled enigmatically. "I work for a rancher in Jacobsville mostly, but I'm also a field medic."

"A medic? Really?" she exclaimed. "That's such a…well, I know it's noble and all that, but it sounds just really boring."

Boring. He was recalling several incidents, trying to treat men under fire and get them evacuated by helicopter or ambulance in trouble spots all over the world. Saving lives. "Maybe not as boring as it sounds," he concluded.

She shrugged. "If you say so." She looked up at him as they danced. "I heard on the news that there was a kidnapping in that town where your rancher boss lives. Was anybody hurt?"

"Carlie was frightened, but they didn't hurt her."

"Shame."

He stopped dancing. "Excuse me?"

"Well, she's a little prude, isn't she?" she said cattily. "Doesn't know how to dance properly, wears cheap clothes. My God, I'll bet she's still a virgin." She laughed heartily at the other woman's stupidity. This woman was annoying. He was beginning, just beginning, to understand how Carlie saw the world. She was blunt and unassuming, never coy, never shallow like this beautiful hothouse flower. Carlie was like a sunflower, open and honest and pretty. The fact that she didn't sleep around was suddenly appealing to him. He hated the implication of that thought. He wasn't going to get trapped. Not by some small-town girl with hang-ups.

"They say her father rescued her," Lanette purred.

"Yes. That's what I heard, too," he said, without adding that he'd been in on the rescue. Not that he'd had much work to do. Jake Blair had done it all.

"One guy against two armed men," she said, almost to herself. "It sounds…incredible. I mean, they were really tough guys. That's what I heard, anyway."

"Not so tough," Carson corrected her. "Blair had them trussed up like holiday turkeys."

She let out a rough breath. "Idiots," she murmured. She saw Carson's sudden scrutiny and laughed. "I mean, whoever planned that kidnapping was obviously not intended for a life of crime. Wouldn't you say?"

"I'd say they'd better be on a plane out of the country pretty soon," he replied. "The FBI got called in."

She stopped dancing. "The FBI? That's no threat. Those people are always in the news for doing dumb things—"

"The local FBI," he interrupted. "Garon Grier. He was formerly with the Hostage Rescue Team. His brother is Jacobsville's police chief Cash Grier. You met him at the dance."

She nodded slowly. "I see."

"So the kidnapper will not be sleeping well anytime soon," he concluded.

"Maybe he'll just have to step up his plans while the local FBI get their marbles together," she laughed.

"That's what bothers me," he replied. "What nobody understands is why someone would try to kill a minister."

"Loads of reasons," she said. "Maybe he's one of those radicals who wants everybody to take vows of chastity or something."

"A political opinion shouldn't result in murder," he pointed out.

"Well, no, but maybe the people who want him dead aren't interested in his opinions. Maybe it's just a job to them. Somebody big calling the shots, you know?"

Somebody big. Big. Like the politician who was finishing out the Texas U.S. senator's term and was campaigning for the May special election to earn his own term.

"What are you thinking so hard about?" Lanette asked.

"Work," he said.

"Oh, work." She threw a hand up. "We're here to have fun. We could dance some more," she said, sliding close to him. "Or we could go back to my apartment…?"

He felt like a stone wall. The thought of sleeping with her had once appealed, but now he felt uncomfortable even discussing it. He thought of all the men Lanette had bragged to him about, the men she'd had. Of course men bragged about their conquests. It was just…when she did that, he thought of Carlie. Carlie!

"Ow," Lanette complained softly. "That's my hand you're crushing, honey."

He loosened his hold. "Sorry," he snapped.

"You are really tense. Please. Let me soothe that ache," she whispered sensually.

"I want to dance." He pulled her back onto the dance floor.

THE NEXT MORNING, just before daylight, he drove back down to Cy Parks's place. He couldn't sleep. He and Lanette had argued, again, about his coldness to her and about Carlie. She was venomous about the small-town girl.

Carson was angry and couldn't hide it. He didn't like hearing her bad-mouth Carlie. He was tired of the city anyway. He just wanted to get back to work.

Cy was working on a broken hoof on one of the big Santa Gertrudis bulls. He filed the broken part down while a tall African-American cowboy gently held the animal in place, soothing it with an uncanny gift.

"That's good, Diamond," the other cowboy murmured softly, using part of the pedigree bull's full name, which was Parks' Red Diamond. "Good old fellow."

Cy grinned. "I don't know what I'd do without you, Eddie," he chuckled. "That bull's just like a dog when you talk to him. He follows you around like one, anyway. Nice of Luke to let me borrow you." He glanced up at Carson. "You've been AWOL," he accused. "Couldn't find anybody to hold Diamond while I filed the hoof down, so I had to call Luke Craig and ask him to lend a hand. He sent Eddie Kells here. Eddie, this is Carson."

Carson nodded politely.

Kells just grinned.

"Kells came down here to a summer camp some years ago that Luke Craig's wife, Belinda, started for city kids in trouble with the law. Didn't know one end of a horse from another. Now he's bossing cowboys over at Luke's place," Cy chuckled.

"Yeah, Mr. Parks here saved my life," Kells replied. "I was in trouble with the law in Houston when I was younger," he said honestly. "I was on Mr. Parks's place trying to learn roping with his cattle, trespassing, and he caught me." He let out a whistle. "Thought I was a goner. But when he saw how crazy I was about cattle, he didn't press charges and Mr. Craig hired me on as a cowboy when I graduated from high school." He smiled. "I got no plans to ever leave, either. This is a good place to live. Fine people."

Carson studied the tall young man. He'd have thought that a place like this would have a lot of prejudice. It didn't seem to be the case at all, not if Kells wanted to stay here.

"You Indian?" Kells asked, and held up a hand when Carson bristled. "No, man, it's cool, I got this friend, Juanito, he's Apache. Some of his ancestors ran with Geronimo. He's hired on at Mr. Scott's place. He's been trying to teach me to speak his language. Man, it's hard!"

Carson relaxed a little. "I'm Oglala Lakota."

"I guess you couldn't speak to Juanito and have him understand you, huh?"

Carson smiled. "No. The languages are completely different."

"Only thing I can manage is enough Spanish to talk to some of the new cowboys. But I guess that's what I need to be studying, anyway."

"You do very well, too," Cy told the young man, clapping him on the shoulder. "That's it, then. You go down to the hardware and get yourself a new pocketknife, and put it on my account," he told Kells. "I'll call and okay it before you get there. Don't argue. I know Luke sent you, but you should have something. That knife's pretty old, you know," he added. Kells was using it to clean under his fingernails.

"Only one I had," Kells said, smiling. "Okay, then, I'll do it. Thanks, Mr. Parks."

They shook hands.

"Nice to meet you," Kells told Carson before he left.

"I had a different concept of life here," Carson told Cy quietly.

Cy chuckled. "So did I. Blew all my notions of it when I moved here. You will never find a place with kinder, more tolerant people, anywhere in the world."

Carson was thinking of some of the places he had been which were far less than that.

"Sorry I didn't get back in time to help," he told Cy. "There's a new complication. I need to talk to Jake Blair. I think I've made a connection, of sorts. I just want to sound him out on it."

"If you dig anything out, tell Garon Grier," Cy replied.

"Certainly." He hesitated. "I'm going to be moving on, soon," he said. "I've enjoyed my time here."

"I've enjoyed having you around." Cy gave him a cynical smile. "I was like you, you know," he said. "Same fire for action, same distaste for marriage, kids. I went all over the world with a gun. Killed a lot of people. But in the end, it was the loneliness that got me. It will eat you up like acid."

"I like my own company."

Cy put a hand on his shoulder. His green eyes narrowed. "Son," he said gently, "there's a difference between being alone and being lonely."

"I'm not lonely," Carson said doggedly.

Cy just chuckled. "Go see Jake. He'll be up. He never was a late sleeper."

"You knew him before?" he asked slowly.

Cy nodded. "He was on special duty, assigned to support troops. We ended up in the same black ops group." He shook his head. "The only person I've ever known who comes close to him is Cash Grier. Jake was…gifted. And not in a way you'd ever share with civilians."

"I heard that from Rourke."

Cy pursed his lips. "Make sure you never share that information with Carlie," he cautioned. "You do not want to see Jake Blair lose his temper. Ever."

"I'm getting that impression," Carson said with a mild chuckle.

It was barely daylight. Carson knew it was early to be visiting, but he was certain Jake would be up, and he needed to tell him what he thought might be going on. Lanette had, without realizing it, pointed him in a new direction on the attempted kidnapping.

When he got to Reverend Blair's house, he was surprised to find Carlie there alone. She seemed equally surprised to find him at her door.

She was wearing a T-shirt and jeans. It was late February and still cold outside. In fact, it was cold in the house. Heat was expensive, and Carlie was always trying to save money. The cold had become familiar, so that she hardly noticed it now.

"What can I do for you?" she asked quietly.

He shrugged. "I came to see your father," he told her.

Her eyebrows arched over wide green eyes. "He didn't mention anything..."

"He doesn't know." He smiled slowly, liking the way her face flushed when he did that. "Is he here?"

"No, but he'll be back...soon," she faltered. She bit her lower lip. "You can come in and wait for him, if you like."

The invitation was reluctant, but at least she made one. "Okay. Thanks."

She opened the door and let him in. Why did she feel as if she were walking into quicksand?

He closed the door behind him and followed her into

the living room. On the sofa was a mass of yarn. Apparently she was making some sort of afghan in soft shades of blue and purple.

"You crochet?" he asked, surprised.

"Yes," she replied. She sat down beside the skeins of yarn and moved them aside. Carson dropped into the armchair just to her left.

"My mother used to do handwork," he murmured. He could remember her sewing quilts when he was very small. She did it to keep her hands busy. Maybe she did it to stop thinking about how violent and angry his father was when he drank. And he never seemed to stop drinking…

Carlie toyed with the yarn, but her hands were nervous. The silence grew more tense by the minute. He didn't speak. He just looked at her.

"Would you mind…not doing that, please?" she asked in a haunted tone.

"Doing what exactly?" he asked with a slow, sensuous smile.

"Staring at me," she blurted out. "I know you think I'm ugly. Couldn't you stare at the— Oh!"

He was sitting beside her the next minute, his hands on her face, cupping it while he looked straight into her eyes. "I don't think you're ugly," he said huskily. He looked at her mouth.

She was confused and nervous. "You said once that you liked your women more…physically perfect," she accused in a throaty voice.

He drew in a breath. "Yes. But I didn't mean it."

His thumb rubbed gently over her bow mouth, liking

the way it felt. It was swollen and very soft. She caught his wrist, but not to pull his hand away.

She hadn't felt such sensations. It was new and exciting. He was exciting. She wanted to hide her reaction from him, but he knew too much about women. She felt like a rabbit walking into a snare.

She should get up right now and go into the kitchen. She should…

His mouth lowered to her lips. He touched them softly, tenderly, smoothing her lips apart so that he could feel the softness underneath the top one. He traced it delicately with his tongue. His hands on her face were big and warm. His thumbs stroked her cheekbones while he toyed with her lips in a silence that accentuated her quick breathing.

He hadn't expected his own reaction to her. This was explosive. Sweet. Dangerous. He opened his mouth and pushed her lips apart. He let go of her face and lifted her across his lap while he kissed her as if her mouth was the source of such sweetness that he couldn't bear to let it go.

Helplessly, her arms went around his neck and she kissed him back, with more enthusiasm than expertise.

He could feel that lack of experience. It made him feel taller, stronger. She had nothing to compare this with, he could tell. He nibbled her lower lip while one big hand shifted down to her T-shirt and teased under the sleeve.

She caught his wrist and stayed it. "No," she protested weakly.

But it was too late. His long fingers were under the sleeve, and he could feel the scars.

She bit her lip. "Don't," she pleaded, turning her face away.

He drew in a harsh breath. "Do you think a scar matters?" he asked roughly. He turned her face up to his. "It doesn't."

Her eyes were eloquent, stinging with tears.

"Trust me," he whispered as his mouth lowered to hers again. "I won't hurt you. I promise."

His mouth became slowly insistent, so hungry and demanding that she forgot to protest, and let go of his wrist. He slid it under the hem of her T-shirt while he kissed her and lifted it, sliding his hand possessively over her small breast and up to the scar.

"You mustn't!" she whispered frantically.

He nibbled her upper lip. "Shh," he whispered back, and quickly lifted the shirt over her head and tossed it aside.

She was wearing a delicate little white lacy bra that fastened in front. Just above the lacy cup was a scar, a long one running from her collarbone down just to the beginning of the swell of her breast.

Tears stung her eyes. She hadn't shown the wound to anyone except the doctor and a woman police officer. She tried to cover it with her hand, but he lifted it gently away and unfastened the bra.

"Beautiful," he whispered when he saw the delicate pink and mauve mound that he'd uncovered.

"Wh...what?" she stammered.

His hand smoothed boldly over her delicate flesh, teasing the nipple so that it became immediately hard. "Your breasts are beautiful," he said softly, bending. "I wonder if I can fit one into my mouth…?"

As he spoke, he did it. His tongue rubbed abrasively over the sensitive nipple while his mouth covered and possessed the pert little mound.

Her reaction was unexpected and violent. She shivered and cried out, and then suddenly arched up toward his lips as he made a slow suction that caused unspeakable responses in her untried body.

"No…nooooo!" she groaned as she felt the tension grow to almost painful depths and then, suddenly, snap. The pleasure was unlike anything she'd ever known in her life. She shivered and shivered, her short nails digging into his shoulders as she held on and convulsed with ecstasy.

He felt her body contort, felt the shudders run through her as he satisfied her with nothing more than his mouth on her breast. His hand went to her hip and ground it into his while he continued the warm pressure of his mouth on her damp flesh. He wanted her. He'd never wanted anything so much!

She was lost. She couldn't even protest. The pleasure swept over her in waves, like breakers on the ocean, on the beach. She arched her back and shuddered as her body gave in to him, hungered for him, ached to have more than this, something more, anything….

Finally, he lifted his head and looked down at her. She lay shivering in the aftermath, tears running down her cheeks. She wept silently, her eyes wide and wet and accusing.

"It's all right," he whispered. He kissed away the tears. "There's no reason to be embarrassed."

She sobbed. She felt as if she'd betrayed everything she believed in. If he hadn't stopped, she wouldn't have been able to. She was embarrassed and humiliated by her own easy acceptance of his ardor. He was a womanizer. God only knew how many women he'd had. And she was so easy…

She pushed gently at his chest.

He let her go, very slowly, his eyes riveted to her taut breasts, to the red marks on the one he'd suckled so hard.

She tried to pull the bra over them, but he prevented her with a gentle movement of his hand. He wasn't looking at her breasts. He was looking at the scar. He traced it, noting the ridge that was forming.

She drew in a sharp breath.

"It was deep, wasn't it?" he asked softly.

She swallowed. He didn't seem repulsed. "Yes."

He traced it tenderly. His finger moved down over her breast to the hard nipple and caressed it. He loved touching her. It was surprising.

"I've never had a virgin," he whispered. "I didn't realize how exciting it would be."

She flushed. "I'm…not perfect physically," she choked, remembering the hurtful things he'd said in her boss's office.

He looked into her eyes with regret darkening his own. "Here," he said quietly. "Show-and-tell."

He unbuttoned his shirt and pulled it away from his broad, muscular chest. He pulled her up into a sitting position on his lap and drew her fingers to the worst scar, where a long, deep wound went just below his rib cage on the side near his heart.

"This was deep, too," she said softly, tracing it.

He nodded. "He came at me with a sword, of all things. I drew him in and guided the blade where it would do the least damage, before I killed him." His eyes were narrow and cold.

She shivered. She could never kill anyone.

"He'd just raped a young woman. A pregnant woman," he said quietly.

Her expression changed. Her eyes went back to the scars. "These are…strange," she said, tracing several small round scars below his collarbone.

"Cigarette burns," he said with a faint smile. "I was captured once. They tortured me for information." He chuckled. "They got my name, rank and serial number. Eventually they got tired of listening to it, but my squad came and rescued me before they killed me."

"Wow," she whispered.

He cocked his head and studied her. "You are…unexpected."

Her eyebrows lifted. "I am?"

His eyes went down to her bare breasts. He drew her against him, very gently, and moved her breasts against his bare chest. She moaned. He bent and kissed her, hungrily, urgently.

"I want you," he murmured.

His hands were on her breasts again, and she was dying for him. She wanted that pleasure again, that he'd given her so easily, so sensually, with just his mouth. But with a harsh moan, she dragged herself away from him and pulled her T-shirt across her bare breasts like a shield.

"Please," she whispered when he started to draw her back into his arms. "Please. I'm sorry. I can't. I just…can't!"

She looked as if he'd asked her to go through the entire catalog of sins at once. Probably she felt that way. She was a person of faith. She didn't believe in quick rolls in the hay. She was innocent.

He felt oddly ashamed. He buttoned his shirt while she fumbled her bra closed and put her shirt back on with tattered pride. As cold reality set in, she was horrified by what she'd let him do. All her principles had flown out the window the minute he touched her.

"I see," he said quietly. "You believe it's the road to hell. And I don't believe in anything," he added coldly.

She met his eyes. "You don't really even like women, do you?" she asked perceptively.

His smile was icy. "She said she loved me," he replied. "We were married for all of a year when she became pregnant. But by then there was another man." His eyes closed, and his brows drew together in pain at the memory while Carlie listened.

"It was almost two days after the wreck before they found the bodies. They thought they could have saved the child, a boy, if they'd found them just a little sooner." His face contorted. "I killed them all…"

"No, you didn't," she said. "You couldn't hurt a woman if you tried."

He looked at her with narrow, intent eyes. "Really? I

scared you to death in your boss's office," he reminded her tautly.

"Yes, but you wouldn't have hurt me. It was the association with the past that frightened me, not you," she repeated softly. She touched his cheek, drew her soft fingers down it. "Some things are meant to be. We don't make those decisions. We can't. God takes people away sometimes for reasons we can't understand. But there's a reason, even if we don't know what it was."

His face hardened. "God," he scoffed.

She smiled gently. "You don't believe in anything."

"I used to. Before she destroyed my life." His eyes were dark with confusion and pain.

"You have to accept the fact that you can't control the world, or the people in it," she continued quietly. "Control is just an illusion."

"Like love?" he laughed coldly.

"Love is everywhere," she countered. "You aren't looking. You're living inside yourself, in the past, locked up in pain and loss and guilt. You can't forgive anything until you can forgive yourself."

He glared at her.

"The key to it all is faith," she said gently.

"Faith." He nodded. His eyes were hostile. "Yours took a hike when I started kissing your breasts, didn't it? All those shiny ideals, that proud innocence, would have been gone in a flash if I'd insisted."

She blushed. Her hand left his face. "Yes. That's true. I never realized how easy it would be to fall from grace." Her wide, soft eyes, wounded and wet, met his. "Is that why you did it? To show me how vulnerable I am?"

He wanted to say yes, to hurt her again. But suddenly it gave him no pleasure. No woman had ever reacted to him that way, been so tender with him, so patient, so willing to listen.

"No," he confessed curtly.

That one word took the pain away. She just looked at him.

He drew her hand to his mouth and kissed the palm hungrily. "I've never told anyone about my wife, except Grier and you, and one other person."

"I never tell anything I know," she replied huskily. She searched his dark eyes. "Ever."

He managed a smile. "You have a gift for listening."

"I learned it from my father. He's very patient."

He touched her soft mouth. "The angle of that wound is odd," he said after a minute, staring at the T-shirt. "Was the attacker very tall?"

"Not really," she confessed. "He reached around my father to do it." She shivered. She could still feel the pain of the knife.

"He'll never do it to anyone else," he assured her.

"I know. He died. They said it took a long time." She touched the scar involuntarily. "I'm sorry that his life took such a turn that he felt he was justified in killing people."

"He was an addict and they offered him product," Carson said coldly. "It works, most of the time."

"I'm sorry for him, for the way it happened. But I'm not

sorry he's gone." She grimaced. "My dad wouldn't like hearing me say that."

"I won't tell him," he said gently. He looked down at her with faint possession. "Don't beat your conscience to death over what happened," he said quietly. "Any experienced man can overcome an innocent woman's scruples if he tries hard enough. And if she's attracted to him," he added gently.

She colored even more. "Yes, well, I…I didn't mean… I don't…"

He put a finger across her mouth. "It's an intimate memory. For the two of us. No one else will ever know. All right?"

She nodded. "All right."

He brought her hand to his mouth and kissed the palm. "Keep your doors locked when your father isn't here," he said.

The tone of his voice was disturbing. "Why?"

"I can't tell you."

She just sighed. As she started to speak, there was a terrible rapping sound against the side of the house.

Carson was on his feet at once, his hand on the hilt of the big bowie knife.

"That's just George."

He scowled. "Who?"

"George. He's my red-bellied woodpecker." She grimaced. "I put nuts out for him at daylight every day. He's telling me he's hungry and I'm late." She laughed. "Listen." There was another sound, like something small bounding across the roof. "That's one of the squirrels. They let

George do the reminding, and then they queue for the nuts." She listened again. There was a loud cacophony of bird calls. "And those are the blue jays. They fight George for the nuts…"

"You know them by sound?" he asked, surprised.

"Of course." She got up, frowning slightly. "Can't everybody identify them from the songs they sing?"

He shook his head. "I don't believe this."

"You can help me feed them if you want to. I mean, if you don't have something else to do," she added quickly, not wanting him to feel pressured.

But he wasn't looking for a way out. He just smiled. "Put on a coat," he said.

She pulled her ratty one out of the closet and grimaced. "This is what it's best for," she sighed. "Feeding birds."

"You should buy a new one."

She gave him a world-weary glance. "With what?" she asked. "We just had to fill up the propane tank again because winter doesn't appear to be leaving anytime soon. New things are a luxury around here."

He was estimating the age of her shoes and jeans. The T-shirt appeared new. He cocked his head. It was black with writing—it had a picture of a big black bird on it. Underneath it read, "Hey, you in the house, bring more birdseed!"

He chuckled. "Cool shirt."

"You like it? I designed it. There's this website. It has nice T-shirts for a reasonable price and you can design your own. This is one of the grackles that come every spring. I haven't seen one just yet."

She led the way, picking up a container of birdseed and one of shelled nuts on the way.

"The pecans came from our own trees," she said. "The farm produce store that sells them has a sheller you can run them through. I did enough to last several weeks."

"Back home, we have ravens," he told her, his hands in his jeans as he followed her out to the big backyard. Towering trees gave way to a small pasture beyond. "And crows." He pursed his lips and grinned. "Did you know that crows used to be white?"

"White?"

He nodded. "It's a Brulé Lakota legend. The crow was white, and he was brother to the buffalo. So he would warn the buffalo when the people came to hunt it. The warriors grew angry that they couldn't get close to the buffalo, so one of them put on a buffalo skin and waited for the crow to come and give its warning. When it did, he caught it by the feet. Another warrior, very angry, took it from him and dashed it into the fire in revenge. The crow escaped, but its feathers were burned. So now the crow is black."

She laughed with pure delight. "I love stories."

"Our legends fill books," he mused. "That's one of my favorites."

That he'd shared something from his culture with her made her feel warm, welcome. She turned to look for the woodpecker. He was clinging to a nearby tree trunk making his usual lilting cry. "Okay, George, I'm here," she called. She went to a ledge on the fence and spread the nuts along it. She filled the bird feeder. Then she motioned to Carson and they moved away from the feeder.

A flash of striped feathers later, George was carting off the first pecan. He was followed by blue jays and cardinals, a tufted titmouse and a wren.

She identified them to Carson as they came in. Then she laughed suddenly as a new birdcall was heard, and started looking around. "That's a red-winged blackbird," she said. "I don't see him."

"I do know that call," he replied. He shook his head, smiling. "I've never known anyone who could listen to a birdsong and identify the bird without seeing it first."

"Oh, I can't do them all," she assured him. "Just a few. Listen. That one's a grackle!" she exclaimed. "Hear it? It sounds like a rusty hinge being moved… There he is!"

She indicated a point high in the bare limbs above. "They're so beautiful. They're so black that they have a faint purple tinge, sort of like your hair," she added, looking at it in its neat ponytail. Her eyes lingered there. He was so handsome that she thought she'd never tire of watching him.

He smiled knowingly and she flushed and averted her eyes. He was wearing that incredible fringed jacket that suited him so. Its paleness brought out the smooth olive tan of his complexion, made him look wild and free. She thought back to what her father had said, that Carson was a lobo wolf who could never be domesticated. The better she got to know him, the more certain she was of that. He'd never be able to stop picking up beautiful women, or looking for the next fight. Her heart felt sick.

She tossed seed onto the ground while the last of the nuts

vanished from the fence. Carson reached into the bucket and pulled out a handful of his own and tossed it.

They stood very close, in the cold light of the morning, feeding the birds. Carlie thought it was a time she'd never forget, whatever came after. Just her and Carson, all alone in the world, without a word being spoken.

It felt…like coming home.

Carson was feeling something similar. He didn't want to think about it too much. His life was what it was. He wasn't going to get married again, settle down and have children. It was too tame for him, for his spirit. He'd lived wild for too long.

He knew she must have hopes. Her physical response to him was purely headlong. She would probably give in to him if he pushed her. He thought about doing that. He wanted her very badly. But no form of birth control was surefire. Carlie was an innocent, and she had strong beliefs. She'd never give up a child she conceived, especially his. It would lead to terrible complications…

He scowled. He was remembering some tidbit of gossip he'd heard. He glanced down at Carlie. She looked up, her eyes full of soft memory.

"Your father married your mother because you were on the way," he said gently. "True?"

She swallowed. "Well, yes. She was like me," she said, lowering her eyes to his chest. "She'd never put a foot out of line, never been…with a man. My father was dashing and exciting, well-traveled and smart. She just went in head-first. She told me once," she recalled sadly, "that she'd ruined both their lives because she couldn't say no, the one time it really counted. She loved me," she added quickly. "She said I made everything worthwhile. But her love for my father, and his for her, never made up for the fact that he'd been pressured into marrying her."

"This isn't Victorian times," he pointed out.

"This is Jacobsville, Texas," she returned. "Or, in my case, Comanche Wells. I live among people who have known my people since the Civil War, when my family first came here from Georgia and settled on this land." She swept a hand toward it. "Generations of us know each other like family. And like family, there are some social pressures on people in terms of behavior."

"Prehistoric ones," he scoffed.

She looked up at him. "Is the world really a better place now that nothing is considered bad? People just do what they want, with anyone. How is that different from what animals do in the wild?"

He was lost for words.

"Everything goes. But the one thing that separates human beings from animals is a nobility of spirit, a sense of self-worth. I have ideals. I think they're what holds civilization together, and that if you cheapen yourself with careless encounters, you lose sight of the things that truly matter."

"Which would be...?" he prompted, stung by her reply.

"Family," she said simply. "Continuity. People get married, have children, raise children to be good people, give them a happy home life so that they grow up to be responsible and independent. Then the next generation comes along and does the same thing."

"Permissive people still have kids," he said drolly.

"They have them out of wedlock a lot, though," she pointed out. "So it's a one-parent family trying to raise the kids. I saw the result in school, with boys who had no fathers around to discipline them and teach them the things men need to know to get along in the world."

He averted his eyes. "Maybe my life would have been happier in a single-parent family."

She recalled what he'd told her, about his father's drinking problem, that he'd beat Carson's mother to death, and she grimaced. "I am so sorry for what happened to you," she said softly. "Except for my grandmother's evil boyfriend, nobody ever hurt me in my life, least of all my parents."

He drew in a long breath. His eyes were solemn as he stared off into the distance. "We attach the same importance to family that you do," he said quietly. "We live in small communities, people know each other for generations. Children are brought up not only by their parents, but by other parents, as well. It's a good way."

"But it isn't your style," she said without looking at him. "You have to be free."

He scowled and looked down at her, but she wouldn't meet his eyes.

"Here, spread the seeds over there, would you?" she asked, indicating another feeder. "I forgot to put up a seed cake for them." She pulled it out of her pocket and took the wrapper off.

In the house, unseen, Jake Blair was watching them with wide, shocked eyes. He turned. "Come here," he told Rourke. "You're not going to believe this."

Rourke followed his gaze out the window and let out

a hoot of laughter. "You're having me on," he chuckled. "That can't be Carson, feeding the birds!"

"Oh, yes, it can." He pursed his lips. "I wonder..."

"I wouldn't even think it. Not yet. He's got a lot to work through before he's fit for any young woman, especially your daughter."

"Men can change. I did," Jake said quietly. "And in my day, I was a harder case than he is."

"You did change," Rourke agreed. "But you don't have the scars he's carrying."

"Tell me," Jake said.

Rourke shook his head and smiled sadly. "I won't do that. It's his story, his pain. He'll have to be the one to tell it."

Jake just nodded. He watched his daughter lead Carson around the yard, saw them laughing together as the birds came very close and they paused, very still, so that they came right up almost to their feet.

That jacket Carson wore was really gorgeous, he thought. Then he compared it to Carlie's old coat and he winced. He'd tried to give her all the necessities. He hadn't realized how difficult it was going to be, living on a minister's small salary in an equally small community. The days of big money were long gone. His conscience wouldn't let him go back to it. He did love his work, anyway.

He turned away from the window, leading Rourke back into his office.

11

CARLIE WENT AHEAD of Carson into the house through the back door. Rourke and her father were just having coffee.

Jake held up the pot and raised his eyebrows.

"Please," Carson said. "I haven't had a cup this morning. Withdrawal symptoms are setting in," he added, deliberately making his hand shake.

The other men laughed.

"Breakfast?" Carlie asked, but she was looking at Carson. "I can make biscuits with scrambled eggs and sausage. Fresh sausage. One of our congregation brought it over yesterday."

"Sounds good to me, pumpkin," Jake said easily. "Make enough for everybody."

"You bet." She could almost float. It was one of the best days of her life so far. She had to make sure she didn't linger over Carson when she looked his way. She didn't want to embarrass him.

"Did you come over to help feed the local wildlife?" Rourke asked with a grin.

Carson chuckled. "No. I made a connection. Actually, I made it from something Lanette said. That whoever planned the kidnapping was sloppy, but that it must be somebody big. So I thought of the politician who's connected to the Cotillo drug cartel across the border."

"Why would he be after you, though?" Rourke asked Jake, frowning. "Have you had any contact with people who know things about the cartel?"

"None," Jake said. He sipped coffee and shook his head. "I have no idea at all why I've been targeted, or by whom." He smiled faintly. "Someone from the old life, possibly, after revenge. But if that's the case, they've waited a long time for it."

"I don't think it's that," Carson said quietly. "It just feels…I don't know, jagged."

The other two men stared at him.

"Jagged?" Rourke prompted.

"A man with a drug habit comes after Carlie, but tries to make it look like he was after you," Carson told Jake. "Now, a kidnapping attempt on Carlie to bring you into the line of fire so they could take you out. Why?"

"Jagged," Jake agreed. "Like someone jumped from one victim to another."

"It's just a thought," Carson continued, "but the man who hired the first assassin was on drugs."

"The man who died in the fire up in Wyoming, who

was trying to kill Dalton Kirk for something he remembered," Rourke told Jake. "I mentioned it to you. The man, Richard Martin by name, was a former DEA agent, a mole who fed information to the drug cartel over in Cotillo. I'm pretty sure he hired the man who came after Carlie, to stop her from remembering what he looked like. With her photographic memory, she was giving out exact information about him. He didn't want that."

"Because he worked for Matthew Helm, a crooked politician who's just been named to the unexpired U.S. Senate seat in Texas," Carson concluded. "We know now why our computer expert Joey was killed and the computer was trashed, and why Carlie was targeted. You see, the killer had murdered an assistant D.A. in San Antonio who was investigating Helm for embezzlement and drug trafficking. He had files that mysteriously disappeared. Every bit of the evidence that could have been used against him is gone, and Lieutenant Rick Marquez of San Antonio PD told Cash Grier that two witnesses in the case have refused to testify. One just left the country, in fact."

"How convenient for Helm," Rourke commented.

"This is pretty big," Jake said, listening intently. "He didn't want his link to Helm to get out, obviously, but why kill a computer tech and try to kill Carlie?"

"Because of the watch and the shirt," Rourke said.

"Excuse me?" Jake asked, wide-eyed.

"The assistant D.A.'s wife was loaded," Carson said. "She'd just bought her husband a very expensive watch that played a song and chimed on the hour. She also bought him an exclusive, equally expensive, designer paisley shirt.

Martin took a shine to both, so he stole them. He didn't want anyone to remember what he was wearing, because it linked his boss to the assistant D.A.'s murder."

Jake exchanged glances with his daughter. "You told me about this."

"Yes," Carlie said. She was deep in thought.

"What happened to the watch and the shirt?" Jake asked Carson.

"I assume whoever ransacked the room Richard Martin was occupying at the local motel took both and destroyed them." Rourke sighed. "It would be insane to keep something so dangerous."

"The watch played a song, but nobody ever told me which song," Carlie said. She looked at Rourke.

He sang it, "I Love Rock 'n' Roll," and grinned because he was totally off-key. "It was a Joan Jett song from—"

"That's it," Carly cried. "I thought I was just reacting to the stuff he knocked me out with, so I didn't say anything. The kidnapper was wearing a cheap suit, but he had this expensive watch on his wrist. It was sort of like the one Calhoun Ballenger wears. You know, that Rolex."

"I know," Jake mused. "I told him once that he could feed a whole third-world country on the proceeds if he sold that thing. He just laughed and said it was two generations old and a family heirloom. He wouldn't sell it for the world." He glanced at Rourke. "He's going to run for that U.S. Senate seat against Helm. He told me yesterday. I ran into him in town."

"He'd be a wonderful senator," Carlie mused. "His brother Justin is dealing with the feedlot and the ranch anyway, since Calhoun's been a state senator for the past few years. He's done so much for our state..."

"He'll be a target, too," Jake said heavily.

"Yes," Carson said. "The other candidates for the temporary appointment ended up arrested on various drug charges. They swore the drugs were planted. I believe them."

"That politician needs to be taken down," Jake said shortly. "Once he has real power, he'll cause untold misery."

"I'm game," Rourke volunteered. "And since I'm officially his gofer, I have the inside track on what he's up to."

"You be careful," Jake told him.

"You know me," Rourke chuckled.

"I do. That's why I made the remark."

Carson was quiet. He was just remembering something. He didn't want to share it with the others. Lanette had excused herself at the theater the night Carlie had been kidnapped. It was a small, insignificant thing in itself and might be quite innocent. But Lanette hated Carlie. She wore expensive clothes, not the sort she could pay for on a meager salary working personnel for a company. A lot of things about her didn't quite add up.

"You're very quiet," Rourke prompted him.

"Sorry." He smiled faintly. "I was thinking about patterns." He glanced at Carlie. "The man who used the chloroform on you, he was wearing the watch?"

She nodded. "I thought I was hallucinating when it chimed. I mean, I've heard musical watches, but that was totally different."

"I'm reliably informed that the price of a new Jaguar convertible is in the same price range," Rourke commented wryly.

"The kidnapper is the connection," Carson said, frowning thoughtfully. "He can link Helm to the assistant D.A.'s murder."

"The watch by itself won't help a lot," Jake commented.

"Yes, but don't you see, the kidnapper has to be working for Matthew Helm. The fact that he has the watch connects him to Helm, through Helm's man, Richard Martin, who killed the assistant D.A.," Carson emphasized. "It's a pattern, a chain of evidence."

"You're right!" Rourke said, drawing in a breath. "I didn't make the connection."

Carson gazed at Carlie quietly, his eyes dark and concerned. "You don't leave the house without the phone in the console of the truck, and not until it's been checked for devices," he told her.

She just nodded.

Jake hid a smile.

"Promise me," Carson added, staring her down.

She grimaced. "Okay. I promise."

Carson's gaze turned to Jake and became amused. "I've learned already that if she gives her word, she'll keep it. You just have to make sure she gives it."

Jake ruffled Carlie's hair. "That's my girl, all right." Carlie grinned.

"One of us needs to go up to San Antonio and talk to Rick Marquez," Rourke said, getting out of his chair. "This is a development he'll enjoy pursuing."

"If he needs to talk to me, I'll go up there, too," Carlie said.

"Not in the Cobra, you won't."

Jake and Carson stared at each other. They'd both said exactly the same thing at the same time, and they burst out laughing.

"Okay, okay," Carlie muttered. "If you're ganging up on me, I'll take the truck if I have to go. Just expect a call for help halfway there because my truck barely makes it to work every day. It won't make it to San Antonio without major engine failure!"

"I'll drive you," Jake told his daughter with a smile. "How's that?"

She grinned. "That's great, Dad."

"Carson, you're the best person to talk to Marquez," Rourke told the other man. "I can't be seen near anyone in law enforcement right now. You can ask if he needs a statement from Carlie," Rourke added. "But he lives in Jacobsville, you know. He could probably take a statement down here."

"I forgot. His mother is Barbara, who runs Barbara's Café," she told Carson, who looked puzzled.

"And his father-in-law runs the CIA," Jake added with a chuckle.

"Nice connections," Rourke said. He glanced at his watch. "I have to get back before Helm misses me. I'll be off, then."

"See you," Jake replied.

Rourke punched Carson on the shoulder and grinned as he walked out.

CARSON FINISHED HIS coffee. Carlie was clearing away breakfast. She glanced at Carson with her heart in her eyes. He looked at her as if she were a juicy steak and he was a starving man.

Jake turned his attention suddenly to Carson and jerked his head toward the office. Carson nodded.

"Breakfast was very good," Carson told her. "You have a way with food."

She smiled brightly. "Thanks!"

Carson followed her father into his study. "No calls for a few minutes, Carlie," Jake called before he shut the door. As an afterthought, he locked it.

Carson drew in a long breath as he studied the man across from him. Jake had been personable over breakfast, but at the moment he'd never looked less like a minister. His long, fit body was almost coiled. His pale blue eyes glittered with some inner fire.

"You're me, twenty-two years ago," Jake said without preamble. "And that child in there is my whole life. I'm seeing connections of my own," he added in a low tone. "I destroyed her mother. I'm not going to stand by and let you destroy her. She deserves better than a womanizing mercenary."

Carson sighed. He slid into a chair beside the desk where Jake sat down, and crossed his legs. "People are not what they seem to be," he began heavily. "You're thinking about the reputation I have with women. Carlie's already thrown it at me. It's why we argued the day I had to take her to the emergency room with the asthma attack."

"I thought as much," Jake replied.

"Six years ago," Carson began, "I was in the last two years of graduate school when I fell in love with a brash, outgoing, beautiful girl at a powwow on the reservation in South Dakota where I grew up. Her name was Jessica and I'd known her for years. I loved her insanely, so she married me. The first year was perfect. I thought it would never end. But my last year in college, she got tired of having me away so much at school. She took a lover. He was one of the most militant men on the reservation," he continued, his eyes cold and haunted. "He had a rap sheet, and the rez police knew him on sight. I tried to get her to come home, but she said she loved him, she wasn't coming back to a boring life as the wife of a college student. She didn't think much of higher education in the first place. So I let her go."

He shifted in the chair. "But I wouldn't give her a divorce. I knew he was beating her. I heard it from my cousins. I talked to her on the phone, and tried to get her to press charges. She said he didn't mean it, he loved her, he'd never do it again." He met Jake's world-weary eyes. "My father gave my mother the same spiel after he beat her up, over and over again," he said coldly. "I was six years old when he hit her too hard and ran. He was prosecuted for murder and ended up in the same prison with one of my mother's brothers. He died not long after that. My uncle had nothing to lose, you see, and he loved my mother."

Jake's face was relaxing, just a little. He didn't interrupt.

"I went to live with cousins. One of my uncles, a rez cop, adopted me as his son since he had no children of his own. I was given all the necessities, but there's no substitute for loving, real parents. I missed my mother." He paused, took a breath and plowed ahead. "Jessie was pregnant and near her due date. She was living with her lover and she swore the child was his. But I had a visitor who knew one of my cousins. He said it was my child, that Jessie lied about it because she didn't want me to drag her into court for paternity tests."

He leaned forward, his eyes downcast. "I finished my last final and flew back to the rez to see her. She was alone at her house. She was afraid of me." He laughed coldly. "She said okay, it was my child, and I could see it when it was born, but she was staying with Jeff no matter what I did. I was about to tell her I'd let her get the divorce, when Jeff drove up. He stormed into the house and accused her of two-timing him. I tried to restrain him, but he blindsided me. While I was getting back up, he dragged Jessie out the door with him. I managed to get outside in time to watch him throw her into the passenger seat. She was screaming. She thought he was going to kill her. So did I."

Jake's pale eyes were riveted to him.

"So I got in my car and went after them. He saw me in the rearview mirror, I guess, because he sped up and started weaving all over the road. I didn't have a cell phone with me or I'd have called the police on the rez and had them pick him up. I followed them around the dirt roads. He started across a bridge that had been condemned. There were spring floods, huge ones, water coming right up over the wooden bridge."

He closed his eyes. "He went through the rotten boards on the side and right into the river. The car, with both of them inside, washed away." He lifted his head. His eyes were cold, dead. "They found the bodies almost two days later. The child was almost full-term, but they couldn't save him." He closed his eyes. "I graduated, joined the military, asked for combat because I wanted to die. That was almost eight years ago."

He felt a hand on his shoulder. He opened his eyes and looked into pale blue ones. "Listen, son," Jake said quietly, "you were trying to save her. In the process, a madman miscalculated his driving skills and wrecked his car. If it hadn't been that, he might have shot her and then shot himself. He might have died in a fight. She might have died from complications of childbirth. But, it would still have happened. When a life is meant to be over, it's over. That's God's business. You can't control life, Carson," he concluded. "It's a fool's game to think you can even try. You're tormenting yourself over something that nobody could have prevented."

Carson averted his eyes. "Thanks," he said huskily.

"How did you end up with Cy?"

His eyes had a faraway look as he recalled that meeting. "I was doing black ops overseas," Carson said. "Political assassination, like Grier used to do." He drew in a long breath. "Cy and Eb Scott and Micah Steele were attached to the unit I was with as independent contractors. We went on missions together, discovered that we worked very well as a group. So I mustered out and signed on with them. It's been…interesting," he concluded with a mild laugh.

"I worked with mercs a time or two," Jake replied. He hesitated. "I also worked in covert assassination."

"I heard some gossip about that," Carson replied, without blowing the whistle on Rourke.

"She can't ever know," he said, nodding toward the other part of the house where Carlie was. "I gave it up for her. I had a crisis of conscience when her mother died. It took me to a bad place. A minister gave me the strength I needed to turn my life around, to do something productive with it." He leaned back with a sigh and a smile. "Of course, I'll starve doing it," he chuckled. "We're always broke, and there's always somebody who wants me fired because I say something offensive in a sermon. But I belong here now. Odd feeling, belonging. I never wanted it in the old days."

"Your wife," Carson said hesitantly. "Was she like Carlie?"

Jake's eyes narrowed with sorrow. "Exactly like Carlie. I didn't believe in a damned thing. I had no faith, no understanding of how people lived in small towns. I wanted her. I took her. She got pregnant." His face was like stone. "I married her to stop gossip. Her mother was a slut. I mean, a real slut. She even tried to seduce me! So everybody locally would have said, 'like mother like daughter,' you know?" He leaned forward on his forearms. "I refused to stay here and be a tamed animal. I provided for her and the child when Carlie was born. I gave them everything except love. It wasn't until Mary was dying that I realized how much I had loved her, how much I had cost her with my indifference. You think you killed your wife? I know I killed mine. I've been trying ever since to find a way to live with it, to make up for some of the terrible things I've done. I'm still trying."

Carson was speechless. He just stared at the older man, with honest compassion.

"If you're wondering," Jake added softly, "this is a moral tale. I'm telling you about what happened to me so that you won't repeat it with my daughter. I think you have some idea of her feelings already."

Carson nodded solemnly. "I don't want to hurt her."

"That makes two of us. You've lived the way I used to. Women were like party favors to me, and I had my share…"

Carson held up a hand. "Slight misconception."

"About…?"

Carson let out a breath and laughed softly. "I pick up women. Beautiful women. I take them to the theater, the opera, out dancing, sailing on the lake, that sort of thing." He hesitated. "Then I take them home and leave them at the door," he said with a rueful smile.

Jake's confusion was evident.

"My wife was my first woman," Carson said with blunt honesty. "After she died, every woman I took out had her face, her body. I…couldn't," he choked out.

Jake put a firm hand on his shoulder, the only comfort he could offer.

"So other guys think I score every night, that I'm Don Juan." Carson laughed coolly. "I'm a counterfeit one. It makes me look heartless, so that honest women won't waste their time on me. But it backfired." He jerked his head toward the kitchen. "She thinks I'm dirty, because of my reputation. Funny thing, a visionary woman up in Wyoming told me that my past would threaten my future. She was very wise."

"Some obstacles can be overcome," Jake commented.

"So, you want me to go out and involve myself intimately with women...?"

"Shut up, or I'll put you down," Jake said in a mock growl. He laughed. "I could do it, too."

"I believe you," Carson said, with true admiration. "You haven't lost your edge."

"Where do you go from here?" Jake continued.

"When we wrap up this mess with Carlie's kidnapper, I don't know," Carson said honestly. "If I stay here, things will happen that will destroy her life, and maybe mine, too. I have to leave."

"For now, or for good?" Jake asked.

Carson drew in a breath. "I...don't know."

"If you graduated, then you got a degree, I take it?" Jake asked.

Carson pursed his lips. "Yes."

"You couldn't go into a normal profession?"

"It would mean a commitment I'm not sure I can make. I need time."

"Most life-changing decisions require it," Jake agreed. "What degree program were you pursuing?"

Carson smiled. "Medicine. I have my medical degree and I keep up my license. I just can't practice without doing the internship." He sighed. "I was going to specialize in internal medicine. I see so many heart patients with no resources, no money."

"On the reservation, you mean?"

"No. Here, in Jacobs County. I was talking to Lou Coltrain. She said they're short on physicians, not to mention physicians who specialize."

Jake searched the other man's face. He jerked his head toward the kitchen. "Going to tell her?"

Carson shook his head. "Not until I'm sure."

Jake smiled. "I knew I liked you."

Carson just laughed.

CARLIE WALKED HIM to the door. "Was Dad intimidating you?" she asked when they were outside on the front porch, with the door closed.

"No. He was listening. That's such a rare gift. Most people want to talk about themselves."

She nodded. "He's talked several people out of suicide over the years."

"He's a good man."

"He wasn't always," she replied. "I've heard a little about his old life, although he won't tell me a thing himself." She looked up at him with raised eyebrows.

"It would be the end of my life to say a single word about it," he said firmly.

"Okay," she said, sighing.

He tilted her chin up and searched her green eyes. "What color were your mother's eyes?" he asked.

"They were brown," she said. "Like the center of a sunflower."

He traced her mouth with a long forefinger. "You're very like a sunflower yourself," he said softly. "Bright and cheerful, shining through storms."

Her lips parted on a surprised breath.

"I'm leaving, Carlie," he said softly.

She started to speak, but he put his fingers across her lips.

"You know how it is between us," he said bluntly. "I want you. If I stay here, I'll take you. And you'll let me," he said huskily.

She couldn't deny it.

"We'll be like your parents, one brokenhearted, one running away until tragedy strikes. I don't want to be the cause of that."

Her hand went up to his hard cheek. She stroked it gently, fighting tears. "You can't live a tame life. I understand."

It sounded harsh. Selfish. He scowled at the look on her face, dignity and courage mixed with heartbreak. It hurt him.

He drew her into his arms and held her, rocked her, in a tight embrace. "It wouldn't work. You know that."

She nodded against his chest.

He drew back finally and tilted her face up to his. It was streaked with hot tears that she couldn't help. He bent and kissed them away.

"I'll be around for a while," he promised. "Until we make sure we have the kidnapper in custody."

"Can they catch him, you think?"

"I believe so," he replied. "Just be careful."

She smiled. "I usually am."

"And if someone shows up and says your dad's been in a wreck…" he began.

She pulled her cell phone out of her jeans. "I'll call him up first."

He grinned. "That's my girl." He bent and brushed his mouth softly over hers, savoring the smile she couldn't help.

He left her on the porch and drove away. She stood there until she couldn't see the car anymore.

ROURKE HAD FINALLY convinced Matthew Helm that it was safe to trust him. He did a few discreet jobs—mostly by warning the people he was supposed to muscle first, and having them cooperate—and was finally handed something useful. Useful for the case against Helm, at least.

"I want you to go talk to Charro," Helm told Rourke. He pursed his lips, deep in thought. "That Ballenger man who's running against me has a following. He's local. People know him and like him. He's got three sons. One of them, Terry, is still in high school. I want you two to find a way to plant some cocaine on him. Put it in his locker at school, in his car and tip off the cops, whatever. I don't care what you do, just make sure you do it. I'll handle the press. I'll have one of my campaign workers release the collar, to make sure it doesn't come directly from me and seem like I'm slinging mud. Got it?"

"Oh, yeah, Boss, I got it," Rourke said with a nod.

"Get going, then."

"You bet."

Rourke was too old a hand to go straight to Calhoun Ballenger or even to Cash Grier's office, much less up to San Antonio to see Rick Marquez. He wasn't trusting his cell phone, either, because Helm could very easily find out who he'd talked to recently.

So he went to Cotillo.

Charro Mendez gave him a careful scrutiny. "So Helm trusts you, does he?" he asked.

"He doesn't really trust anybody," Rourke replied. "Neither do I," he added, hands in his jeans pockets. "It doesn't pay, in this line of work. But he trusts me enough to relay messages, I believe."

"And what message does he wish you to bring me?" Mendez asked, propping his booted feet on his own desk in the mayor's office.

"He wants some product planted in a particular place," he replied, leaning back against the wall.

"Ah. Something to do with a rival in the political arena, *sí?*"

"Exactly."

"This is not a problem. Who does he expect to perform this task, *señor,* you or me?"

"He didn't say," Rourke replied. "He told me you'd supply the product. I assume that means I'll have to plant it."

"I see." The man grinned, displaying gold-filled teeth. "I would assume that he would not expect a man in my position to perform such a menial chore, however."

"Exactly," Rourke said, nodding.

"Excellent! I will have the…product," he said, "delivered to you across the border. When?"

"He didn't tell me that, either. But it would be convenient to do two Saturdays from now," Rourke continued. "There's going to be a dance at the high school. I can sneak it into the glove compartment of the boy's vehicle while he's inside the building."

"I could almost feel sorry for his father. I also have sons."

His face darkened. "I would kill someone who did that to me. But these rich men in Texas—" he waved a hand "—they can buy justice. I have no doubt the politician can have the charges dropped. The publicity, however, will be very damaging I think."

"I agree."

"Give me a cell phone number where my man can reach you," Charro said.

Rourke handed him a slip of paper. "It's a throwaway phone," he told the other man. "I'll answer it this once and then toss it in a trash bin somewhere. It will never be found or traced to me."

"A wise precaution."

"I try to be wise, always," Rourke replied.

"Then we agree. I will have my man contact you within the week."

"I'm certain my boss will express his appreciation for your help."

"Indeed he will," Charro returned thoughtfully. "Many, many times, whenever I ask." He smiled coldly. "I will have him, how do you say? over a barrel."

"A big one," Rourke chuckled.

"Very big. Yes."

12

ROURKE COULDN'T RISK being seen with any law enforcement official, or overheard talking to one, not with things at this critical juncture. He called Carson.

"Have you been to see Marquez yet?" he asked quickly.

"Well, no," Carson replied. "Something came up over at Cy's ranch…"

"This is urgent. I want you to go see Marquez right now. I've got some news."

So Carson drove up to San Antonio to relay the information Rourke had transferred over to another throwaway phone, a pair he and Carson had arranged at an earlier time.

Rick Marquez did a double take when he saw Carson. The other man was almost his age, with the same olive complexion and long, black hair in a ponytail.

"Lieutenant Marquez?" Carson greeted the other man when the clerk showed him in.

"That would be me. Amazing," Rick mused. "We could almost be twins."

Carson smiled faintly. "Only if you turned out to be from South Dakota."

He shrugged. "Sorry. Mexico. Well, that's where my father was born. He's now president of a small Latin American nation. Sit down." He offered his visitor a chair.

"I assume you have regular checks for bugs in here?" Carson asked, glancing around.

"My father-in-law runs the CIA," Rick told him as he dropped into his aging desk chair. "He might bug us, but nobody else would dare. What can I do for you?"

"There have been some new developments that you might not have heard about," Carson began.

"Jake Blair's daughter was kidnapped, you and her father freed her and took out two guards, the kidnapper got away," Rick rattled off. "I know everything."

"Not quite," Carson replied. He pursed his lips. "How about coffee?"

"We've got a pot right over there…"

Carson shook his head. "Real coffee. Come on."

Rick was puzzled, but he caught on pretty quickly that Carson didn't trust telling him in the office.

They drove to a specialty coffee shop and moved to a corner table.

"Sorry, I know you think it's secure in your office, but this information could get Rourke killed if it slips out somehow. He's working for Matthew Helm and there's a plot underway. But let me tell you this first. Carlie Blair's kidnapper was wearing a watch. An expensive watch that chimed an old Joan Jett rock tune—"

"You're kidding!" Rick exploded. "We thought the watch burned up with the man who was wearing it, in Wyoming!"

"No," Carson replied. "I was there when he died. There was no watch on him. The local police were trying to back-track him to any motels he'd stayed at. I assume his boss's men got to the room first."

"What a stroke of luck," Rick said with a short laugh. "That watch, if we can get our hands on it, is the key to a murder and perhaps the end of a truly evil political career."

"The problem is that we don't know where the watch is. The kidnapper has vanished into thin air."

"We have to find him."

"I agree. Rourke's working on it. He's wormed his way into the political process. That's why I'm here."

"Okay. Shoot."

"Helm sent Rourke over the border today to arrange for the delivery of some cocaine. Enough to charge someone with intent to distribute. The idea is for Rourke to plant it in the glove compartment of Calhoun Ballenger's youngest son, Terry, at a school dance in two weeks."

Rick's face hardened. "What a low-down, dirty, mean…"

"All of the above," Carson agreed grimly. "But we know it's going down, and when, and where. Believe me, this is going to send Helm up the river. All we have to do is set a trap and spring it."

"Why isn't Rourke here?" Rick asked.

"Because he's being watched, and probably listened to,

as well. We used throwaway phones to communicate, just to exchange this much information."

"And you think my own office isn't secure?" Rick sounded a little belligerent.

"This man has ex-cops working for him," Carson explained. "They'll know all the tricks. It isn't far-fetched to assume he has a pipeline into your office. The missing evidence the assistant D.A. had on Helm, for example, that was destroyed right here in impound?"

Rick let out a heavy sigh. "I get your point. I've been careless."

"Don't sell yourself short. Helm has some pros on his team. His main enforcer is gone, but he's got others. One is an ex-cop who got fired for using excessive violence. Carlie's kidnapper. He knocked a perp down the stairs when he caught him beating a child."

"Know where?" Rick asked suddenly.

"Carlie said the kidnapper had an accent, like you hear in those old gangster movies of the '30s and '40s."

"Chicago, maybe, New Jersey, New York…" Rick's eyes were thoughtful. "I can send out some feelers to people I know in departments there, ask around. Some of the veterans might remember something."

"Good idea. Meanwhile, Rourke's on the job."

"Should we warn Calhoun Ballenger?" Rick wondered aloud.

"If he knows, he'll warn his son, and his son might mention it to a classmate," Carson replied. "It's better to keep him in the dark. We'll make sure his son is watched and protected."

"Don't toss any hand grenades around," Rick warned.

Carson sighed as he stood up. "My past will haunt me."

"Actually, if it was up to me, you'd get a medal," Rick said. "So many dead kids because rich men want to make a profit off illegal drugs." He shook his head. "Crazy world."

"Getting crazier all the time."

"Thanks for the heads-up," Rick said, shaking hands with the other man. "By the way," he added, "nice hair-style." He grinned. Carson grinned back.

FRED BALDWIN WAS WORRIED. Mr. Helm had promised that he was going to protect him, that he was in no danger of getting arrested for kidnapping Carlie Blair. But he knew from painful experience that Mr. Helm didn't keep many of the promises he made. That was, unless he promised to get you for crossing him. He kept all those promises.

He fingered the expensive watch that he still had, that Mr. Helm didn't know about. He knew why the watch was important. It had belonged to Richard Martin, who burned up in Wyoming after trying to kill two women. He'd killed an assistant prosecutor for that watch. But Martin was dead. And Fred had the watch.

Mr. Helm didn't know that he hadn't destroyed it. He liked the watch. That chime it sounded wasn't a song he knew, but it was okay. It was the two-tone gold on the timepiece, very expensive, and that made him feel good. His father had been a low-level worker at an automobile plant in Detroit. His mother had kept a day care in their home. There were four kids and never enough money. His father drank it up as fast as he got paid.

Two of his brothers were in jail. His oldest brother had died last year. His mother had finally left his father, and went to live with a sister in California. He hadn't heard from her in a long time. She'd loved her oldest child best, the one who died. She hadn't wanted the others. She thought they were too stupid to be her kids. She said so, often.

The only time she'd liked Fred was when he became a policeman. Finally, one of her kids besides her favorite might actually amount to something.

Then he got arrested and fired and she turned her back on him. Well, it was no surprise.

Fred didn't like women much. His mother was cold as ice, heartless. Maybe his father had made her that way. Maybe she was that way to begin with.

He liked that little woman he'd kidnapped, though. She should have hated him. He'd terrified her. But she'd been sorry for him when he told her about his father beating him up. He felt bad that he'd scared her. He was glad to know she'd escaped, that her father hadn't been killed.

Luckily for him, the two would-be assassins got blamed for the screwup. Mr. Helm hadn't hired them in person, so he wouldn't be connected with them.

On the other hand, Fred had hired them for the person who was contracted by Richard Martin to kill Reverend Blair, on Mr. Helm's orders. If they talked, Fred was going to be the one who'd go to prison.

Well, that little woman knew what he looked like, and he had no reason to believe she wouldn't have told the law about him. He knew from something Mr. Helm had let slip once that Carlie Blair had a photographic memory.

Mr. Helm said not to worry about it, that he'd make sure Fred was okay. But Fred had seen what had happened to the man Richard Martin had hired to kill Carlie Blair, the same woman he'd kidnapped. Martin had poisoned the would-be killer, right under the cops' noses, and apparently on Mr. Helm's orders.

Funny, that he'd been ordered to kidnap Carlie, when Richard Martin had been ordered to hire somebody to kill her. Not only that, when the first killer failed, Martin had hired someone else to finish the job. But the person he was taking orders from had sent him to kidnap Carlie to draw the reverend out to be killed.

Why did Mr. Helm want the preacher dead? As far as Fred knew, the preacher didn't have anything on Mr. Helm at all. And what Carlie knew didn't matter before, because she remembered Richard Martin and he was dead.

She'd remember Fred now, though. That would be a motive. But they were trying to kill her father!

Well, his opinion was that Richard Martin had been so high on drugs that he hadn't made it clear who was supposed to be the victim. And his hire, to put it politely, was as crazy a person as Fred had ever met. He'd been sent to kidnap Carlie on that person's orders, to strike at a time when she was unprotected at her home. He shook his head. It was nuts. Worse, he was the one who was being set up to take the fall.

He looked at the watch again. He'd never been tempted to talk about it. But after what he'd just overheard Mr. Helm say to his new enforcer, that South African guy, he had to do something. The South African man was going to plant drugs on the son of a politician who was the only serious contender for the U.S. Senate seat. If the man had been a stranger, he might not have cared. But Fred knew Calhoun Ballenger.

He'd seen the cattleman a few months ago, coming out of a downtown hotel where some cattlemen's conference was being held. Two men were waiting in the shadows. One of them was armed. When Mr. Ballenger started down the street, they jumped him.

He was a big man, and he handled himself well, but the man with the gun struck him in the head.

Fred didn't like bullies. He'd never been one, for all his size, and he hated seeing anybody pick on an unarmed man. It was why he'd become a cop in the first place years ago. So without really thinking about it, he jumped in, subdued the man with the pistol and knocked out his accomplice.

He'd left them in the alley and dropped a dime on them while he took Mr. Ballenger down the street to the emergency room of a local hospital.

He didn't dare tell the cattleman who he was, but Mr. Ballenger had wanted to do something for him, to pay him back for the kindness. He'd looked at Fred with admiration, with respect. Those were things sadly lacking in his life. It had made him feel good about himself for the first time in years. He'd waved away the older man's thanks and left the hospital without identifying himself.

Mr. Ballenger's son was going to be targeted by Matthew Helm, and Fred didn't want to be any part of it. But how was he going to warn the man without incriminating himself and his boss? Mr. Helm would turn on him, make sure he went to prison for the kidnapping if he lifted a finger.

He couldn't go to the law, as much as he'd have liked to. But there was one other possibility. This watch was important. The right people could do good things with it. And suddenly, right in front of him, was the very girl he'd kidnapped…

CARLIE WAS PUTTING her groceries into the back of the pickup truck when she came face-to-face with the man who'd kidnapped her.

"Don't scream," Fred said gruffly, but he didn't threaten her. He was wearing a raincoat and a hat, looking around cautiously. "You got to help me."

"Help you? You kidnapped me!" she blurted out.

"Yeah, I'm sorry," he said heavily. "I got in over my head and I can't get out. I can't go to the law. They're always watching. Mr. Helm is going to plant drugs on Mr. Ballenger's youngest son," he said hastily, peering over the truck bed to make sure nobody was nearby. "He's going to try to get him out of that Senate race."

"Terry?" she exclaimed. "He's going to try to set Terry Ballenger up?"

"Yeah. That South African guy who works for him, he's going to plant the evidence," he said quickly. "You got to tell your boss."

She was absolutely dumbfounded. She couldn't even find words. He didn't know that Rourke was working with the authorities and she didn't dare tell him. But he was risking his very life to try and save Calhoun's son from prosecution. It really touched her.

His dark eyes narrowed. "I'm so sorry for what I done," he said, grimacing. "You're a nice girl."

Her face softened. "Why do you work for that rat?" she wondered.

"He's got stuff on me," he explained. "I can't ever get another job. But I can help you." He took off the watch, looked at it admiringly for just a few seconds and grimaced. "Never had nothing so fancy in my whole life," he said, putting it in her hands. "He told me to bust it up and throw it away. I couldn't. It was so special. Anyway, that watch belonged to some prosecutor that had evidence on Mr. Helm. Richard Martin killed him. It was his watch. Martin took the watch and then killed people who remembered he had it."

"He tried to have me killed," she told him.

"Yeah, and then he hired somebody to kill your dad." He shook his head. "See, Martin was high on drugs, out of his mind. I think he got confused, gave the contract out on the wrong person. I think it was supposed to be you, again, but we got sent after your dad."

"You know who's behind it," she said, surprised.

He nodded solemnly. "Mr. Helm's behind it. But the contract was given out by Martin."

"Who's got it?" Carlie asked. "Please?"

He searched her eyes. "Some pretty blonde woman up in San Antonio. I didn't know until a day ago. Funny, she didn't even know about my connection to Mr. Helm. She asked around for some muscle to help with a hit, and the other guys got hired. One of them was a man I knew, he said I could do it on the side and Mr. Helm would never have to know." He laughed coldly. "Well, Mr. Helm knew already. He just didn't tell us."

"Blonde woman…?"

"Yeah. She used to work for Mr. Helm, years ago, when he started out in the local rackets."

Blonde woman. Hit woman. Contract killer. Somebody who knew that Carlie would be home alone on that Friday night. Somebody with ties to Jacobsville.

"Do you know her name?" Carlie asked.

He frowned. "Funny name. La…La…something."

Carlie's blood froze. "Lanette?"

"Yeah. That's it. How'd you know?"

Now wasn't the time to fill him in on personal information. But it meant that Carson could be in real danger if Lanette suspected that he might blow her cover. She'd be in jeopardy if her link to the kidnapper here was ever found out.

She slid the watch into her pocket, gnawed her lower lip. She looked up into his broad, swarthy face. "They'll kill you if they find out you gave me the watch."

His dark eyes were quiet and sad. "I don't care," he said. "I never done anything good in my whole life except for being a cop, and I even fouled that up. You were nice to me." He forced a smile. "Nobody ever liked me."

She put a small hand on his arm. "How do you feel about small towns?"

He frowned. "What do you mean?"

"You have to trust me," she said quickly.

"Why?"

"Because I'm going to do something that will seem crazy."

"Really? What?"

She threw back her head and screamed.

"JUST RELAX," CASH GRIER told his prisoner under his breath. "This isn't what it seems. You may think she sold you out, but we're trying to save you. Your boss will think you're being arrested for assault."

Fred Baldwin went along, stunned but willing to cooperate on the off chance that he might not have to spend his whole life in federal prison. "Okay, boss," he said. "It's your play."

Cash marched him out to the police car, put Carlie in front beside him, and left a patrolman to take her truck home and explain things to her father.

ONCE THEY WERE in the police station, Cash took Fred into his office and removed the handcuffs. He put Fred's automatic in his desk drawer and locked it. Carlie produced the watch out of her pocket.

"And I've got you filing," Cash said, shaking his head at her. "You should be wearing a badge, kid."

"No, no," she protested. "He—" she pointed at Fred "—just turned state's evidence. So to speak. He can make the connections. But we have to get word to Carson," she added quickly. "His girlfriend is the woman who hired Fred and the other two guys to kidnap me and kill my dad."

“Why did you give Carlie the watch?” Cash asked Fred. “You had everything to lose!”

“She was nice to me,” he murmured, glancing at Carlie. “They tried to kill her dad, with my help. And now they’re trying to frame Mr. Ballenger’s son. I took down two hoods who jumped him in San Antonio. Never seen a rich man so grateful for just a little help. I liked him. It’s not right, to punish a man’s son because the father’s just doing something good for the community. I got tired of being on the wrong side of the law, I guess. I thought if I gave her the watch, she’d give it to you and maybe you could stop Mr. Helm before he hurts somebody else.”

“I’ll stop it, all right,” Cash said. He frowned. “But it’s suicide on your part. You think Helm wouldn’t know who gave us the watch?”

Fred smiled sadly. “I ain’t got no place to go, nobody who cares about me. I thought, maybe I could do one good thing before he took me out.”

“You’re not going anywhere,” Cash told him firmly.

“And you do have somebody who cares about you,” Carlie said firmly. She took the big man’s hand in her own and held it. “Right here.”

Incredibly, tears ran down his wide cheeks.

“Now, don’t do that, you’ll have me doing it, too,” Carlie muttered. She pulled a tissue out of her pocket and wiped his eyes and then wiped her own.

“I’m Italian,” Fred muttered, embarrassed. “We don’t hide what we feel.”

“You’d better let me get this on paper,” Cash said, smiling. “Coffee?”

"Thanks."

"I'll make a pot," Carlie said. She glanced at Cash. "Carson..." she began.

"I'm two steps ahead of you," Cash promised, picking up the telephone.

CARSON HAD HIS phone turned off, which was a pity. Lanette had already heard from an informant that Fred Baldwin was in custody down in Jacobsville, Texas, for apparently confronting that pitiful little secretary that Carson was so crazy about.

She was livid. Fred was stupid. It was why she'd hired him, because he was expendable and too dumb to realize she was setting him up to take the fall for her when she killed Jake Blair.

But somewhere along the line, he'd had a flash of genius. He was probably spilling his guts. They'd be after her in a heartbeat. That little secretary would be gloating, laughing, feeling so superior to the beautiful woman who was obviously her superior in every single department.

Fred had flubbed his assignment. His cohorts were in jail. Now he'd been arrested, too. She'd been paid for a job that she hadn't completed. Word would get around that she was incompetent. She'd never get another contract. Worse, Fred would implicate her to save himself. She'd be running from the law for the rest of her life. The perks of her profession, all that nice money, her spectacular wardrobe, everything would be lost because her own plan had backfired on her.

Even Matthew Helm had refused to help her. Oh, he made promises, but his back was to the wall right now, and he was trying to save his own skin. He had to know that Fred would rat on him.

Well, she reasoned, at least she was going to have one bit of satisfaction on the run. That stupid little hick in Jacobsville wasn't going to get to gloat. Her feelings for Carson were so apparent that a blind woman could see them. Carlie loved Carson. So Lanette would go to prison for kidnapping and assault and conspiracy, and little Carlie would end up with Carson.

No way. If she lost Carson, for whom she had a real unrequited passion, Carlie wasn't going to have him. She'd make sure of it.

She reached into the purse she carried to make sure the automatic was where it was supposed to be.

"I can't stay long," she told Carson, who was impatient to be gone and seemed surprised and irritated to have found her at his apartment door when he arrived.

"Just as well," he said curtly, "because I have someplace to go and I'm already late."

"Couldn't we have just one cup of coffee first?" she asked, smiling softly. "I found out something about that attempt on the preacher."

"You did? How?" he asked, instantly suspicious.

"Well, let's just sit down and talk, and I'll tell you what I know," she purred.

CASH PHONED ROURKE, using the number Rourke had sent him. "Carson's in danger," he told the other man. "His blonde girlfriend is the contract killer Richard Martin hired to take out Reverend Blair."

"What!" Rourke exploded.

"I don't have time to go into the particulars," Cash said. "Suffice it to say I have a witness," he glanced at Fred, who was smiling as Carlie handed him a mug of black coffee, "and no time to discuss it. Do you know where he is?"

"At the apartment he rented," Rourke said, shell-shocked. "In San Antonio."

"Can you get in touch with him?"

Rourke let out a breath. "No. Not unless I do it in the open."

"Rourke will have to blow his cover to call Carson, they're monitoring his phone," Cash said aloud.

"I'll do it," Carlie said urgently. "Give me the number."

"Rourke, give me the number," Cash said.

He did. Cash scribbled it down and handed it to Carlie.

"What's this written in, Sanskrit?" she exclaimed.

Cash glared at her, took it back and made modifications. "It's just numbers, for God's sake," he said irritably

"Sir, your handwriting is hands-down, without a doubt, the worst I ever saw in my life," she muttered as she pushed numbers into her cell phone.

"Hear, hear!" Rourke said over the phone. "I have to go. I'll let you know about Ballenger's son as soon as I have word." He hung up.

Carlie held her breath as the phone rang once, twice, three times…

"Hello?"

Carlie recognized the voice. It wasn't Carson's. It was hers. Lanette's.

She swallowed, hard. "I want to speak to Carson," she said.

"Oh, do you? I'm sorry," Lanette said in a silky sweet tone. "I'm afraid he's indisposed at the moment. Really indisposed." She laughed out loud. "I can't have him. But, now, neither can you, you little backward country hick! And you can spend hours, days, just watching him die!" She cut off the connection.

"She's with him," Carlie said with an economy of words. "You have to get someone to him, quick!"

Cash was already punching in numbers.

While her boss worked to get a medical team to Carson, Carlie hovered, tears running down her cheeks.

"You sit down," Fred said softly. "They'll get there in time. It will be all right. Everything will be all right."

She just looked at him, her face that of a terrified child. It hit him in the heart so hard that he let out a breath, as if it had been a blow to his stomach.

He put down his coffee, got up, picked her up and sat down with her in his lap, wrapped up in his big arms, sobbing her heart out on his broad shoulder. He patted her back as if she were five years old, smiling. "It's okay, honey," he said softly. "It's okay."

Cash watched them and mentally shook his head. What a waste. That man had a heart as big as the world, and he was going to take the fall for that crooked politician unless Cash could find him a way out. That might just be possible. But first he had to save Carson. And that mission had a less hopeful outcome.

THE PARAMEDICS HAD to wait while San Antonio PD broke down a door to get inside, on Lieutenant Marquez's orders. Once the way was clear, they rushed in with a gurney. They found Carson in the kitchen, facedown on the floor. He was unconscious and bleeding from a wound in his chest. There was a lump on his head, as well.

One paramedic looked at the other and winced. This was not going to be an easy run. He keyed his mike and started relaying medical information. It was complicated by the fact that the victim apparently had no ID on him.

BECAUSE FRED BALDWIN could make all the right connections to Matthew Helm, and because they knew about the fate of the former failed hit man, Cash Grier refused to turn him over to the authorities in San Antonio, where Helm would have to be arrested and tried.

"You'll get him over my dead body," Cash assured Rick Marquez on the telephone. "I'm not risking his life. He's too valuable. You come down here and take a deposition, bring all the suits you need and add your district attorney to the list. I'll give you free access. But he is not, under any circumstances, leaving Jacobsville!"

Rick drew in a breath. "Cash, you're putting me in a tough spot."

"No, I'm not. My cousin is still the state attorney general. He'll pull some strings for me if I ask him," Cash added. "Besides that," he said with a whimsical smile, "I have a few important connections that I don't talk about."

"You and my father-in-law would get along," Marquez

chuckled. "All right. I'll get the process started. But I'm going to need that watch."

"No way in hell," Cash said pleasantly.

"It's state's evidence!"

"Yes, it is. And evidence doesn't walk out of *my* property room," he added, emphasizing the "my."

"Rub it in," Rick muttered. "Carson already did, in fact." He sobered. "They have him in intensive care."

"I know. My secretary is up there with him. Or as close as she can get," Cash said heavily.

"So I heard. She's parked in the corridor next to the emergency room surgical suite and won't move."

"Stubborn."

"Yes, and very much in love, apparently," Rick replied solemnly. "It won't end well. I know the type, and so do you. Even if he makes it out of the hospital, he'll never settle down."

"Are you a betting man?" Cash mused.

"Why?"

"Because several years ago, you'd have laid better odds that I'd never marry and live in a small Texas town. Wouldn't you?"

Rick laughed. "Point taken." He hesitated. "Well, can we at least see the watch and photograph it?"

"Mi casa es su casa," Cash said smugly. "My house is your house."

"I'll bring an SUV full of people down. May I assume that the state crime lab has already dusted the watch for prints?"

"Our own Alice Jones Fowler did the job herself. She

does still work as an investigator for state crime," Cash reminded him, "although she lives here with her husband, Harley, on their ranch. She's not only good, she's unforgettable."

"Nobody who ever met Alice would forget her," Rick agreed. "She even makes autopsies bearable."

"No argument there. Anyway, the watch is adequately documented, even for a rabid prosecutor. And you're going to need the best you've got for Helm," he added quietly. "The man is a maniac, and I don't mean that kindly. He'll sacrifice anybody to save himself. Even assistant district attorneys."

"You don't know how much I'd love to tie him to that murder," Rick said. "The watch is the key to it all. Good luck for us that it wasn't destroyed."

"Even better luck that the man wearing it decided to also turn state's evidence. He can put Helm away for life."

"You've got him in the county jail, I hope?"

Cash hesitated. "Someplace a little safer."

"Safer than the lockup?" Rick burst out laughing. "What, is he living with you and Tippy and Tris?"

"Let's just say that he's got unique company. I'll give you access with the D.A. when you get down here."

"This is going to be an interesting trip," Rick predicted. "See you soon."

"Copy that."

THE HOSPITAL WAS very clean. Carlie noted that the floors must be mopped frequently, because when she got up to use the ladies' room, the back of her jeans didn't even have dust. She knew she was irritating the staff. Security had talked to her once. But she refused to move. They could throw her out, but that was the only way she was leaving. Her heart was in that intensive care emergency surgery unit, strapped to machines and tubes, fighting for his life. They could put her in jail, after, she didn't care. But she wasn't moving until they could assure her that Carson would live. And she told them so.

13

The neurologist on Carson's case, Dr. Howard Deneth, paused at the nurses' station in ICU, where they'd taken Carson an hour ago, and glanced toward the cubicle where Carson was placed.

"She's still there?" he mused.

The nurse nodded. "She won't leave. The nurses called security, but she said they'd have to drag her out. She wasn't belligerent. She just stared them down, with tears rolling down her cheeks the whole time."

"Unusual in these days, devotion like that," the doctor remarked. "Are they married?"

"Not that we know. Of course, we don't know much, except what she was able to tell us. He doesn't carry identification."

"I noticed. Some sort of covert work, I imagine, classified stuff."

"That's what we thought."

Dr. Deneth looked down at the nurse over his glasses. "He's deteriorating," he said heavily. "The wound was superficial. There was minor head trauma, but really not enough to account for his condition. However, head injuries are tricky. Sometimes even minor ones can end fatally." He pursed his lips. "Let her in the room."

"Sir?"

"On my authority," he added. "I'll write it on the chart, in case you have any flak from upper echelons. They can talk to me if they don't like it."

The nurse didn't speak. She just smiled.

CARLIE HELD HIS HAND. She'd been shocked when the nurse came to tell her that she could have a comfortable chair beside Carson's bed. One of the other nurses had been curt to the point of rudeness when she tried to make Carlie leave the hall.

She guessed that nurses were like policemen. Some were kindhearted and personable, and some were rigorously by-the-book. She worked for a policeman who'd thrown the book away when he took the job. He believed in the rule of law, but he wasn't a fanatic for the letter of it. Case in point was big Fred Baldwin, who was now living in a safe but undisclosed location, so that he didn't end up dead before he could testify against his former boss.

No arrests had been made yet, that she was aware of. She did know that they had an all points bulletin out for the blonde woman who'd left Carson in this condition. She really hoped the woman resisted arrest, and then she bit her tongue and said a silent apology. That wasn't really a wish that a religious person should make.

Her father had come to see Carson a few minutes ago. The nurses had at least let him into the room. But when he came out he was somber and although he tried to get Carlie to come home, he understood why she wouldn't. He'd done the same when her mother was in the hospital dying. He'd refused to leave, too.

Carlie supposed he'd seen cases like Carson's many times. Judging by the look on his face, the results had been fatal. He reminded Carlie that God's will had precedence over man's desires. He wanted to stay with his daughter, but she reminded him that having two people in the corridor to trip over would probably be the straw that broke the camel's back for the nursing staff. He went home, leaving Carlie's cell phone—which she'd forgotten—with her so that she could keep him posted.

Unknown to her, one of Rourke's buddies was nearby, posing as a family member in the intensive care waiting room. Just in case Helm had any ideas about hurting Carlie. It was a long shot, but nobody wanted to leave anything to chance.

Meanwhile, the forces of good were coalescing against Matthew Helm. He knew they had Baldwin in custody, and the man was probably spilling his guts. But his attorney could take Baldwin apart on the stand. The man had a criminal record, which is how he was pressured into taking Helm's jobs in the first place. He had a conviction for assault when he was a cop in Chicago. That could be used against his testimony.

After all, Helm's hands were clean. He'd never broken the law. They might have Baldwin and a lot of hearsay evidence, but there was nothing that could connect him to the murder of the assistant D.A. He'd made sure of it.

So now he was free of that worry, and he could concentrate on the Senate race. He was in Washington, D.C., of course, learning his way around, making contacts, making use of all the connections that Charro Mendez had in the country's capital. He liked the power. He liked the privilege. He liked bumping elbows at cocktail parties with famous people. Yes, he was going to enjoy this job, and nobody was taking it away from him in that special election in May!

What he didn't know was that Fred, like Carlie, had an excellent memory for dates and places. With it, the authorities could check telephone records, check stubs, gas receipts, restaurant tickets, even motel logs to see where Helm was at particular times and with particular people. They could now connect him directly to the assistant district attorney's murder through Richard Martin because of the theft of the watch. It went from the assistant D.A.'s body to Richard Martin, who worked for Helm, to Fred Baldwin whom Helm had sent to retrieve it, right back to Helm himself.

The San Antonio D.A.'s office put together a network, a framework, that they were going to use to hang Matthew Helm from. The watch was going to put Helm away for a very long time. Added to Baldwin's testimony, it would be the trial of the century. It had all the elements: intrigue, murder, politics, kidnapping—it was almost a catalog of the deadly sins. And now, with Rourke ordered to set up

Calhoun Ballenger's youngest son—with cocaine provided by Charro Mendez—a concrete link between the two men had been formed. The trap was about to spring shut.

Fred had been kept in the dark about Rourke's true allegiance. What he didn't know, he couldn't accidentally let slip.

"TONIGHT'S THE NIGHT," Rourke told Cash Grier on a secure line. "Seven o'clock. Helm himself ordered the plant and I have it on tape."

"Sheer genius," Cash announced. "We're going to catch you in the act." He groaned. "Calhoun Ballenger is going to use me for a mop when he finds out that his son was the bait."

"I'll save you," Rourke promised. "But it's what we need to make the case."

"Good thing we spoke to Blake Kemp about this before you agreed to do it," Cash added.

"Yes, the Jacobs County D.A. should be in on such matters. Just to keep yours truly out of the slammer," Rourke chuckled. "Don't be late, okay? I'm not absolutely sure that Helm won't assign backup in case I get cold feet or he suspects I'm not reliable."

"No worries. We've got one of Eb Scott's men watching you, and one with Carlie up in San Antonio."

"How is he?" Rourke asked.

"No change," Cash said heavily. "Well, one change. They finally let Carlie into the room with him."

"Probably because they got tired of tripping over her in the hall," Rourke remarked. "Stubborn girl."

"Very." Cash's voice lowered. "It doesn't look good. Head injuries…well, you know."

"Any luck turning up that deadly blonde?" Rourke added coldly.

"Not yet, but I'm told they have a lead. She ordered the kidnapping. That's a federal offense. It means my brother gets involved." There was real pride in his tone. "Nobody gets away from Garon."

"Maybe they'll hit her over the head and shoot her while she's lying helpless," Rourke said icily.

"In real life, it doesn't go down like that." Cash sighed. "Pity."

"Yeah. Okay, I'll see you later."

"Be careful," Cash cautioned.

"Always."

CARLIE HELD CARSON's hand tightly in both of her small ones. He had beautiful hands, the skin smooth and firm, the nails immaculately clean and neatly trimmed. No jewelry. No marks where jewelry might ever have been. She remembered the feel of his hands on her skin, the tenderness, the strength of them. It seemed like an age ago.

The neurosurgeon had come in to check Carson's eyes, and how his pupils reacted to light. He was kind to Carlie, telling her that sometimes it took a little time for a patient to regain consciousness after a blow like the one Carson had sustained. If they were lucky, there wouldn't be too much impairment afterward. He didn't add that the head trauma didn't seem damaging enough to account for the continued unconsciousness. That bothered him.

The head trauma being the predominant condition, Carson was in the ICU on the neurological ward. The gunshot injury, by comparison, was far less dangerous and had a better prognosis. That damage had been quickly repaired by the trauma surgeon.

She only half heard him. She wanted him to tell her that Carson would wake up and get up and be all right. The doctor couldn't do that. Even he, with his long experience, had no guarantees. At the moment, they weren't certain why he was still unconscious.

Carson had been in shock when they transported him, but now he was still breathing well on his own, his levels were good, BP was satisfactory. In fact, he should be awake and aware. But he wasn't. They'd done a CT scan in the emergency room. It did not show extensive brain injury. There was some minor bruising, but nothing that should account for the continued unconsciousness.

Blood had been sent to the lab for analysis, but it was a busy day and a few patients in far worse shape were in the queue ahead of him.

The doctor asked, again, if Carson had any next of kin in the area. She shook her head. Carson was from the Wapiti Ridge Sioux Reservation in South Dakota, but she didn't know anything about that part of his life. Neither did anybody else locally.

He suggested that it might be wise to contact the authorities there and inquire about relatives who might know more about his health history. So Carlie phoned Cash Grier and asked him to do it. She was too upset to talk to anyone. His medical history would certainly be useful, but he was fighting for his life from a set of circumstances other than illness. She prayed and prayed. Please let him live, she asked reverently, even if he married some pretty sweet young woman from his hometown and Carlie never saw him again.

She whispered it while she was holding Carson's hand. Whispered it over and over again while tears ran hot and salty down her pale cheeks.

"You just can't die," she choked, squeezing his hand very hard. "Not like this. Not because of that sick, stupid, beautiful blonde female pit viper!" She swallowed, wiping tears away with the tips of her fingers. "Listen, you can go home and marry some nice, experienced girl who'll be everything you want, and it will be all right. I want you to be happy. I want you to live!" She sniffed. "I know I'm not what you need. I've always known it. I'm not asking for anything at all. I just want you to live until you're old and gray-headed and have a houseful of kids and grandkids." She managed a smile. "You can tell them stories about now, about all the exotic places you went, the things you saw and did. You'll be a local legend."

He shifted. Her heart jumped. For an instant she thought he might be regaining consciousness. But he made a soft sound and began to breathe more deeply. Her hands tightened around his. "You just have to live," she whispered. "You have to."

While she was whispering to him, the door opened and a woman with jet-black hair and black eyes came into the room. She was wearing a white jacket and had a stethoscope around her neck. She glanced at Carlie and smiled gently.

"No change, huh?" she asked softly.

Carlie swallowed. Her eyes were bloodshot. She shook her head.

The newcomer took something out of her pocket and removed Carlie's hand, just for a few seconds, long enough to press a small braided circle with a cross inside into Carson's palm.

"What is it?" Carlie asked in a whisper. "It looks like a prayer wheel…and those are Lakota colors…"

"You know that?" the visitor asked, and the smile grew bigger. "It is a prayer wheel. Those are our colors," she added. "Red and yellow, black and white, the colors of the four directions."

"It may be just what he needs," Carlie replied, folding his hand back inside both of hers, with the prayer circle inside it. "Are you a *wicasa wakan?*" she added, her eyes wide with curiosity as she referenced a holy person in the tribe who could heal the sick.

"A *wasichu,* and you know that?" she laughed, using the Lakota word that referred to anyone outside the tribe. She grinned from ear to ear. "No. I'm not. But my grandfather is. He still lives on the rez in Wapiti Ridge Sioux Reservation. It's where I'm from. Somebody called the rez to find a relative who knew him, so my cousin answered their questions and then he called me. We've got family all over," she added with a twinkle in her eyes. "Even in South Texas."

Carlie smiled. "Nice to know. It's like where I live, in Comanche Wells. I know everybody, and everybody knows my family for generations."

She nodded. "It's that way back home, too." She looked

at Carson. "Cousin Bob Tail is praying for him. Now he is a *wicasa wakan,*" she added.

"I believe in prayer," Carlie replied, looking back at Carson. "I think God comes in all colors and races and belief systems."

The visitor laid a hand on her shoulder and leaned down. "Cousin Bob Tail says he's going to wake up soon." She stood up and chuckled. "Don't you tell a soul I said that. They'll take back my medical degree!"

"You're a doctor," Carlie guessed, smiling.

"Neurologist," she said. "And I believe in modern medicine. I just think no technology is so perfect that it won't be helped by a few prayers." She winked, glanced at Carson again, smiled, and went out.

"You hear that?" she asked Carson. "Now you have to get better so people won't think Cousin Bob Tail is a fraud."

EVEN SHE, WITH no medical training, could tell that Carson was getting worse. She got up and bent over him, brushing back the unruly long black hair that had escaped the neat ponytail he usually wore it in.

She leaned close to brush her mouth over his. She stopped. Frowned. There was a fleeting wisp of memory. Garlic. He smelled of garlic. She knew he hated it because he'd once told Rourke he couldn't abide it in Italian dishes and Rourke had told her, just in passing conversation.

Another flash of memory. Wyoming. Merissa Kirk. She'd been poisoned with the pesticide malathion disguised in capsules by Richard Martin, who'd substituted it in her migraine headache capsules. A cohort of Martin's, a woman, had tried again to poison Merissa when she was in the hospital. The woman, on Martin's orders, had put malathion in a beef dish that Merissa had for supper. It had smelled of overpowering garlic! Cash Grier had told her all about it. She let go of Carson's hand and rushed out the door. The doctor, the Lakota neurologist, was standing at the desk.

"Please, may I speak with you?" she asked hurriedly.

"Yes..."

Carlie pulled her into Carson's cubicle. While she was walking, she was relaying the memories that had gone through her head. "Smell his breath," she asked softly.

Dr. Beaulieu caught her breath. "Poison?" She was thinking out loud. "It would account for the deterioration better than the slight head injury..."

"The woman who did it, she answered the phone when I called Carson. She said I'd get to watch him die slowly, over days!"

"Poison," the doctor agreed, black eyes narrowed. "That could explain it."

SHE WENT OUT. They came and took Carson out of the cubicle and wheeled him quickly back to the emergency surgical suite.

"It will be all right," Dr. Beaulieu assured her as she went by. "We're running a blood screen for poison right now, and I have a phone call in to the doctor whose name you gave me in Wyoming." She pressed Carlie's arm with her hand. "I think you may have saved his life."

"Cousin Bob Tail will be happy," Carlie said with just a hint of a smile.

"Oh, yes."

It seemed to take forever. Carlie sat in the waiting room this time, as close to the door as she could get, her legs pressed tightly together, her hands clenched in her lap, praying. She didn't have the presence of mind to call anyone. She was too involved in the moment.

She remembered Carson being so hostile to her in the beginning, antagonizing her with every breath, flaunting Lanette in front of her, insulting her. Then he'd frightened her, and with incredible skill, he'd treated her, taken her to the emergency room and then to have lunch by a flowing stream in the woods.

Afterward, in his arms, she'd felt things she'd never known in her young life. They'd fed the birds together and he'd told her the Brulé legend of the crow and how it became black. At the end, he'd told her it would never work out for the two of them and he was going to have to leave.

Now, there was the danger. She knew he wasn't tame. He would never be tame. He wouldn't marry her and settle down in Comanche Wells, Texas, and have children with her. He was like her father. Jake Blair had overcome his own past to change and transform himself into a man of God, into a minister. But Carson was different.

She looked at her hands, tightly clenched in her lap. Ringless. They'd be that way forever. She was never going to get married. She would have married Carson, if he'd asked. But nobody else. She'd be an old maid and fuss in her garden. She smiled sadly. Maybe one day Carson would marry someone and bring his children to visit her. Maybe they could at least remain friends. She hoped so.

The door to the surgical suite opened and Dr. Beaulieu came out. She sat beside Carlie and held her cold hands.

"We were in time," she said. "They've just finished washing out his stomach. They're giving him drugs to neutralize the effects of the poison. Your quick thinking saved his life."

Tears, hot and wet, rolled down Carlie's pale face. "Thank you."

"Oh, it wasn't me, honey," she laughed. "I just relayed the message to the right people. I only do head injuries, although I've put in my time in emergency rooms." She smiled sadly. "Back home, there are so many sick people with no money, no way to afford decent health care. I tried to go back and work there, but I was just overwhelmed by the sheer volume of people. I decided I needed more training, so I specialized and came here to do my residency. This is where my life is now. But one day, I'll go back to the rez and open a free clinic." She smiled, showing white teeth. "That's my dream."

"You're a nice person."

"You really love that man, don't you?" she asked with a piercing gaze.

Carlie smiled sadly. "It doesn't help much. He's a wolf. He isn't tameable."

"You know, that's what I said about my husband." She chuckled. "But he was. I have three kids."

"Lucky you."

"I am, truly." She cocked her head. "You know, Carson's great-great-grandfather rode with Crazy Horse. His family dates back far beyond the Little Big Horn."

The knowledge was surprising. Delightful. "Like mine in Comanche Wells," Carlie said softly.

"Yes. You both come from villages where families grow together. We aren't so very different, you know."

"He doesn't…love me," Carlie replied sadly. "If he did, I'd follow him around the world on my knees through broken glass."

"How do you know he doesn't?"

"He was leaving when this happened. He said it would never work out."

"I see." The other woman's face was sad. "I am truly sorry."

"I'm happy that he'll live," Carlie replied. "Even if he marries someone else and has ten kids and grows old, I'll still be happy."

Dr. Beaulieu nodded slowly. "And that is how love should be. To wish only the best for those we love, even if they choose someone else."

"When can I see him?"

"They'll take him out to a room very soon," she said, smiling. "We had him in ICU because he wasn't improving. But while they still had the tube down his throat he woke up and began cursing the technician." She chuckled. "I think they'll be very happy to release him to the poor nurses on the ward."

Carlie grinned. "He's conscious?"

"Oh, yes." She stood up. "Now will you relax?"

"I'll try." She stood up, too. *"Pilamaya ye,"* she said softly in Lakota. The feminine form of *thank you.*

Dr. Beaulieu's eyes widened . "You speak Lakota?"

"Only a few words. Those are my best ones, and I imagine my accent is atrocious."

"I've been here for two years and not one person has ever spoken even one word of Lakota to me," the other woman said with pursed lips. "However few, I appreciate the effort it took to learn them." She nodded toward the emergency suite. "Does he know you speak them?"

Carlie hesitated and then shook her head. "I was afraid he'd think I was, well, doing it just to impress him. I learned it when I was still in school. I loved reading about Crazy Horse. Of course, his mother was Miniconjou Lakota and his father was part Miniconjou, but he was raised Oglala Lakota…"

Dr. Beaulieu put her hand on Carlie's shoulder. "Okay, now you have to marry him," she said firmly. "Even on the rez, there are some people who don't know all that about Crazy Horse." And she laughed.

CARSON WAS MOVED into a room. Carlie had phoned her father and her boss to tell them Carson was out of danger.

She was allowed in when they got him settled in the bed and hooked up to a saline drip. He was sitting up, glaring, like a wolf in a trap.

"You look better," she said, hesitating in the doorway.

"Better," he scoffed. He was hoarse, from the tube. "If you agree that having your stomach pumped with a tube down your throat is better!"

"At least you're alive," she pointed out.

He glared at her. "What are you doing here?"

She froze in place. Flushed. She wasn't certain what to say. "I phoned you for Rourke and Lanette answered..."

"Lanette." He blinked. "We were having coffee. I was about to tell her that I'd never tasted worse coffee when she came up behind me and hit me in the head. A gun went off." He shifted uncomfortably. "She shot me!" He glanced at Carlie. "Where is she?"

"They have a BOLO for her," she replied, using the abbreviation for a "Be on the lookout." "She hasn't surfaced yet. Fred Baldwin, who kidnapped me, is in custody in Jacobsville, along with the watch that Richard Martin stole from the assistant prosecutor he killed. He's turned state's evidence against Matthew Helm. They should be at his door pretty soon."

Carson was staring at her. "That doesn't answer the question. Why are you here?"

"Nobody else could be spared," she lied. "My father came by earlier. The others will be along soon, I'm sure."

His black eyes narrowed. He didn't speak. He didn't offer her a chair or ask her to sit down.

"There's a neurosurgeon here. A Dr. Beaulieu. She's Lakota. She said your cousin Bob Tail was praying for you, and that he said you'd live."

"Cousin Bob Tail usually can't even predict the weather," he scoffed.

"Well, he was right this time," she said, feeling uncomfortable. She twisted her small purse in her hands.

"Was there anything else?" he asked, his eyes unblinking and steady on her face.

She shook her head.

"Then I imagine visiting hours are over and you should go home before it gets dark."

"It's already dark," she murmured.

"All the more reason."

She nodded.

"They'll have someone watching you," he said.

"I guess."

"Don't go down any back roads and keep your phone with you."

"It's in my purse."

"Put it in your coat pocket so that you can get to it in a hurry if you have to," he continued curtly.

She grimaced, but she took it out and slid it into her coat pocket.

"Good night," he said.

She managed a faint smile. "Good night. I'm glad you're okay."

He didn't answer her.

She walked out, hesitated at the door. But she didn't look back when she left. She didn't want him to see the tears.

THEY'D GIVEN HIM something for pain. The gunshot wound, while nonfatal, was painful. So was his throat, where the tube had gone down. He was irritated that Carlie had come to see him out of some sort of obligation. Nobody else was available, she'd said. It was a chore. She hadn't come because she was terrified that he was going to die, because she cared. She'd come because nobody else was available.

Yet he was still concerned that she was driving home alone in the dark, when there had been attempts on her life.

He'd wanted to phone Cash and ask him to watch out for her. Then he laughed inwardly at his own folly. Of course Cash would have her watched. He probably had somebody in the hospital the whole time, somebody who would keep her under surveillance even when she drove home.

He fell asleep, only to wake much later, feeling as if he had concrete in his side where the bullet had hit.

"Hurts, huh?"

He looked up into a face he knew. "Sunflower," he said, chuckling as he used the nickname he'd hung on her years ago. Dr. Beaulieu had been a childhood playmate. He knew her very well, knew her family for generations.

She grinned. "You're looking better."

"I feel as if a truck ran through my side," he said, grimacing. "They pumped my stomach."

"Yes. Apparently the woman who shot you also hit you on the head to show us an obvious head injury. But she poisoned you first. The poison was killing you. If it hadn't been for your friend from Comanche Wells, you'd be dead. We were treating the obvious injuries. None of us looked for poison because we didn't expect to see it." She hesitated. "We did blood work, but it was routine stuff."

"My friend?" He still felt foggy.

"Yes. The dark-headed girl who speaks Lakota," she replied. "She smelled garlic on your breath and recalled that you hated it and would never ingest it willingly. Then she remembered a poisoning case in Wyoming in a hospital there, a woman who was given malathion in a beef dish…"

"Merissa Kirk," Carson said heavily. "Yes."

"So we checked with the attending physician there for

verification. I was involved only peripherally, of course, since my specialty is neurology. We thought you were unconscious because of the head wound."

"The coffee," Carson recalled. "The coffee tasted funny."

She nodded. "She told the dark-haired girl that she would get to watch you die slowly. When she smelled your breath, she remembered what the woman told her."

"Lanette." His face tautened. "I hope they hang her. If they'll let me out, I'll track her down, wherever she goes."

Dr. Beaulieu was smiling. "She said you were like a wolf, that you could never be tame. She said it didn't matter, that she only wanted you to be happy, even if it was with some other woman." She shook her head. "She thanked me in Lakota. It was a shock. Most *wasicus* can't speak a word of our language."

"I know."

"She even knew that Crazy Horse's mother was Miniconjou," she said.

"Where's my cell phone?" he asked.

She raised both eyebrows. "Cell phone?"

"Yes. Wasn't it brought in with me?" he asked.

"Let me check." She phoned the clerk at the emergency room where he was brought in. They checked the records. She thanked them and hung up. "There was no cell phone with you when you were admitted," she said.

He grimaced. All his private numbers were there, including Carlie's, her father's and Rourke's. If Lanette had taken it…

"Will you hand me the phone, please? And tell me how to get an outside line…"

CARLIE WAS NO sooner back home than her phone rang while she was opening the front door. She answered it.

There was nobody there. Only silence.

"Hello?" she persisted. "Look, tell me who you are or I'm calling the police."

There was a dial tone.

It worried her. She went inside to talk to her father. But he wasn't there. A note on the hall table said that he'd been called to a meeting of the finance committee at the church. He wouldn't be long.

Carlie hung up her old coat. She started upstairs when she remembered that she'd left her cell phone in her coat. She went to get it just as there was a knock on the door.

14

"WHAT DO YOU MEAN, you can't get her on the phone?" Carson raged at Cash Grier. "Get somebody over there, for God's sake! Lanette has my cell phone. It has Carlie's number and Rourke's real number on it!"

"Will you slow down and calm down?" Cash asked softly. "I've got people watching Carlie's house. Believe me, nobody's touching her."

"Okay. How about her father?"

"At a church meeting. We have someone outside."

"Rourke?"

Cash laughed. "I arrested Rourke two hours ago in the act of placing cocaine in the glove compartment of Calhoun Ballenger's son's truck."

"Arrested?"

"You've been out of the loop," Cash told him. "Blake Kemp, our district attorney, was on the scene, along with agents from the DEA, ICE and several other agencies. We had to make it look good, in case Helm slips through our fingers and Rourke has to go undercover again."

"All right." Carson's head was throbbing. His wound hurt. "Carlie said she came because nobody else was available to sit with me—"

"Really? You should talk to the staff. She sat in the corridor outside the E.R. and refused to budge. When they got you to ICU, she did the same thing. They even called security. She sat where she was and cried. Finally, the neurosurgeon on your case took pity on her and let her in."

"Dr. Beaulieu?" he asked.

"No, it was a man. Anyway, she smelled garlic on your breath. She connected you with the Wyoming case, told Dr. Beaulieu, and the rest is history. Saved your life, son," he added. "You were dying and they didn't know why. I assume your blonde friend hit you on the head and shot you so that they wouldn't think of looking for poison until it was too late."

"I don't remember any of this."

"I guess not. I had Carlie call you at your apartment because Rourke couldn't risk having his number show up on your phone, assuming that it was bugged by Helm's men. Lanette answered it. She told Carlie that you'd be a long time dying and she'd have to watch you suffer. Almost came true."

"Almost." His heart lifted like a bird. Carlie had lied. She'd been with him all the way, all the time. She did care. Cared a lot.

"So just get well, will you? We've got everything covered down here."

"Okay." He drew in a breath. "Thanks, Cash."

"You'd do it for me."

"In a heartbeat."

He hung up the phone and closed his eyes. He should call Carlie. He wanted to. But that was when the pain meds they'd been shoveling into him took effect. He went to sleep.

CARLIE OPENED THE DOOR. Just as she did it, she realized that she shouldn't have done it. She had no weapon, her phone was in her coat, she was vulnerable. Just like when she'd answered the door and Fred Baldwin had carried her off.

Her father stared back at her with set lips. "How many times do I have to tell you to make sure who's at the door before you answer it?" he asked.

She smiled sheepishly. "Sorry, Dad." She stared at him. "Why did you knock?"

He grimaced. "Forgot my keys."

"See? It's genetic," she told him. "You lose your keys, I lose my phone. It's catching, and I got it from you!"

He chuckled. "Heard from Carson?"

"He's sitting up in bed yelling at people," she said.

He let out a relieved whistle. "I wouldn't have given a nickel for his chances when I saw him," he replied. He smiled. "I wouldn't have told you that. You still had hope. I guess they've got some super neurosurgeons in that hospital."

"It wasn't the head injury," she said. "Or the gunshot wound. It was poison. She put malathion in his coffee."

"Good Lord!" he exclaimed. "That's diabolical!"

"Yes. I hope they catch her," she said doggedly. "I hope they lock her up for a hundred years!"

He hugged Carlie. "I can appreciate how you must feel."

She hugged him back. "Carson sent me home," she said, giving way to tears. "I think I made him mad by just going up there."

He grimaced. "Maybe he's trying to be kind, in his way, Carlie. You know he's probably never going to be able to settle in some small town."

"I know. It doesn't help."

She drew back and wiped her eyes. "How about some coffee and cake?"

"That sounds nice."

"Did you just try to call me?" she added on the way.

"Me? No. Why?"

"Just a wrong number, I guess. Somebody phoned and hung up." She laughed. "I'm probably just getting paranoid, is all. I'll make a pot of coffee."

TWO DAYS LATER, Carson was out of the hospital. He was a little weak, but he felt well enough to drive. He went to his apartment first, looking for the missing cell phone. He knew he wouldn't find it. He hoped they could catch Lanette before she managed to get out of the country. She probably had several aliases that she could refer to if she was as competent at her job as he now believed she was. A contract killer, and he'd been dating her. All the while she'd been hell-bent on killing Carlie's father. He felt like an idiot.

He drove down to Jacobsville to Cash Grier's office. As soon as he opened the door, he looked for Carlie, but she wasn't at her desk. He went on in and knocked at Cash's door.

"Come in."

He opened the door, expecting Carlie to be taking dictation or discussing the mail. She wasn't there, either.

"You look like hell," Cash said. "But at least you're still alive. Welcome back."

"Thanks. Where's Carlie?" he asked.

"Bahamas," he replied easily.

He frowned. "What's she doing in the Bahamas?"

"Haven't a clue," Cash said heavily. "She and Robin took off early yesterday on a red-eye flight out of San Antonio. She asked off for a couple of days and I told her to go ahead. She's had a rough time of it."

"I tried to call her. I didn't get an answer."

"Same here. I don't think her cell phone is working. Her father's still looking for it. She said she left it in her coat pocket, but then they noticed there's a hole in the pocket. Probably fell out somewhere and she didn't notice. She was pretty upset over you."

"I heard." He was feeling insecure. He thought Carlie cared. But she'd gone to the Bahamas with another man. He'd heard her speak of Robin with affection. Had he chased her into the arms of another man with his belligerent attitude? He should have called her father when he couldn't reach her, called the house phone. The damned drugs had kept him under for the better part of two days!

"Why did she go to the Bahamas with a man?" he asked shortly.

Cash frowned. "I don't know. She and Robin have always been close, from what I've heard. And he took her to the Valentine's Day dance." He hesitated. "It didn't seem like a love match to me. But..."

"Yes. But."

Cash could see the pain in the other man's face. "I'm sorry."

"So am I." He managed a smile. "I'm leaving."

"Today?"

He nodded. "I'm going home. I have some ghosts to lay."

Cash got up, went around the desk and extended his hand. "If you ever need help, you've got my number," he told the younger man.

Carson returned the pressure. He smiled. "Thanks."

"Keep in touch."

"I'll do that, too." He glanced out at the empty desk where Carlie usually sat.

"What do you want me to tell her?" Cash asked.

Carson's face set into hard lines. "Nothing. Nothing at all."

CARLIE STOOD UP with Robin and his fiancée, Lucy Tims, at their secret wedding in Nassau.

"I hope you'll be very happy," she told them, kissing both radiant faces.

"We will until we have to go home and face the music,"

Robin chuckled. "But that's not for a few days. We're going to live in paradise until then. Thanks so much for coming with us, Carlie."

"It was my pleasure. Thanks for my plane ticket," she added gently. "I sort of needed to get away for a little while."

"Stay for a couple of days anyway," Robin coaxed.

She shook her head. "Overnight was all I can manage. The chief won't even be able to deal with the mail without me," she joked. "I'm going back tonight. You two be happy, okay?"

"Okay." They kissed her again.

She didn't want to say, but she was hoping that Carson might come to see her when he was out of the hospital. It was a long shot, after his antagonistic behavior, but hope died hard. She went home and wished for the best.

SHE MISSED HER cell phone. She knew it had probably fallen through the hole in her pocket and it was gone forever. It was no great loss. It was a cheap phone and it only had a couple of numbers in it, one was her father and the other was Cash Grier.

But it was like losing a friend, because Carson had carried it around with him before he brought it to her. It had echoes of his touch. Pathetic, she told herself, cherishing objects because they'd been held.

It had been several days. She was getting used to the idea that Carson was gone for good. Chief Grier had told her that Carson had come by the office on his way out of town. But he hadn't had a message for Carlie. That was all right. She hadn't really expected one.

She disguised the hurt on the job, but she went home and cried herself to sleep. Wolves couldn't be tamed, she reminded herself. It was useless to hope for a future that included Carson. Just useless.

ROURKE WAS BAILED out by Jake Blair. They had a good laugh about his imminent prosecution for breaking and entering, possession of narcotics and possible conspiracy.

They laughed because Rick Marquez and the San Antonio assistant D.A. working the case finally had enough evidence to arrest Matthew Helm. It made headlines all over the country, especially when Rourke gave a statement to the effect that Mr. Helm had ordered him to plant narcotics on Calhoun Ballenger's son Terry and that Charro Mendez had supplied them.

There was an attempt to extradite Mendez to stand trial in the U.S. on drug charges, but he mysteriously vanished.

Helm wasn't so fortunate. He, his senior campaign staff and at least one San Antonio police officer were arrested and charged with crimes ranging from attempted murder to theft of police evidence and narcotics distribution.

It came as a shock when Marquez released a statement heralding Fred Baldwin as a material witness in the case. Fred, who was turning state's evidence, was being given a pardon by the governor of the state in return for his cooperation.

That news was pleasing to Eb Scott, whose kids had become great playmates of the big, gentle man who lived with them while Helm was under investigation. Eb wanted to give Fred a job, in fact, but Cash Grier beat him to it. Fred was wearing a uniform again, having been cleared of all charges against him in Chicago, his record restored, his reputation unstained, his former partner now under investigation for police corruption.

He was Jacobsville's newest patrol officer, and his first assignment was speaking to children in grammar school about the dangers of drugs. He was in his element. Children seemed to love him.

Carlie went about her business, working diligently, keeping up with correspondence for the chief. But the sadness in her was visible. She'd lost that impish spark that had made her so much fun to be around. Her father grieved for her, with her. He understood what she was going through as she tried to adjust to life without Carson, without even the occasional glimpse of him in town. He was long gone, now.

AUTUMN CAME TO Jacobs County. The maples were beautiful and bright, and Carlie was filling her bird feeders for the second time, as the migrating birds came from the north on their way to warmer climates. Cardinals and blue jays were everywhere. The male goldfinches were losing their bright gold color and turning a dull green, donning their winter coats.

Carlie was still wearing her threadbare one with the hole in the pocket sewn up. Her phone had miraculously reappeared, brought in by a street person who found it and traded it to a soup kitchen worker for a sandwich. The worker had turned it in to police, who returned it to

Carlie. She had the phone in her pocket even now. It was safe enough with the hole mended.

The birds usually stayed nearby while she filled the feeders, but they suddenly took off as if a predator was approaching. It was an odd thing, but she'd observed it over the years many times. Sometimes, for no apparent reason, birds just did that. Flew up all together into the trees, when Carlie saw nothing threatening.

This time, however, there was a threat. It was standing just behind her.

She turned, slowly, and there he was.

She tried valiantly not to let her joy show. But tears stung her eyes. It had been months. A lifetime. She stood very still, the container of birdseed held tight in her hands, her eyes misting as she looked at him.

He seemed taller than ever. His hair wasn't in a ponytail. It was loose around his shoulders, long and thick and as black as a grackle's wing. He had something in a bag under one arm. He was wearing that exquisite beaded jacket that was so familiar to her.

"Hello," he said.

"Hello," she said back.

He gave her coat a speaking look. "Same coat."

She managed a smile. "I was going to say the same thing."

He moved closer. He took the seed canister out of her hands and placed it on the ground. He handed her the bag and nodded.

She opened it. Inside was the most exquisite coat she'd ever seen in her life, white buckskin with beading, Oglala Lakota colors of the four directions, in yellow, red, white and black patterns on it. She gasped as she pulled it out of the bag and just stared at it.

He held out his hand. She took off her ratty coat and gave it to him to hold while she tried on the new jacket. It was a perfect fit.

"It's the most beautiful thing in the world," she whispered, tears running down her cheeks.

"No, Carlie," he replied, dropping her old coat on top of the birdseed canister. "You're the most beautiful thing in the world. And I've missed you like hell! Come here…!"

He wrapped her up against him, half lifting her so that he could find her lips with his hard, cold mouth. He kissed her without a thought for whoever might see them. He didn't care.

He was home.

She held on for dear life and kissed him back with all the fear and sorrow and grief she'd felt in the months between when she thought she'd never see him again. Everything she felt was in that long, slow, sweet kiss.

"I love you," she choked.

"I know," he whispered into her mouth, the words almost a groan. "I've always known."

She gave up trying to talk. It was so sweet, to be in his arms. She was probably hallucinating and it wasn't real. She didn't care. If her mind had snapped, it could stay snapped. She'd never been so happy.

Eventually, he stood her back on her feet and held her away from him. "You've lost weight."

She nodded. She studied him. "You look…different."

He smiled slowly. "At peace," he explained. "I had to go home and face my demons. It wasn't easy."

She touched his hard face. "There was nothing you could have done to stop it," she said softly.

"That's what his own brother said. I made peace with his family, with her family."

"I'm glad."

"I had my cousin make the jacket. I'm glad it fits."

She smiled. "It's beautiful. I'll never take it off."

He pursed his lips. "Oh, I think you might want to do that in a week or so."

"I will? Why?"

He framed her face in his big, warm hands. "I'm not wearing clothes on my honeymoon. And neither are you."

"How do you know what I'll be wearing?" she asked, brightening.

"Because we'll be together." The smile faded. "Always. As long as we live. As long as the grass grows, and the wind blows, and the sun sets."

Tears rolled down her cheeks. "For so long?" she whispered brokenly.

"Longer." He bent and kissed away the tears. "I would have been here sooner, but I stopped by to talk to Micah Steele."

"Micah?"

He nodded. "I still have to do an internship. I'm arranging to do it here. Afterward, a year or two of residency in internal medicine, here if possible, San Antonio if not. Then I'll move into practice with Lou and Micah."

She was standing very still. She didn't understand. "You're going to medical school?"

He laughed softly. "I've already been to medical school. I got my medical license. But I never did an internship so I couldn't, technically, practice medicine." He smoothed her hand over his chest. "I did keep my medical license current. I guess I realized that I'd go back to it one day. I have some catching up to do, and I'll have to work late hours, but—"

"But you want to live here?" she asked, aghast.

"Of course," he said simply. "This is where your tribe lives, isn't it?" he teased.

Tears were falling hot and heavy now. "We're going to get married?"

He nodded. "I'm not asking, by the way," he said with pursed lips. "We're just doing it."

"Oh."

"And I don't have a ring yet. I thought we'd go together to pick them out. A set for you, and a band for me."

"You're going to wear a ring?" she asked.

"It seems to go with the position." He grinned.

She hesitated, just for a second.

"You're thinking of my reputation with women. I took them home, kissed them at the door and said good-night," he said, reading her apprehension. "It was a nice fiction, to keep homebodies like you from getting too interested in me." He shrugged. "I haven't had anybody since I was widowed."

She pressed close into his arms, held on for dear life. "I would have married you anyway."

"I know that."

"But it's nice that you don't know a lot more than I do…"

"And that's where you're wrong," he whispered into her ear. "I'm a doctor. I know where ALL the nerve endings are."

"Gosh!"

"And the minute your father pronounces us man and wife, I'll prove it to you. When we're alone, of course. We wouldn't want to embarrass your father."

"No. We wouldn't want to do that." She pressed close into his arms, felt them fold around her, comforting and loving and safe. She closed her eyes. "You didn't say good-bye."

His arms contracted. "You went to the Bahamas with another man."

She jerked back, lifting horrified eyes. "No! I went to be a witness at his wedding to Lucy Tims!" she exclaimed.

He grimaced. "I know that, now. I didn't at the time. I tried to call you, but I never got an answer."

"I lost my phone. Some kind person turned it in at a soup kitchen in San Antonio."

He sighed, tracing her mouth with a long forefinger. "A comedy of errors. I felt guilty, too. I'd sent you packing without realizing that you'd saved my life. I was still confused from the blow on the head and the drugs. I was worried that you'd be on the road alone in the dark." He leaned his forehead against hers. "Lanette was still on the loose. I was afraid for you. I should never have let you leave the hospital in the first place—"

"I was okay," she interrupted. "Cash Grier had people watching me all the time. Dad, too. Just in case."

"I hurt you. I never meant to." He closed his eyes as he rocked her in his arms. "I wasn't sure, Carlie. I had to be sure that I could settle down, that I could give up the wild ways. Until I was sure, I wasn't going to make promises."

She drew away. "And are you? Sure, I mean?"

He nodded. "That's why I went home." He smiled. "Cousin Bob Tail says we're going to have three sons. We have to name one for him."

"Okay," she said, without hesitation and with a big grin.

He laughed. "He wants us to name him Bob. Just Bob."

"I wouldn't mind." She searched his black eyes. "Our sons. Wow."

"Just what I was thinking. Wow." He chuckled.

"I haven't been playing online for a while."

"Neither have I," he confessed. "I missed you so much that I really wanted to. But I had to be sure, first." He sighed. "I guess if push comes to shove I can make an Alliance toon and we can run battlegrounds on the same side."

"Funny, I was just thinking I could make a Horde toon for the same reason."

He smiled. "We're on the same side in real life. That's enough."

"So," she asked, her green eyes twinkling, "when are we getting married?"

"Let's go and ask your father when he's free," he said.

She slid her hand into his and walked back into the house with him. Her father didn't even have to ask. He just grinned.

THEY WENT TO Tangier for their honeymoon. Carlie was horrified at the expense, but Carson just laughed.

"Honey, I've got enough in foreign banks to keep us going into our nineties," he said complacently. "I work because I enjoy working. I could retire tomorrow if I felt like it. But I think practicing medicine will occupy me for many years to come. That, and our children."

"You told Rourke you wanted to be an attorney," she recalled.

"Yes, well, if you tell somebody you gave up law they don't care. If you tell them you gave up medicine, that's a whole other set of explanations I didn't want to make. As it happens, I did a double major in undergraduate school in biology and chemistry, but I minored in history and anatomy. History and law do go together."

"I wouldn't know. Will it matter to you that I haven't been to college?"

"You're kidding, right?" he teased. "You can speak Lakota and you know who Crazy Horse's mother was. That's higher education enough to suit me."

"Okay. Just so you're sure," she laughed. "And you don't mind if I go on working for the chief?"

"He'd skin me if I tried to take you away," he said with a sigh. "He'd never find a stamp or a potato chip, and some new girl would surely find out about the alien files he's got locked up in his office and call the Air Force. So, no, you can go on working. I intend to."

She smiled. "Dr. Farwalker. Sounds very nice."

"I thought so myself."

TANGIER WAS AN amazing blend of old and new. There were high-rise apartment buildings near the centuries-old walled marketplace. Carlie found it fascinating as they drove through the city at night in the back of a taxicab.

It had been a very long flight, from San Antonio to Atlanta, Atlanta to Brussels, Brussels to Casablanca, Casablanca to Tangier. They'd arrived in the dead of night and Carlie was worried sick about being able to find a way to get into the city as they waited endlessly to get through passport control and customs. But there were cabs sitting outside the main building.

"Told you so," he chuckled.

"Is there any foreign city you haven't been to?" she wondered.

"Not many," he confessed. "You'll love this one. I'll take you around town tomorrow and show you where the pirates used to hang out."

"That's a deal."

CARLIE WAS SO tired by the time they got into the hotel, registered and were shown to their room that she almost wept.

"Now, now," he said softly. "We have our whole lives for what you're upset about missing. Sleep first. Then, we explore."

She smiled shyly. "Okay."

He watched her undress, with black eyes that appreciated every stitch that came off. But when she was down to her underwear, he moved close, pulled out a gown and handed it to her.

"First times are hard," he said gently. "Go put on your gown. I'll get into my pajamas while you're gone. Then we'll get some sleep before we do anything else. Deal?"

She smiled with relief. "Deal. I'm sorry," she started to add.

He put his fingers across her lips. "I like you just the way you are," he told her.

"Hang-ups and all?"

He smiled. "Hang-ups and all."

She let out the breath she'd been holding and darted into the bathroom, chiding herself for her wedding night nerves. It was natural, she supposed, despite the fact that most people had the wedding night long before the wedding. She and Carson must be throwbacks, she decided, because he'd wanted to wait as much as she had.

The lights were out when she came back into the room. The shutters were open, and moonlight filtered across the bed, where Carson was sprawled under the sheet. He held out his arm. She darted into bed and went close, pillowing her cheek on his hard, warm chest.

"Oh, that feels good," she whispered.

"I was about to say the same thing. Happy?"

"I could die of it."

"I know exactly what you mean." He closed his eyes, tucked her close and fell asleep almost at once. So did she. It had been a very long trip.

SHE WOKE THE next morning to the smell of coffee. She opened her eyes. Carson was sitting on the side of the bed in his pajama bottoms holding the cup just over her head.

"What a wonderful smell," she moaned.

"Sit up and have a sip. They serve a nice buffet breakfast downstairs, but I thought you might like coffee first."

"I would." She sat up, noticing at once how much of her small breasts were visible under the thin gown. He was looking at them with real interest, his eyes soft and hungry.

The way he looked at her made her feel beautiful. Exciting. Exotic.

"Tangier," she murmured, putting the cup down on the side table. "It makes me feel like I should be wearing a trenchcoat or something." Breathlessly, she slid the straps of the gown down her arm and let them fall.

Carson's expression was eloquent. He didn't even hesitate. He moved across the bed, putting her down on it, while his mouth opened and fed on her firm, soft breasts.

She arched up, shyness vanishing in the heat of sudden passion. She felt his hands go down her back, sliding fabric out of the way. She felt him move and then his body was moving on hers, bare and exciting.

He eased between her legs, his mouth poised over hers. He teased her lips while his body teased hers. He was smiling, but there was heat and passion in the smile. "Lift up," he whispered. "Seduce me."

"Gosh, I don't have…the slightest idea…I'm sorry…I…!" A tiny, helpless moan escaped her as his hand moved between them. "Carson, oh, gosh!"

"Yes, right there," he murmured at her lips. He chuckled softly. "It feels good, doesn't it? And this is just the beginning."

"Just the…?" She cried out again. Her body arched,

shivering. What he was doing was shocking, invasive, she should be protesting or something, she should be… "Carson," she sobbed against his mouth. "Please…don't stop!"

"Never," he breathed against her lips. "Move this leg. Yes. Here. And that one. Now lift. Lift up, baby. Lift up… that's it…yes!"

There was a rhythm. She'd never known. In all her reading and covert watching of shocking movies, she'd never experienced anything like this.

It was one thing to read about it, quite another to do it. He knew more about her body than she did, apparently, and used that knowledge to take her to places she'd never dreamed about. The sensations piled upon themselves, growing and multiplying, until she felt as if she had the sun inside her and it was going to explode any second. The tension was so high that it was like being pulled apart in the sweetest sort of way.

She dug her nails into his hips as he strained down toward her, his powerful body arched above her as he drove down one last time.

She heard herself sobbing as she fell and fell, into layers of sweet heat that burned and burned and burned. It was like tides, rippling and falling, overwhelming and falling, crushing and falling, until finally she burst like fireworks and shuddered endlessly under the heavy, hard thrust of his body.

She heard him cry out at her ear, a husky sound that was so erotic, she shivered again when she felt his body cord and ripple and then, quite suddenly, relax.

He was heavy. His skin was hot, damp. She held him, smoothed the long, thick hair at his back, loving him.

"Everybody says it hurts the first time," she murmured.

"Oh? Did it?"

She laughed secretly. "I don't know."

He chuckled, the sound rippling against her hard-tipped breasts. He moved on her, feeling her instant response. He lifted his head and looked into her wide, soft eyes. "You will never get away," he promised her. "No matter how far, how fast you run, I will find you."

"I will never run," she said with a sigh. "Everything I want or love in all the world is right here, in my arms."

He bent and kissed her eyes shut as he began to move. She shivered gently.

"How long do you want to wait?" he whispered at her mouth.

"How…long? For…what?" she gasped, moving with him.

"To make a baby," he whispered back.

Her eyes opened. She shivered again. The look on her face was all the answer he needed. He held her gaze as he moved, tenderly, enclosing her in his legs, bending them beside her, so that they were locked together in the most intimate position she'd ever experienced.

"Oh…my…goodness," she said, looking straight into his eyes.

His hands framed her face. His was strained, taut, as he moved expertly on her body.

"I can't bear it," she managed to say.

"Yes, you can," he whispered. His eyes held hers. "I love you. This is how much..."

He shifted, and she cried out. The pleasure was beyond words, beyond description. She held on and sobbed with each slow, deep, torturous movement of his hips as he built the tension and built it and built it until she exploded into a million tiny hot pieces of sheer joy.

He groaned, almost convulsing, as the pleasure bit into him. "Never," he whispered hoarsely. "Never, never like this!"

She couldn't even manage a word. She just clung to him, enjoying the sight of the pleasure in his face, in the corded muscles of his body, in the sweet agony that echoed in the helpless movements of his hips.

Long after they felt the last ripple of pleasure, they clung to each other in the bright stillness of the morning, unable to let go.

"I think I dreamed you," he whispered finally.

"I know I dreamed you," she replied at his ear, still holding tight.

He rolled over so that she was beside him, but still joined to his body.

"I didn't know it felt like this," she confessed shyly. "I feel hungry now in a way I didn't before."

He smiled, brushing his mouth over hers. "You can't miss what you've never had."

"I guess so." She drew in a breath and looked down.

He smiled to himself and pulled away, letting her look. Her eyes were as wide as saucers when he moved away.

"Show-and-tell," he teased.

She blushed. "Men in racy magazines don't look like that," she whispered. "I only saw one and he was, well, he was…" She cleared her throat. "He wasn't that impressive."

He chuckled. He pulled her to her feet, enjoying her nudity. "I have an idea."

"You do? What?" she asked, looking up at him with a smile.

"Let's have a shower, and then breakfast and go look for pirates."

"I would like that very much."

He led her toward the bathroom.

She hesitated at the door.

He raised an eyebrow.

"What you said." She indicated the bed. "Was it just, I mean, did you really mean it?"

He pulled her close. "I want children very much, Carlie," he said softly. "They'll come when it's time for them to come." He smiled. "If it's this year, I don't mind at all. Do you?"

She laughed and hugged him close. "Oh, no, I don't mind!"

"Then let's have a shower and go eat. I'm starving!"

LIFE WITH CARSON was fascinating. They found more in common every day. They moved into a house of their own and Carson went to work at Jacobsville General as an intern. It was long hours and hard work. He never complained and when he got home, he told Carlie all the interesting things he'd learned that day. She never tired of listening.

Fred Baldwin had coffee with her when he started out on his patrols. He'd turned into a very good cop, and he'd have done anything for Cash Grier. He'd have done anything for Carlie, too. He told her that her father was going to have to share her with him because he didn't have a daughter of his own. She'd almost cried at the tenderness in his big brown eyes.

Lanette had been found, but not in a condition that would lead to trial. She took a flight to a small South American country that had no extradition treaty with the United States, but had the misfortune to run into the brother of a man she'd killed for money. Since she had no living family, they buried her in an unmarked grave in South America.

Matthew Helm was arrested, prosecuted and convicted on so many felony counts that he'd only get out of prison when he was around 185 years old. Or so the jury decided.

His cohorts went with him. The wife of the murdered assistant district attorney was in the courtroom when the sentence was pronounced.

Calhoun Ballenger won the special election and went to Washington, D.C., with his wife, Abby, as the junior United States senator from the grand state of Texas. Terry, having just graduated from high school, was off to college with his two brothers, Ed and Matt.

Calhoun had given Fred Baldwin a musical watch that played an Italian folk song when he learned about Fred's role in preventing the potential criminalization of his son Terry. Fred wore the watch to work every day.

Charro Mendez was still on the run. But people across the border were watching and waiting for his return.

Two months after Carlie and Carson were married, she was waiting for him at the front door when he came home from a long day at the hospital. She was holding a small plastic device in her hands. She handed it to him with an impish grin.

He looked at it, read it, picked her up and swung her around in his arms, kissing her the whole while and looking as if he'd won the lottery.

Seven months later, a little boy was born at Jacobsville General Hospital. They named him Jacob Allen Cassius Fred Farwalker, for his father, his grandfather and his two godfathers. Officer Fred Baldwin held him while he was baptized. He cried.

★★★★★

Don't miss Diana Palmer's next book in October—
TEXAS BORN!
Coming to you from Harlequin Special Edition,
TEXAS BORN is the romance between
Gabriel Brandon and Michelle Godfrey!